ALLEGRA HAD
TO CHOOSE...

For a young lady who wanted to live her own
free and independent life, Allegra suddenly
found herself beseiged by men who wanted
to join their lives with hers.

There was the Baron de Lempriere. He was
dashing, good-looking, impulsive, witty,
eloquent, and passionate—in short, so
disconcertingly *French*.

There was Sir Arthur Huddleston. He was
sound, respectable, honest, dependable,
devoted, and persistent—in short, so reliably
English.

And then there was Sir Derek, arrogant,
elegant, stubborn, domineering, virile, and
handsome—in short, so infuriatingly *male*.

Allegra could not make up her mind—and
then her heart took over. . . .

**"AS BUBBLY AND REFRESHING AS
GOOD CHAMPAGNE!"**
                              —PUBLISHERS WEEKLY

Big Bestsellers from SIGNET

Allegra

by
Clare Darcy

A SIGNET BOOK

NEW AMERICAN LIBRARY

TIMES MIRROR

SIGNET TRADEMARK REG. U.S. PAT. OFF. AND FOREIGN COUNTRIES REGISTERED TRADEMARK—MARCA REGISTRADA HECHO EN CHICAGO, U.S.A.

SIGNET, SIGNET CLASSICS, MENTOR, PLUME AND MERIDIAN BOOKS are published by The New American Library, Inc., 1301 Avenue of the Americas, New York, New York 10019

First Printing, February, 1976

1 2 3 4 5 6 7 8 9

PRINTED IN THE UNITED STATES OF AMERICA

Allegra

Chapter One

THE MORNING callers, having dutifully enquired for Lady Warring, looked not in the least disappointed upon being informed that her ladyship was from home but that the Dowager Lady Warring would receive them, and followed the butler sedately up the stairs to the apartments that had been set aside at Questers for the latter lady's use. Once inside the door of the bright sitting room, however, Miss Herington cast decorum aside and flew across to her ladyship's waiting arms, while her younger sister Hilary looked on with the negligently proprietary air of a cat who has just deposited a particularly fine mouse at her mistress's feet for her approval.

"I *told* you I should bring her the very instant she arrived," Hilary said, plumping herself down in a winged armchair in a manner scarcely befitting the newly acquired young ladyhood of which she was exceedingly proud. "Aunt Colbridge and Charlotte are as mad as Bedlam, for they were planning to go to Huntingdon this morning to change the ribbons on Charlotte's new muslin, only the nursery-governess said she had had quite enough of being ordered about like a sweep and went off home to her mother last night in a flood of tears and Charlotte's best embroidered petticoat—at least it is missing this morning and they cannot think *I* took it any longer, after having been through all my things—so that left me to look after the children. Only when Allie arrived I said I could not stay, of course, for I had promised to bring her here to

1

you—and oh, Lady Warring, she says it was quite as bad with Aunt Hatherill in Bath as it is here with Aunt Colbridge, so what in the *world* are we to do now?"

Having delivered herself of this speech in a pell-mell, optimistic manner that quite belied its dire content, Miss Hilary Herington looked expectantly at Lady Warring, who had heard no more than half of it, between kissing the elder Miss Herington and replying with enthusiasm to her greetings. However, when Miss Herington had taken a seat beside her on the sofa Lady Warring turned her attention to Hilary and thanked her warmly for bringing her, in spite of Mrs. Colbridge and Charlotte.

"I am sure they will understand," she said, "when they consider that it has been the better part of a year since I have seen Allegra—"

"A year! It seems like a century, and I am sure it must have seemed even longer to Hilary," said Miss Herington, who in her own way was quite as outspoken as her sister, though twenty-five to Hilary's seventeen. It was in fact, the only point of resemblance between them, for Miss Herington was tall, with a head of flaming cropped curls and a kind of beautiful, aloof angularity that the spare high-waisted gowns fashionable in this year of 1815 became to admiration, while Hilary was small and rounded as a kitten, all enormous dark eyes and vivacity. "I consider," Miss Herington went on roundly, "that the way Aunt Colbridge has behaved towards her has been quite disgraceful. It is perfectly clear that she has been trying for months to goad that unfortunate nursery-governess into leaving so that she may tell my uncle she cannot find a proper one to take care of the children, besides its being quite unnecessary now that Hilary is old enough to be trusted with them. And she has not the least notion, it appears, of taking Hilary to London with her next month so that she may make her come-out along with Charlotte—which she faithfully promised me she would do when I agreed to leave Hilary with her at Chatt Park."

Lady Warring, who as Miss Herington's godmother had been acquainted with her from her cradle and knew what the ominously calm tone in which she had been reciting her sister's wrongs portended, said hastily, in a pacifying voice, that she dared say Mrs. Colbridge did not mean to be unkind.

"Yes, she does," said Allegra, not compromising in the least. "She has meant to be unkind to Hilary and me ever since we were in short-coats, probably because she thought that snubbing us would make people forget that her father was a wool-merchant—only it did not signify, of course, as long as Papa was alive. But it signifies a great deal now, and I will *not* have her turning Hilary into a drudge for those overbearing children of hers, so that she never so much as meets an eligible gentleman or has the least chance to make a suitable marriage!"

Lady Warring said, again with pacific intent but now with a slight agitation for which neither Allegra nor Hillary could account—which was not surprising, as they were quite unaware of the matter occupying her ladyship's mind—that perhaps it need not come to that.

"Well, if you are thinking of Aunt Hatherill," said Allegra, referring to the redoubtable dowager with whom she herself had been spending the eleven months since her father's death, "you had as well give over, darling God-mama, for you know that she can't endure Hilary and says it gives her the headache merely to be in the same room with her. And if you must know the worst," she went on, with the air of one triumphantly clinching her point, "I have had a furious quarrel with her over her odious Pug, whom she accused me of trying to give an inflammation of the lungs to by taking him for a walk when it was coming on to rain, and we went all through my dreadful want of conduct again in refusing Sir Dugald Macdougal, to say nothing of my lack of forethought in having been born a wretched female instead of a boy, so that I could not inherit Rolveston when Papa died. And the upshot of it is that she says she wishes to have no more to do with me. Which is a very good thing, as I have been moped to death all these months in Bath, doing nothing but playing whist, and taking Pug for his airings, and listening to that interminable Bath gossip!"

Lady Warring said, "Oh, dear!" rather faintly, but was obliged to admit that Allegra's words scarcely came in the nature of a surprise to her. When Sir Thomas Herington had died unexpectedly some eleven months before, leaving his daughters with no more than a very small trust fund to provide for them, his estates being entailed upon a distant cousin whom he had seen but once in his life, she had had the direst premonitions concerning the arrangements that hastily had been made for them—their maternal uncle, Mr. Colbridge of Chatt Park, having offered Hilary the shelter of his roof, much against the advice and wishes of his wife, a stout, underbred woman dotingly absorbed in her own large family, and Allegra going to the home of Sir Thomas's sister, Lady Hatherill, in Bath.

If it had been possible, Lady Warring would have offered them both a home at Questers; but she was a pensioner there herself since the death of her husband some half dozen years before, and she knew well that her son's wife, its present mistress, would never countenance such a scheme. The younger Lady Warring, who was given to a ferocious piety that expressed itself chiefly in bullying her husband's tenants and wearing all her new bonnets first in church, considered the plight in which Sir Thomas had left his daughters a direct judgment upon him for a misspent life—though to say the truth the worst of his excesses had been to keep a fine stable of hunters, which he could not afford—and would no doubt have looked upon any attempt to alleviate the lot of his daughters as something akin to flying in the face of Providence.

This point of view, Lady Warring was aware, was shared by both Mrs. Colbridge and Lady Hatherill, the latter's animus against her improvident brother being directed as well against her elder niece, Allegra, whom she had agreed, in a moment of unusual generosity seven years before, to take under her wing for a Season in London, the young lady's mother being then dead.

Allegra Herington, at eighteen, with a coltish eagerness imperfectly concealed beneath a set of brittle, rather haughty, and faintly absurd mannerisms that were a cloak for a shyness with which few people credited her, had made something of a stir in London Society, for, though not a Beauty, she *was* an original, and she had received offers from no fewer than three very eligible gentlemen before the Season was at an end.

But, to the fury of Lady Hatherill and the dismay of her friends, she had refused them all to bestow her affections upon an impecunious young lieutenant in a Line regiment, to whom Sir Thomas—never able to deny anything to either of his daughters—had reluctantly allowed her to become betrothed. However, this weakness upon his part had fortunately (in Lady Hatherill's eyes, at least) not culminated in the marriage of the two young people, for Lieutenant Neil Alland had been killed at Talavera in the following year. A month later Lady Hatherill was posting up to Cambridgeshire to press upon Allegra the suit of the Scottish baronet who, although rebuffed by her in London, still had hopes of gaining her hand. Miss Herington's recalcitrance upon this occasion had involved not only herself and her aunt, but also Sir Thomas and even the gentle Lady Warring, in a battle-royal, the latter being driven to inform Lady Hatherill plainly that no one of the slightest sensitivity could expect a girl in the first throes of grief over the death of her lover to accept the suit of another man.

The upshot of the matter was that Lady Hatherill had washed her hands of her brother's family and had gone back to Bath, and Allegra was left to devote what she considered—but never acknowledged—to a be a blighted life to her father, her younger sister, and Rolveston. No further thoughts of marriage appeared to have entered her mind, although even in the restricted circle in which she lived she had received, during the ensuing years, a pair of offers—one from the local vicar, a dedicated classical scholar, who admired her quick wit and intelligence, and the second from a hard-drinking military gentleman, a hunting companion of her father's, who, inspired by the stylish manner in which she had taken a regular rasper one November morning, had proposed to her immediately after the kill.

Now, at twenty-five, she seemed quite reconciled to the thought of being "on the shelf," as her cousin, Miss Charlotte Colbridge, with the superior air of a blonde and lovely seventeen, had described the outspoken, slender young lady in the *démodé* pelisse and plain bonnet who had descended upon Chatt Park that morning. But Allegra had not the least idea, Lady Warring saw—not with surprise, for she knew her goddaughter's strong loyalties and warm affections—of allowing Hilary's life to follow the same pattern as her own. This was a fact which Lady Warring, nourishing her own secret schemes for Allegra, felt was in her favour, for what Allegra would not do for herself she would do for Hilary, and thus might be brought to act, for once, in a manner serving her own interests.

Lady Warring bided her time, however, before bringing these schemes to light, enquiring instead whether Allegra had enjoyed the attentions of any gentlemen in Bath. This brought a wickedly humorous smile to Miss Herington's lips, and she said, with a marked access of the fashionable drawl which many people, including her aunt Colbridge, found so exasperatingly incomprehensible in a young lady whose manners were otherwise almost unbecomingly off-hand, that she had indeed enjoyed the attentions of several.

"There was General Brindle," she said, "whose gout

was so bad, poor man, that he required to be wheeled about in a Bath-chair; I believe he thought that I should make an excellent nurse-companion at the small cost of a wedding ring and a gown or two a year. And Mr. Oxtoby—a very worthy gentleman, I assure you, and not above thirty years older than I am myself—was, I think, on the very point of screwing up his courage and asking a lady's hand in marriage for the first time in his life, now that his mama had finally passed to her reward, when the unfortunate contretemps over Pug occurred and I was obliged to leave Bath."

Lady Warring smiled and said, "Now do—*do* be serious, Allegra dear. I realise that you were not able to go into Society on any large scale at Bath because of your being in mourning, but I *did* think that, since you at last had an opportunity to meet a considerable number of gentlemen, which you have never had here in the country—"

"Oh lord, Godmama, don't you know I am at my last prayers?" Allegra interrupted, without the slightest embarrassment. "Ask Charlotte; she did not scruple to tell her mama, without taking the trouble to be sure that I was out of hearing, that I was a positive antidote!"

Lady Warring said, with what was, for her, unusual asperity, that Charlotte Colbridge was a very thoughtless and ill-bred young woman. "And you are *not* an antidote, Allegra," she said. "Indeed, if you had only the proper clothes to set you off, I am sure you would be handsomer than you were at eighteen, for you have a great deal more countenance and manner than you had then."

Allegra laughed, but Hilary said loyally that it was quite true, and she expected there were any number of dukes and marquises who would be glad to marry Allegra, if only they might somehow get to know her.

"Not dukes, my dear," said Lady Warring, who was rather literal-minded. "There is only Devonshire, and he is quite deaf, I hear. But certainly there are gentlemen of unexceptionable birth and position who would consider themselves fortunate to obtain such a wife. There are few families in England, I believe, who can say that they have held their estates since the year 1125, when there is record that the first Herington settled at Rolveston, and Allegra has *all* the accomplishments, owing to Mlle. Jusseau, who I believe was an excellent preceptress, although a Frenchwoman."

This compliment made Allegra laugh again, and then ask if Lady Warring had any particular gentleman in mind to whom she intended to recommend her as a wife. Somewhat to her surprise, this sally caused Lady Warring to colour up and look exceedingly self-conscious; but before Allegra could enquire what she had said to put her godmother to the blush, Hilary had plunged into the conversation to say it was very odd that Lady Warring should have mentioned Cherry just then because, while walking to Questers, Allegra had disclosed the most exciting plan to her, and it was exactly their old governess who was involved in it.

Lady Warring shook her head in slight disapproval. "*Not* Cherry, dear Hilary," she said, "even though Mlle. Jusseau *is* unfortunate enough to have been christened with the quite inappropriate—and, I believe, unchristian—name of Cerise. She always disliked very much your calling her so, you will remember. And what can *she* have to say to anything, at any rate? I understand she has returned to Brussels."

"Oh yes, she has!" Hilary said eagerly. "But she has written to Allie and says she has opened a school there now, and she has offered her a position as English mistress. Isn't it splendid? Allie says we shall go abroad at once, and I need never live with Aunt Colbridge again."

"Oh no!" The exclamation broke distressfully from Lady Warring. She turned to Allegra. "*Not* a schoolmistress, my dear! You *shan't* dwindle to that!"

Allegra shrugged her shoulders, laughing again. "Dar-

ling Godmama pray do not be making a Cheltenham
tragedy of the matter!" she said. "It is a very good offer,
you know; Cherry appears to be getting on famously, and
has her house quite full of pupils, she says—all of them
jeunes filles de familles riches et élégantes."

"I don't care how rich and elegant they are!" Lady
Warring declared, with an unwonted lack of elegance on
her own part. "You are *not* to go to Brussels, Allegra!
You really cannot! Even if things were not so upset on the
Continent as they are just now, with Bonaparte returned
to France from Elba, it is quite out of the question!"

"But where *am* I to go then?" Allegra asked, looking
slightly puzzled and a little amused at her godmother's ve-
hemence. "Dear ma'am, do try to look at the matter sensibly! I cannot go back to Aunt Hatherill, and as to accepting my uncle's hospitality indefinitely, it really would
not do, even if Aunt Colbridge were not sure to think of
some scheme to have me out of the house before many
months had passed. And Hilary and I cannot possibly afford to set up an establishment of our own."

"Of course you cannot! That is not at all what I was
thinking of!" said Lady Warring. "But—but if you were
to marry—"

"Marry? Marry whom?" Allegra enquired in astonishment. "Good God, surely you have not taken seriously
that nonsense I spouted about General Brindle and Mr.
Oxtoby!"

"No, of course I have not! But if you were to receive
another offer—an offer for a very eligible gentleman
of good fortune and unexceptionable personal endow-
ments—"

"A gentleman of—Darling Godmama, what in the
world are you talking of? There is no such gentleman."

"Yes, there is!" declared Lady Warring, driven to the
wall. "I had not meant to speak to you of it quite yet, but
Derek Herington—that is, he is *Sir* Derek now, of course,
as your papa's heir—intends to make you an offer, and

... Oh dear! This is not at all the proper way to tell you, but don't you see what a splendid thing it would be for you, and that you cannot possibly go to Brussels now!"

Chapter Two

FOR A MOMENT after Lady Warring had finished speaking neither Allegra nor Hilary said a word; each was staring at her with an expression of the blankest incredulity upon her face.

It was Hilary who recovered herself first. "Oh, that is famous! Now we can go back to Rolveston and live there just as we did when Papa was alive!" she exclaimed, apparently considering the matter, in spite of her new grown-upness, exclusively from the point of view of her own and her sister's domestic arrangements. "Only are you *quite* sure," she continued, a slight anxiety entering her manner, "that he really does wish to marry Allie, Lady Warring? Because you know he has seen her only once, and that was years and years ago."

Lady Warring, made nervous by Allegra's continued silence, said that she knew that and naturally the matter could not in any sense be considered as settled, but that Sir Derek was inclined to look very favourable upon it in view of the fact that he had been the cause of their being thrown quite unprovided for upon the world.

"Not, of course," she said, "that that was in any way *his* fault, but at any rate he often heard me speak of Allegra while we—that is, Sir Archibald and I—were in St. Petersburg when Sir Archibald was attached to the Embassy there and he—Sir Derek, that is, only naturally he was *Mr.* Derek Herington then—was a junior secretary. And then when he came here," she continued, feeling more and more guilty under the accusing gaze of Allegra's fine eyes, "he called upon me and I told him even more about you, and—and, in short, my dear—"

Here Lady Warring, though a woman of sense and considerable intelligence, became so hopelessly entangled in her own explanations that she faltered and then fell silent altogether. But this did not help matters, either, for Allegra continued to look reproachfully at her, and it was Hilary, who, also finding her sister's behaviour somewhat unusual, finally enquired practically what the matter was.

"Do you mean that you don't want to marry Sir Derek?" she asked acutely, looking at Allegra. "Of course I don't remember much about his coming to visit us at Rolveston, because that was ages ago and I was still in the nursery, but I know you and Papa didn't like him above half. Only he really *is* very handsome, you know, though rather old, for he must be quite thirty-three or -four, and rich enough to buy an Abbey, Aunt Colbridge says, and I must say that those Welsh-bred horses he drives are perfect movers. You'd like them, Allie; really you would."

If Allegra had been in a mood to be sarcastic she would have said that it was not Sir Derek's horses, Welsh-bred or otherwise, who were proposing to marry her, so that whether she liked *them* or not really did not signify. But she was still too stunned by Lady Warring's disclosure to have a great deal of coherence in her mental processes, and was only conscious of a flaming resentment at the fact that she was apparently considered by Sir Derek as another of the chattels he had inherited along with Rolveston, coupled with the horrid anguish one feels upon having one's heart's desire dangled before one's eyes at a price one is not prepared—though able—to pay. More than anything in the world she wanted Rolveston and a chance for Hilary to have a happy, prosperous life, and both, it appeared, might shortly be hers if she would only swallow her pride and meekly accept the charity that was being offered her.

But the remembered vision of a very arrogant and very handsome young man in exquisitely cut coats and boots polished with such loving care by the highly superior valet who had accompanied him to Rolveston that one could see one's face in them, a young man who had scarcely troubled to conceal his amusement at their plain country ways and who had appeared frankly bored both with his thirteen-year-old cousin Allegra and with the company invited to meet him, made her think—at this moment, at least—that even the Colbridges would be preferable to him as the source of her daily bread. Not, she told herself, rationality suddenly intruding upon those dire reflections, that it was at all probable that she would even be offered the choice. It was more than likely that what had actually happened had been that Lady Warring, led on by her deep affection for her goddaughter, had hinted at the suitability of such a match to Sir Derek, and then had taken the vague civility with which a man of fashion might have put down the impertinence of such a suggestion as a tacit acquiescence to her plans.

Considering the matter in this light, her displeasure with Lady Warring abated and she felt sorry for her for being so taken in. But she could not forbear saying to her with some severity that she really should not have made such a suggestion to that poor man.

"But I *didn't* make the suggestion. *He* did," Lady Warring defended herself. "And as for being poor, I don't know why you should call him so, my dear, for his grandfather left him a really splendid fortune—his father, you know, died when he was quite young—and Sir Archibald often told me that he had a brilliant future before him in the diplomatic service as well, only he has decided to give that up, at least for the present, so that he may put Rolveston to rights again."

Allegra disregarded the latter part of this speech, being already quite aware that Sir Derek's grandfather had succeeded in increasing the handsome fortune his own father had amassed in the East India trade to the point that his death, some half dozen years before, had made his grandson what Sir Thomas had sarcastically called "the richest Herington ever to wear shoe leather." She directed her words instead, with some incredulity, to Lady Warring's insistence that it had been Sir Derek himself who had broached the subject of the marriage.

"Surely you are mistaken, ma'am!" she argued. "Sir Derek can have no wish to marry me. He scarcely deigned to notice me when he visited Rolveston when I was a girl, and there has been no communication between us since, except on the most necessary matters of business arising after my father's death. You must have misinterpreted something he said—read too much significance into a chance remark—"

"But it was *not* a chance remark! I tell you, we discussed the matter for a quarter hour at the least!" Lady Warring said, with what was, for her, unusual asperity. "You need not think me such a perfect wigeon, my dear, as not to be able to distinguish in a matter of such importance whether a man is in earnest or not! He came here as soon as he heard you were returning to Chatt Park to consult me on the subject, said he felt his responsibility, as the last of his name, to marry, and enquired whether your affections were otherwise engaged—"

"Oh, *did* he!" Allegra interrupted, her wrath rising once more. "How *very* considerate of him, dear ma'am! I should rather have imagined that—whether they were engaged or not—he would have expected me to forget such a paltry matter as that, once *he* had thrown his handkerchief at me!"

Lady Warring looked at her in some perplexity. "But

really, my dear, I cannot see why you are putting yourself into such a taking!" she protested. "Naturally he cannot be expected to suppose that a young lady in your situation in life would refuse such an eminently suitable offer! He is, as you must know yourself, a very personable man, with an excellent understanding and easy, unaffected manners; his fortune is unexceptionable, and his birth quite equal to your own—"

"He is also, apparently," Allegra said bitingly, "if you will forgive my pointing it out to you, ma'am, a conceited coxcomb to believe that I should jump at his offer, no matter *how* rich and personable he is. As for his feelings—I should wonder very much if he had any, to be approaching the matter of marriage in this gothic manner! This is not the eighteenth century, you know; even the Princess Charlotte was not obliged to go through with an arranged marriage, and *she* is the heiress to the throne!"

Lady Warring, who had never until this moment had the least sympathy with Lady Hatherill in regard to the affair of Sir Dugald Macdougal, suddenly began to feel that there was something to be said, after all, for that redoubtable lady's position. That a young woman in such dire straits as Allegra was in now should be contemplating refusing so advantageous an offer of marriage, on the grounds of missish scruples about feelings, quite passed her comprehension. Lady Hatherill, she remembered, had said that she would like to shake her niece, and, though Lady Warring had no idea of doing such a thing herself, it did occur to her that a gentleman of Sir Derek Herington's athletic physique would be quite capable of carrying out such an assignment, and that her headstrong goddaughter might not be the worse for it.

Sir Derek, however, was not present to press his suit or to enforce Allegra's compliance by the rather stringent methods Lady Warring had in mind, and matters were made even worse at this moment, from her point of view, by Hilary's entering the fray with the loyal statement that if Allegra thought Sir Derek horrid, of course she need not marry him, and it would probably be much jollier in Brussels, at any rate.

But to her surprise and relief this statement of support, instead of confirming Allegra in her obstinate course, had the opposite effect. She suddenly stopped looking angry and began to look thoughtful; after a moment she even looked a little guilty.

"Oh, dear!" she said ruefully. "I daresay I am being a perfect ninnyhammer and losing my temper as usual, when I ought to be folding my hands and looking meek and grateful, and saying, 'Yes, sir; as you please, sir,' like a well-trained housemaid who knows her place."

"Allegra!" Lady Warring expostulated, laughing in spite of herself. "You know nothing of the sort is expected of you. But all the same, to be flying up into the boughs because Sir Derek has it in mind to do something perfectly proper and sensible—"

"Perhaps he will think better of it when he sees me," Allegra said hopefully. "After all, you cannot have told him about my *curst disposition,* ma'am, or he would surely have taken fright and hedged off at once. And as a man of fashion he will no doubt object to marrying such a worri-crow as—according to Charlotte—I have become."

"You have become no such thing!" Lady Warring said indignantly. "But I *do* wish, my dear," she added after a moment, "that you will not feel it necessary to keep to your blacks when you meet him, for it is quite proper, you know, so many months after your poor papa's death, for you to go into something ligher, which would be far more becoming to you."

This was a statement that could not be considered entirely just, however, as black set in startling relief the dazzling fairness of Allegra's complexion and the flaming crown of her hair in a way that grey or lavender quite failed to do. But Lady Warring had the old-fashioned prejudice against hair the colour of well-burnished copper, which she privately considered fit for no female except one of easy virtue, and she could never be brought to admit that Allegra's was anything but a sedate auburn.

The subject of clothes, however, was one that all three ladies could enter into as a happy escape from the disagreement that had so unfortunately marred their meeting, and in a discussion of the enormous Oldenburg hats that had become all the crack since the visit of the Tsar's sister, the Grandduchess of Oldenburg, to London during the past Season. Sir Derek and his intentions were temporarily forgotten.

It was, in fact, only as Allegra and Hilary arose to take their leave that Lady Warring broached the subject again, enquiring rather nervously if it would be convenient for Allegra to call upon her the following day, as she believed it might be more comfortable for her to meet Sir Derek for the first time at Questers rather than in the company of Mrs. Colbridge and Charlotte at Chatt Park.

"Though I am sure he will be very happy to wait upon you there if you should prefer it," she added a trifle anxiously, seeing Allegra's expression of sudden hauteur, which still represented her response to inner uncertainty or embarrassment, exactly as it had when she was eighteen.

But to Lady Warring's relief the expression vanished almost at once as Allegra, wickedly mischievous once more, said lightly, "Dear me, Godmama, surely you don't expect the man to make an offer the instant he claps eyes upon me!" But she agreed with no further argument to come to Questers on the following day at any hour that would be convenient to Lady Warring, and then went away with Hilary.

The road back to Chatt Park led past Rolveston, the eastern lands of which lay adjacent to Questers. Allegra, passing by the great iron gates beside the lodge where, as a child, she had often been called in to be regaled with hot gingerbread by old Mrs. Binter, looked nostalgically at the drive curving away inside them and thought what she would give to be able to follow it up to the elegant seventeenth-century raspberry-brick house that had replaced the Tudor manor built by earlier Heringtons and then walk inside as she had been used to do, amid the shabby Chippendale furniture and faded Chinese scenic wallpaper she knew so well.

But it did no good to think of that unless she also thought of marrying Sir Derek Herington, who by this time had probably used a small part of his enormous wealth to rehang all the saloons with imported velvets and damasks and replace the Chippendale furniture with pieces in the currently fashionable Egyptian style, including sofas with crocodile legs, japanned bamboo chairs, and lamps made to resemble huge water lilies. So she gave herself a little mental shake and asked Hilary, who had been indulging in an agreeable monologue ever since they had left Questers on the horridness of her aunt Colbridge and the difficulties of choosing between the delights of going to Brussels and living at Rolveston again, where the Binters were now.

"The Binters?" Hilary said. "Oh, they have gone to live with their married daughter in Cambridge."

Allegra stopped short, her brow darkening abruptly. "I daresay," she said ominously, "that Sir Derek has turned them off?"

"Well—yes," Hilary acknowledged, looking at her sister in some surprise.

"Without provision?"

Hilary's eyes widened even further. "Good gracious, you *don't* like him very much, do you, Allie?" she said. "Well, I should think that settles the matter then, and we really had better go to Brussels. But as to the Binters," she added, fair-mindedly, "Sir Derek *didn't* turn them off without a penny, if that is what you mean, for they came to say good-bye to me before they left and Mrs. Binter told me that he had behaved *very handsome* towards

them and they were to have a pension for as long as either of them lived. So at least he is *not* a nip-squeeze, if
that is what you have been thinking."

She then took the bloom off this compliment by adding
conversationally that nobody in the neighbourhood liked
Sir Derek, at any rate, which caused Allegra, who had
come to an irrevocable decision to die rather than show
sufficient interest in Sir Derek to ask questions about him,
to betray her better self and enquire why not.

Hilary shrugged. "Well, of course the village people all
dislike him because he has got Rolveston instead of us,"
she said, considering the matter. "And Lizzie Morford
and Charlotte don't like him because they were making
sheep's eyes at him in church last Sunday and he paid
them not the least attention. And Mr. Brownridge detests
him because his horses quite take the shine out of his—
oh, but Hubert *does* like him," she added, referring to her
cousin, Mr. Hubert Colbridge, aged twenty, "because he
says that his cravats are slap up to the nines, and that if
only he can succeed in learning his style of tying them he
will be the envy of all the Town Tulips when he goes to
London next month. Only I don't think he will—succeed,
that is—because he is driving the laundry-maids to dis-
traction, ruining half a dozen neckcloths every day before
he is able to tie one to suit him, and even so his never
look in the least like Sir Derek's."

Allegra was obliged to admit that the reasons alleged
for Sir Derek's being held in dislike in the neighbourhood
were scarcely sufficient to blacken his character, and
found her own disapproval inclined to dwell more particularly upon the single virtue that had been attributed to
him—that of having a skilled hand with a neckcloth—as
evidence that he was still the foppish exquisite she
remembered from a dozen years past. But she discovered,
to her great disappointment in herself, that her curiosity
concerning Sir Derek was not content to satisfy itself with
these crumbs of information, and led her instead to

enquire in an offhand manner whether he was then a proud, disagreeable sort of man, that he was held in such universal disfavour.

"Oh, no!" said Hilary equably. "In fact, I thought he was perfectly agreeable when he came to Chatt Park to return Uncle's call—though he *did* treat me," she added with some slight resentment, "as if I were a child, and said I was quite unlike what he remembered *you* to have been at my age. I told him that I was seventeen, and that I was certain *you* could have been no more than thirteen when he had seen you."

This brought a laugh from Allegra, who said, "Poor Hilary!" and then, drawing her arm through her sister's, walked on, determining to dismiss the subject of Sir Derek from her tongue and mind.

But this turned out to be a matter that presented a good deal of difficulty, as the Colbridges were all full of discussion of Rolveston and Sir Derek at dinner. She was obliged to receive a complete account of that gentleman's carriages (from Charlotte), cravats (from Hubert), and expenditures (from Mr. Colbridge), and from her aunt a discussion of the inordinate length of time it had taken after her father's death before he had so much as set foot in Rolveston—"eight full months, my dear, and though everyone knows he was in Brazil when your papa died and so could not have been expected to attend his funeral, it *does* appear that he might have arranged his affairs so that he could have come sooner, for it is very bad for the neighbourhood when an estate is left with no one but an agent to look after it. And Mr. Rudwick is growing quite past his work, you know."

Mr. Colbridge, a stout, severe-looking man, said that Rudwick should have been pensioned off long since—a statement to which Allegra, who had determined not to enter into the discussion, took exception both on Sir Thomas's account and on Mr. Rudwick's, for the old agent had been a part of her life as long as she could remember, and held in much affection and esteem by Sir Thomas. So she discarded her resolution and said warmly that her father had known very well that it would break Mr. Rudwick's heart if he were dismissed from his post, and that Mr. Rudwick knew more about Rolveston and its lands than any man in the county, which store of knowledge she hoped Sir Derek would have the good sense to value.

"Well, he hasn't turned him off," said Mrs. Colbridge, "which I must say is a great surprise to me, for he has not kept any other of your papa's people on—not," she added, "that there were many left to keep, dear knows, when your papa died, for I always did say that he cared nothing about the house as long as his stables were in proper order, and not even keeping a housekeeper, so that everything fell upon *you,* Allegra, and only three maids in a house that needs at least six, I will always maintain, for Rolveston is not at all a convenient house like Chatt Park—everything so old-fashioned, and not even a good closed stove in the kitchen."

And she glanced around complacently at her own dining room, where everything was the latest, the largest, and the most ornate specimen of its kind that money could buy. For Mr. Colbridge's modest house had undergone constant enlargements and refurbishings ever since he had married his wealthy wool-merchant's daughter some twenty-odd years before—much to the dislike of his late brother-in-law, Sir Thomas Herington, who remembered it as it had been when he had courted Mrs. Colbridge's sister there, a pleasant, sturdy stone manor house surrounded by cornfields and sheep-walks and making no pretence at being a Gothic castle or anything else but an honest country gentleman's residence.

Allegra and Hilary, who were inured to slighting references to Rolveston from their aunt and cousins but would probably have sprung to its defence anyway if they had not just been made to feel so acutely that it no longer be-

longed to them, looked at each other, and Allegra contented herself with saying tersely that they liked Rolveston
just as it was.

"Well then, I daresay you won't like it now at all," said
Miss Charlotte Colbridge triumphantly, for she was the
sort of girl who, in spite of her angelic fairness, was never
happier than when she was scoring a point off someone,
"because John-coachman says he has heard at the Rolveston Arms that Sir Derek intends bringing a positive army
of workmen from London to refurbish it, and I expect, as
he is a man of fashion, he will wish to furnish it in the
style of Chatt Park, which you and Hilary are always turning up your noses at, though you don't *say* anything."

Allegra sat bolt upright, saying—as Charlotte had truly
observed—nothing at all, for she had been far too well
brought up by her very proper governess, Mlle. Jusseau,
to let her tongue loose upon the clothes, houses, or ap-
pearances of people who annoyed her, except under ex-
treme provocation. And, at any rate, the person she
would have liked to attack at that moment was not her
cousin Charlotte but Sir Derek Herington, who was the
one responsible for turning the home she loved into what
would probably be a haven for every monstrous fashion in
home furnishings to take the fancy of what Sir Thomas
would unequivocally have called a damned caper-mer-
chant. Thinking about this, she scarcely had the patience
to sit quietly through her aunt's fretful animadversions
upon Sir Derek's not choosing to seek her counsel in the
matter of refurbishing Rolveston.

"For I told him when he called," she said, with an
injured air, "that, as we had all been through the same
sort of thing with Chatt Park, *we* were in the very best
position to advise him as to how to go about the matter. I
even offered to give him the direction of the silk ware-
house in Huntingdon where I purchased the material for
the green-striped draperies in the Green Saloon, but he
went away without taking it and so, as I said to Mr.

Colbridge, he will be properly served if Rolveston is not in the highest kick of fashion when the work is done, for being out of the country as he has been for so many years he cannot be expected to know what the mode is."

Allegra, listening to her aunt rambling on, felt that it was something in Sir Derek's favour that he had at least not allowed himself to be bullocked into accepting her advice about Rolveston, but then thought gloomily that he had probably too many horrible ideas of his own as to what was to be done with it to need to borrow any from Mrs. Colbridge, and wished that her aunt would choose some other subject of conversation.

But when she did, it scarcely improved matters, for she turned her attention from Sir Derek only to start the topic of the expense to which she would be put by having not one niece now, but two, added to her household. This was a subject in which her husband could enthusiastically join, for both—happily for the domestic harmony of Chatt Park—belonged to that class of persons who are quite willing to lay out considerable sums on ostentatious display but grudge any expenditures that do not advance their consequence in the world.

So Allegra and Hilary were treated to a thorough discussion of the high price of candles at sevenpence the dozen and butcher's meat at sevenpence the pound, causing Hilary to declare to her sister, when they retired later that evening to her small north bedchamber, into which a second bedstead had been introduced to accommodate Allegra as well, that she felt as if every mouthful she ate were being weighed up and added to some monstrous total of indebtedness to her aunt.

"I know," said Allegra, standing at the window and looking out with an intense expression upon her face, as if she were coming to some momentous resolution—which indeed she was. "I truly don't think I can bear it—and even if I could for myself, I can't for you. I shall simply have to marry that wretched man, I expect. It would be folly not to, for if I go schoolmistressing in Brussels there is no telling that I shall ever be able to do anything more for you than to put you to following in my footsteps there, to say nothing of things being so upset on the Continent just now that I have been wondering if I am mad even to think of taking you there. Whereas if I marry Sir Derek, we shall be rich and comfortable and may send Aunt Colbridge and her butcher's meat to the devil forever!"

At which agreeable prospect Hilary applauded, and even Allegra looked gratified for a moment.

"Only," she added, gloom descending upon her once more, "when I think of his walking in Papa's shoes at Rolveston and turning the house into something just as hideous as this one is—"

"Perhaps," Hilary said hopefully, "if you marry him you can make him change it back."

But Allegra, who had few illusions about the influence of a bride married for convenience, said that she did not think so and that they would probably have to settle just for being able to live at Rolveston, no matter what horrible things Sir Derek had done to it, and then went to bed but not to sleep, having entirely too many matters of importance upon her mind to be able to settle herself for peaceful slumber.

Chapter Three

ON THE FOLLOWING morning Allegra, with an appearance of calm that quite belied a violent inner reluctance, set off for Questers and her meeting with Sir Derek. She had

prevailed upon Hilary to remain at Chatt Park, feeling
that the addition of her outspoken sister to the party
would only add to the embarrassment of what she considered to be a visit of inspection by her prospective
bridegroom; but she might not have succeeded in carrying
the day in this regard had it not been for Mrs. Colbridge's
insistence that Hilary was needed to look after the nursery
while she and Charlotte paid morning calls in the neighbourhood.

So Hilary had been obliged to content herself with su-
pervising her sister's toilette, advising the addition of an
ostrich plume preserved from more prosperous days to
the sage-green bonnet that had been Allegra's latest purchase before Sir Thomas's death, and a relaxation of the
severity with which her elder sister usually attempted to
restrain the tendency of her thick cropped hair to curl
about her face.

"And I _do_ wish you hadn't allowed Miss Minifie to
make that frock for you," she had added, looking disap-
provingly at the sage-green walking dress, with its rows
of ruching and knots of ribbon, that had been made for
Allegra by the local dressmaker more than a year before,
"because she has not the least idea of à la modality! In
fact, if you want my opinion, Allie, that gown is downright _deedy!_"

"Well, it is my best, so if I am not to wear black, it will
have to do," Allegra had replied philosophically, affecting
a nonchalance that she did not at all feel; for being obliged
to appear before Sir Derek Herington, whose ideas of
fashion she could not conceive to be anything but of the
highest particularity, in an outmoded frock seemed to her
at the moment the horridest fate that could befall her.

But there was no help for it, and summoning up, to
bolster her self-assurance, all her remembrances of Sir
Thomas's disdain of the elegant stripling who had visited
them at Rolveston years before, she went off to Questers
in the despised sage-green gown.

It is bad enough, when one has screwed up one's courage to the point of doing something one wishes abominably one had not to do, to find, upon arriving at the sacrificial spot, that it can be done immediately, with no further time available for reflection on the disagreeable scene to be enacted. But when one is obliged to sit waiting, so to speak, for the axe to fall, as Allegra had to do for an interminable quarter hour in Lady Warring's sitting room, indignation is apt to get the better of dread. It was not surprising, therefore, that by the time Sir Derek was shown into the room her feelings had been worked into such a state that she was able to control them only by adopting the pose of rather absurdly chilly hauteur that had served to hide a fierce shyness at London *ton* parties more than half a dozen years before.

"Allegra, my dear," said Lady Warring, addressing her goddaughter rather nervously when Sir Derek had exchanged civilities with her, and sternly repressing a tendency to flutter at this inauspicious start of the romance she was fostering, "I daresay you may not recognise your cousin after so many years, but this—this is Sir Derek Herington, and, Sir Derek, this is my dear Allegra."

Sir Derek bowed and took the hand that was extended to him, saying civilly how happy he was to meet Miss Herington again. He did not look particularly happy, however; Lady Warring, who knew him fairly well, would have said rather that he looked startled and even a trifle daunted for a moment, in spite of his excellent control over his features, and hoped that Allegra would not be able to read his expression as accurately.

But to say the truth Allegra was in no case at the moment to take in anything at all about Sir Derek except the rather overwhelming fact that he was one of the handsomest men she had ever seen—tall, dark-haired, bronzed, and broad-shouldered, carrying himself with an easy, athletic grace, and possessing an intent, humorous smile that was calculated to make even the severest damsel's heart give a disturbing little jump.

Allegra's heart gave that little jump and then, in self-defence—for she was feeling more disastrously inadequate than ever, before all that lazy, assured male charm—settled down immediately to try to find some flaw in it with which to build her own self-confidence a little. Sir Derek's neckcloth served for a beginning—as elegantly and intricately arranged as she remembered Mr. Brummell's to have been when she had been privileged to meet that famous dandy during her London Season. And one could go on to the mulberry coat, so exquisitely fitting that it was impossible to imagine that its owner could have got into it without the assistance of his valet, the buckskins that displayed to advantage a well-formed leg, and the mirror-polished boots with their fashionably long white tops. He had not changed in the least, she told herself—knowing full well at the same time that there was nothing of the self-centred arrogance of the youth she had known in this calm, attentive stranger, that what she was seeing now was a man of sense and experience, not a wilful, overindulged boy.

Sir Derek was saying politely that he had already had the pleasure of renewing his acquaintance with Miss Hilary Herington at Chatt Park, and had been looking forward to the elder Miss Herington's return to that part of the country. This promising attempt to open the conversation, however, met with only the briefest of smiles from Allegra, accompanied by a slight inclination of the head that would have done credit to Royalty, but that actually represented only her firm conviction that Sir Derek had by this time already set her down as a provincial dowdy and was keenly regretting the impulse that had led him to consider making her an offer of marriage. It was Lady Warring who was obliged to step into the breach with a remark to the effect that she had always considered it a great pity that Sir Derek had never had the opportunity to become better acquainted with his Cambridgeshire cousins.

"I entirely agree with you, Lady Warring," Sir Derek said frankly. "But the fact seems to be that my grandfather unfortunately had such a bitter quarrel at one time with Miss Herington's grandfather—over, I believe, a hideous gold watch the size of a large turnip that each of them expected to inherit from a mutual uncle—that they never spoke to each other again and weren't very willing to have their descendants do so, either."

This anecdote, unexpectedly dropped into the conversation, caused Allegra to forget her discomfort for a moment and exclaim interestedly, "Oh, is *that* what it was about? Papa never quite knew; he said he had only been told by my grandfather that *your* grandfather was a shocking rogue who had cheated him out of some sort of inheritance. I daresay that means your grandfather got the watch?"

"Yes, I believe he did," Sir Derek admitted, observing with some appearance of interest upon his own part the sudden sparkle of animation that had momentarily lit up Allegra's hazel eyes and was giving her face the special eager radiance that had ensnared so many susceptible gentlemen in London seven years before.

But the next moment the radiance had vanished and he saw again only the aloof young woman in the sage-green frock decorated at all the wrong places to set off properly her slender figure, who was looking at him as if she despised him. Which she did, in truth, although chiefly at the moment she was despising herself.

Lady Warring said helpfully that family quarrels were so unfortunate, and usually over the most ridiculous causes.

"You *must* have got on with Sir Thomas if you had known him, I believe," she said to Sir Derek. "You both are—were—which should I say?—so very fond of horses."

She then despised herself, in turn, for speaking so
inanely, and all three of the participants in this very halt-
ing conversation sat in silence for several moments, each
racking his or her brain for something to say next and all
wishing they were somewhere as far away as possible
from where they were.

Sir Derek, who as a diplomat was the most used to
dealing with situations in which momentous matters had
to be settled without anyone's being permitted to make
the least reference to them, was the first to recover
himself and said that he had observed that the stables at
Rolveston had been kept in excellent condition, and that
he remembered having been very handsomely mounted by
Sir Thomas on the occasion of his visit there. He looked
at Allegra as he spoke, upon which Lady Warring, seeing
that that unco-operative young lady showed no signs of
taking up this conversational gambit, said in the slightly
exasperated tone of a fond mama prompting an obstinate
child, "Allegra is a splendid horsewoman herself, Sir
Derek, and was always used to hunt with Sir Thomas."

She then looked expectantly at Allegra, who, sitting
bolt upright in her chair, her hands clasped in her lap and
a vengeful look upon her face, said nothing at all. She
felt, in fact, very much like an applicant for a housemaid's
post being invited to expatiate upon her skill in dusting
and polishing and turning out a grate, and, like the independent Cambridgeshire countrywomen among whom
she had grown up, would have none of such self-display
and so remained mute.

Lady Warring, in desperation, and feeling more and
more that Lady Hatherill had been quite right in calling
her niece—as she had upon one memorable occasion—a
plague sent from heaven on her, began to talk about St.
Petersburg.

A quarter of an hour later Allegra, so sunk by this time
in a sense of the enormity of her behaviour that she was
incapable of saying anything even in answer to a direct

question except by concealing her feelings behind a mask of brittle artificiality, rose abruptly and said that she must go.

"Oh, dear—must you?" said Lady Warring, not knowing whether to feel relieved or furious.

"Yes," said Allegra uncompromisingly. She looked at Sir Derek, who had risen upon her doing so, and hated him for being so tall, and so coolly collected, and more than anything for the look of faint amusement she saw in his dark eyes. "Too, too delightful to meet you again, Sir Derek," she said to him in a tone of entirely unconvincing patronage, and bestowed a brilliant smile upon him that was meant to convey her utter indifference as to whether he wished to marry her or not.

She then walked out of the room, and was half-way down the stairs, with a hot flush of mortification at her own stupidity upon her face, when she became aware, to her dismay, that her aunt Colbridge and Charlotte were standing in the lower hall in conversation with Lady Warring's granddaughter, Susan Warring.

All three were regarding her with the most intense interest.

"Here she is now," said Miss Susan Warring, aged seventeen, and Charlotte's most intimate friend that year; and she giggled expectantly.

"Yes, indeed!" said Mrs. Colbridge, managing to sound envious and patronising at the same time. "Well, Allegra, I must say, you are a sly thing! Never breathing a word of all this to us last night!"

"Never breathing a word of what?" asked Allegra, feeling that she had undoubtedly gone mad from the strain of the past half hour and that if she did not find an opportunity quickly to go off alone somewhere and put her shattered self back together again she would inevitably fall into strong hysterics.

"Why, Sir Derek, of course!" said Mrs. Colbridge. "Susan has just been telling us that he intends making you an offer. Well, well, I daresay you are in high croak over it, though I *will* say that I should never have expected such a thing myself, as high a form as he sets himself on, so that I made up my mind from the start it was an earl's daughter at least he'd throw his handkerchief to, which his own mother was, you know—"

"Dear ma'am," Allegra interrupted, quite aghast at this monologue, in Mrs. Colbridge's relentlessly penetrating voice echoed clearly through the large hall, "pray do not be jumping to conclusions! I don't know what Susan may have told you—"

"Oh, you need not bother to deny it!" Mrs. Colbridge said, with a knowing little laugh. "Susan chanced to be outside old Lady Warring's sitting room yesterday while she was telling you and Hilary about Sir Derek's intentions, and you won't try to make us believe you have not been upstairs with him just now, for we know better— don't we, Susan?" she asked, with meaning archness.

Susan, looking self-conscious all over her large, highly coloured face, said defensively that she had just happened to be passing by her grandmama's sitting room and couldn't help hearing, and that everyone knew Sir Derek's phaeton and horses and she couldn't help, either, seeing them standing outside.

Allegra took firm hold of herself. "Well, that is no excuse for spreading such *untrue* gossip," she said to Susan, in the most minatory tone she could manage. "I wish that you will make your apologies to anyone you may have repeated it to, and tell them there is not a word of truth in it!"

"But I heard Grandmama say it herself," Susan said mulishly. "I couldn't be mistaken!"

Charlotte cast a superior glance at her cousin's unbecoming frock and bonnet. "Perhaps," she said pertly, "Sir Derek means to cry off, now he has seen you, Allie. Is that it?"

But Mrs. Colbridge said, nonsense, gentlemen who

married for convenience did not put their hearts in their eyes, as other gentlemen did, and she had heard of such cases before, where the heir had felt himself obliged to do something for a daughter left unprovided for on his predecessor's death.

"Which is very proper of him, I am sure," she said, "and you must be excessively grateful to him, Allegra, for offering you such a splendid position in life, which you certainly could never have aspired to otherwise."

And to Allegra's horror she said she would go upstairs at once and ask Sir Derek to come to dinner at Chatt Park on the very first day that suited him, evidently feeling that the blessed prospect of having both her nieces taken off her hands compensated for her chagrin at seeing Allegra walk off with such a prize as Sir Derek while Charlotte was still unmarried.

Nothing that Allegra could say would induce her to relinquish this scheme. The younger Lady Warring, upon whom Mrs. Colbridge and Charlotte had come to call but whom they had not found at home, walked into the hall at that moment, returning from a shopping excursion, and was at once drawn into the discussion. Allegra, with all the sensations of being in a nightmare in which events too dreadful to contemplate were tumbling over one another in their haste to happen to her, gave up the battle and ignominiously fled.

Half an hour later, her face burning from rapid walking and the remembrance of the scenes through which she had just passed, she burst in upon Hilary, who was preparing to take the nursery party for a walk, and demanded her instant attention.

"Good gracious, what is the matter? Whatever has happened?" asked Hilary, looking in astonishment at her sister's stormy face.

She sent the children, to their rebellious wails of protest, back to the nursery, and dragged Allegra into their small bedchamber.

"Now, what *is* it?" she asked again. "You look as if the world had fallen upon you! Was it very dreadful?"

"Oh, it was *awful!*" said Allegra, jerking her bonnet-strings apart and throwing that unbecoming article of apparel upon the bed. "I have never had anything more dreadful happen to me in my life! That wretched little Susan Warring was listening at the door yesterday when Lady Warring was telling us about Sir Derek's having it in mind to offer for me, and she has told Aunt and Charlotte about it, and her mother, and will certainly spread it all over the county as fast as she can. And Aunt intends to ask him here to dinner, and—oh, Hilary, what in the world am I to do?"

And to Hilary's intense concern—for she had come to look upon her sister as a fount of unfailing wisdom and a rock of strength—she turned a harassed face of appeal upon her.

Hilary, who had a great deal of character though not as yet much sense, immediately rose to the occasion.

"Well, the first thing you must do is to sit down and tell me quickly what has happened," she said, "for if I know those odious little monsters, they will be down upon us in five minutes or else have set the house afire by that time. Did you see Sir Derek?"

Allegra's face, already somewhat flushed, grew pinker. "Yes," she said, and stopped.

"Well, *yes* what?" Hilary asked impatiently. "Didn't you like him?"

Allegra shrugged her shoulders and said after a moment, with an unsuccessful attempt at airiness, that she dared say he was very handsome.

"Of course he is handsome," Hilary said, her impatience increasing. "But did you *like* him?"

"No," said Allegra. The airiness vanished suddenly and she said in a despairing voice, "He thinks I'm a dowd—which I am—and a fool—which I was, all the while he was trying to talk to me—and he doesn't in the least wish to marry me, now that he has seen me. Only he will probably feel he must, with every prattle-box in the county knowing of it now. And that's all there is to it. I shall go to Brussels."

She then sat down, looking as if she were prepared to go to the stake before abandoning this determination, but immediately complicated matters by asking Hilary in rather uncertain tones whether that was what she thought she ought to do.

"No, I don't," said Hilary firmly. "I mean to say, if it's only Aunt Colbridge and Charlotte and that sneaksby Susan Warring that have upset you, I shouldn't let *them* thrust a spoke in my wheel. They were bound to behave like cats as soon as they heard of it, anyway, for you know they will be eaten up with envy when you are Lady Herington and have so much pin money and carriages and jewels that you will cast them all quite in the shade. Only," she added, looking more doubtfully at her sister as she saw something suspiciously like tears in Allegra's eyes, "of course, if you have taken Sir Derek in aversion—"

"I haven't taken him in aversion," said Allegra, taking her handkerchief from the reticule and blowing her nose defiantly. "There was nothing *to* take in aversion. He behaved perfectly properly; *I* was the one who made a show of myself!" She said bitterly, *"No* one would wish to marry a female who never opened her mouth except to say something idiotish, and who looked as if she had never so much as *seen* a fashionable frock in her life!"

"Well, I told you about that dress," Hilary said resignedly, "but you *would* wear it. But *do* be sensible, Allie! This was only the first time, you know. When you meet him again, things may go off better."

"Not if it's here, at dinner with Aunt Colbridge," Allegra said, with a shudder. "Good God, you know that she is bound to save up all the awkward things she can think of to say for an occasion like that!"

Which made Hilary laugh, and then Allegra laughed too, and the morning's tragedies suddenly seemed much less soul-searing than they had a moment before.

They then began to discuss the possibility of purchasing some really *nice* ribbons, before Mrs. Colbridge's dinner party for Sir Derek took place, to replace the sad primrose-coloured ones that drooped all over Allegra's frock —a discussion continued while they both took the nursery party on its walk, but considerably interrupted by Master Humphrey Colebridge's getting into a violent altercation with his sister, Miss Cecelia Colbridge, and requiring the attention of both young ladies to keep the peace between them from that time out.

Chapter Four

As ALLEGRA had predicted, forty-eight hours had not passed before the news that Sir Derek Herington had it in mind to offer for her had spread through the neighbourhood, to the point that, when she called in at the receiving office in the village to ask for the letter she was expecting from Mlle. Jusseau, even Mrs. Tansill, the elderly postmistress, had a meaning word and smile for her on the subject of the changes shortly to be expected at Rolveston.

"For haven't we all been saying, miss," she remarked to her, "that it didn't make a bit of sense for a single gentleman to be putting out such a deal of money on the place just for himself like, with no plans for the future?"—and then told everyone afterwards, with a great deal of satisfaction, how Miss Allegra had coloured up like a poppy and all but snatched the letter from her hand and run off.

This was quite true, for Allegra was by this time in such a state of nerves over the highly anomalous situation in which Sir Derek's intentions and Miss Susan Warring's disclosures had placed her that she had felt quite incapable of silencing Mrs. Tansill with the cool competence she would ordinarily have used if such an insinuation had been made to her.

In the same way she found herself powerless to halt the plans being made at Chatt Park by Mrs. Colbridge for the dinner party to which she had bidden Sir Derek—plans which included the importation of a group of musicians from Huntingdon to play for the dancing that she intended the younger members of the party to enjoy after dinner. Allegra, seeing her aunt's list of guests growing to include every eligible family in the vicinity, and looking forward in the liveliest dismay to a gathering at which each word or gesture of hers or Sir Derek's would be scrutinised with ruthless curiosity by everyone present, fled to her godmother for support, quite forgetting for the moment that she was avoiding Lady Warring's company for fear of finding Sir Derek in it.

But to her great relief she learned from Lady Warring, when she arrived at Questers, that Sir Derek had gone to London for a few days upon business, and was not expected back until the very day of Mrs. Colbridge's dinner party.

"He is putting himself to a great deal of trouble over the estate, you know," said Lady Warring, looking at Allegra with the anxious air of a parent who is wondering if a favourite child is going to be difficult over something meant entirely for its own good and rather expecting that it will be. "I daresay it must be irksome for him at times, having to deal with hiring workmen and matters of that sort, because he has no proper agent, of course, with Mr.

Rudwick being so old. And then I understand some of the village people have been quite unaccommodating, because naturally they all remember your papa, and appear to feel it very much that Sir Derek has stepped into his room while you and Hilary have had to leave Rolveston."

Allegra, inspired by the devil, said that no doubt the thought of such inconveniences had weighed with Sir Derek when he had decided to make her an offer of marriage, and added that if he chose to take the alterations he was making in the house and estate out of Mr. Rudwick's hands he was properly served to find himself in difficulties.

"I am only surprised," she went on, "that he has not turned Mr. Rudwick off entirely. But I daresay he does not care to make himself *quite* odious to the neighbourhood by doing that."

Lady Warring, looking even more anxious at the militant sound of this speech, said that Mr. Rudwick's rheumatism had been troubling him a good deal during the past winter, and then, unable to control herself, although she knew quite well she would later wish that she had, asked Allegra if she did not think Sir Derek a very personable man.

"Very," said Allegra, with the disinterested air of one to whom the subject was of only the most infinitesimal concern.

"I particularly admire his manners," Lady Warring persevered, driven by her own demon. "So open, so easy—they cannot fail to please. His understanding, too, is excellent; Sir Archibald often remarked to me on his grasp of the most complicated matters, and I believe the Duke of Wellington himself was hoping to have him with him in Vienna when he returned from Brazil—but of course your papa's death changed all that."

Allegra looking perversely unimpressed by this tribute to Sir Derek from the Hero of Salamanca and Talavera, said she dared say Sir Derek must find a small Cambridgeshire village very dull indeed after spending so much time in the capital cities of countries all over the world, and thereupon rose to take her leave, having neglected entirely to broach the question that she was burning to ask—namely, whether Sir Derek had confided to Lady Warring his impressions of the young lady he was considering taking as his bride.

But it turned out to be quite unnecessary for her to do this, for, coming upon Miss Susan Warring in the hall, she was accosted by that young damsel at once and desired to say if she wished to hear what Sir Derek had said to her grandmother about her before he had left Questers on the occasion of his last visit.

"No!" said Allegra, honourably and even almost truthfully, for she had a dire suspicion, from the smug look upon Susan's face, that the information she had to impart was scarcely flattering. "Were you on the listen again, you odious little wretch? I wonder what your mama would say if she knew!"

"Well, you won't tell her," Susan said, with the comfortable reliance of the criminal nature upon other people's rectitude. "I say, don't you really want to know? He said you were a rather formidable young woman and not at all the way he remembered you."

"I have told you, I haven't the least desire to hear anything that Sir Derek said," Allegra said, furious with herself to find that she was colouring, and she walked on down the stairs, hearing Susan giggling above her.

After that, any charitable feelings she might have had towards Sir Derek went away entirely, and she said to Hilary when she returned to Chatt Park that she believed it would be best after all if she wrote to Mlle. Jusseau at once and told her that she had decided to accept her offer to employ her as English mistress at the Pensionnat Jusseau.

"Did you see Sir Derek at Questers?" asked Hilary, who had suddenly found herself obliged to become very

astute and grown-up, owing to the remarkably foolish way
in which her elder sister had been behaving ever since the
subject of Sir Derek's offering for her had been broached.

"No," said Allegra. "He is gone to London."

"Well, that's all right then," Hilary said with satisfaction. "You can't have taken him any more in aversion if
you haven't seen him again. If you want my advice, you'll
wait until you've got to know him a little better before
you make up your mind about it one way or the other,
because I have been thinking about it and it seems to me
that it is only right we should have Rolveston back again.
So it would be particularly silly for us to lose the chance,
unless Sir Derek turns out to be an archfiend or something like that."

Allegra, who was feeling at the moment that *archfiend*
was too good a name for a man who had called one "a
formidable young woman," no doubt in that odiously cool
manner that Lady Warring admired so much, yet found
herself for some reason unable to confide this latest evidence of Sir Derek's perfidy to her sister and was obliged
to brood over it in secret. But as Mrs. Colbridge's plans
for her forthcoming dinner party included turning over
most of the work involved in it to her elder niece she really had not much time for brooding—which was perhaps
as well, considering the state of her affairs.

On the evening of the dinner party she was obliged to
dress in great haste, owing to having to go down to the
kitchen at the last moment and cope with the cook, who
was close to hysterics over an impending disaster to the
jelly of marasquino forming one of the dishes of the
lengthy second course that Mrs. Colbridge had ordered.
As a result, her cheeks were wearing a becoming colour
and her bright curls were escaping in a fetchingly rebellious manner from the high knot in which she had hurriedly dressed them when she came downstairs to greet
the arriving guests.

Sir Derek was one of the first of these, having made up

his mind, it seemed, to be agreeable and atone for any slights the Chatt Park ménage might feel he had previously cast upon it. Apparently for this purpose also he had attired himself in the satin knee-breeches and long-tailed coat which, although indispensable for an evening party in town, were sometimes discarded by younger gentlemen in the country in favour of more casual dress. And his scrupulous observance of this point of etiquette was indeed quite successful, for it resulted in Mrs. Colbridge's being made happy by what she considered a tribute to the tonnishness of her party, and in young Mr. Hubert Colbridge's being set in so much awe of the mastery that had achieved such an intricately elegant style of tying a cravat that he was almost stunned, and scarcely touched his dinner while trying to puzzle out exactly how Sir Derek had done it.

Sir Derek, however, seemed quite oblivious both of the burning envy his sartorial elegance was arousing among the younger male members of the party and of the equally burning interest being displayed by the ladies in his manner towards Miss Herington. The latter, conscious of appearing to excellent advantage that evening in a gown of amber crape and the topaz set that had once belonged to her mother, was able to behave almost normally towards him during dinner, where she had of course been placed beside him by Mrs. Colbridge. And although Sir Derek's manners, as Lady Warring had truly said, were too excellent for him to make it obvious that he was surprised and pleased by the change he saw in her from the young woman to whom he had been presented on their disastrous first meeting, she had the distinct impression that he was feeling interested, which she found for some reason quite exhilarating.

So she told him about her stay with her aunt Hatherill in Bath, which city she was happy to find he disliked as cordially as she did, and learned that he even knew her aunt Hatherill as well, having been presented to her, he said, at a London party many years ago, when she had quite depressed his pretensions by remarking that he had not the look of any Herington she had ever seen or heard of.

"She made me feel as if my parents had not been properly married, at the least," he said, "or even worse, as if my poor mama, who I understood was the soul of propriety though I never knew her, had engaged in sordid intrigue in wholesale lots, with the result that it was hardly to be wondered at that I had such a distinctly un-Herington appearance." Allegra choked and he looked at her in kindly enquiry. "I beg your pardon, ought I not to have said that?" he asked. "If so, consider it unsaid, but there is a look in your eyes, besides what Lady Warring has told me about you, that made me rather believe you don't care a great deal for Mrs. Grundy."

"Oh, I don't!" Allegra said, finding this description of herself a great deal more satisfactory than being called "a formidable young woman," and smiling at him. "And I know *exactly* what you mean about Aunt Hatherill. She always makes me feel as if I belong in a home for fallen women if I so much as go shopping in Milsom Street without taking along a footman or a maid. And, after all, I *am* five-and-twenty, you know."

At which staggering acknowledgement from an unmarried female Sir Derek said, "Really?" very gravely, but with a look in his dark eyes that made her feel he was laughing at her.

But it was not unkind laughter and she would have gone on talking to him very happily if Mrs. Colbridge on his other side had not claimed his attention at that moment. And then, looking around the table, she saw, with a sudden return to the dire realities of her situation, that she was being observed by a score of pairs of eyes all pretending to be doing so quite by accident, and devoted herself at once with ferociously single-minded attention to Mr. Brownridge on her right, who talked to her at very boring length about a splint he thought his new hunter was throwing out.

As the dinner—a highly elaborate one, wending its way inexorably through soup, fish, removes, entrées, roasts, and entremets to a Savoy cake and coffee creams in cups of almond paste—went on for a good two hours, it required some ingenuity upon her part to prevent her conversation with Sir Derek during this time from becoming interesting enough to draw the attention of the other diners down upon them. But by dint of perseveringly giving only monosyllabic answers to all his most promising conversational attempts she managed to do so, and Mr. Brownridge, whom everyone disliked for his habit of boring on forever about his horses and horsemanship, was agreeably surprised to find out how Miss Herington hung on his words and told his wife later that her stay in Bath had certainly improved her a great deal.

Allegra herself, conscious of having puzzled and snubbed Sir Derek, disappointed her aunt's guests, and incurred Hilary's severe disapproval, evidenced by several meaning frowns directed at her by that young lady across the table, escaped at the meal's end with a harried feeling of relief to the drawing room. But her relief was short-lived: the drawing room had already been cleared for dancing, and as the musicians tuned their instruments preparatory to striking up the first set, she saw Sir Derek approaching her with the unmistakable air of a gentleman bent upon asking a lady to dance. She turned about hastily, almost colliding with her aunt as she did so.

"Merciful heavens, Allegra!" said Mrs. Colbridge peevishly. "*Do* look what you are about! You have trod upon my lace, I do believe!"

Allegra hurriedly begged her pardon, and was about to move away when her aunt, suddenly perceiving Sir Derek bearing down upon them, took her arm and prevented her from doing so.

"Why, my dear," she said, in a voice quite altered for

Sir Derek's benefit, "wherever are you off to in such a hurry? Here is Sir Derek coming to ask you to stand up with him for the first set, I'll be bound!"

And she gave Sir Derek an arch look that made Allegra want to kill her, particularly as she appeared to believe that she should be grateful to her for what she had done.

Sir Derek said civilly that it had indeed been his intention to ask Miss Herington to do him the honour of standing up with him for this set, though looking at her so quizzically as he did so that she immediately transferred her ire to him.

"Oh, no!" she disclaimed, finding to her fury that she was colouring and speaking in a somewhat disjointed fashion. "That is—I mean to say—should you not rather ask Charlotte—Miss Colbridge?"

But Charlotte's mama at once disposed of any claim her daughter might have to expect Sir Derek to lead her, instead of Allegra, into the set.

"Lord, my dear, it's not Charlotte Sir Derek is casting out lures to!" she said, with what Allegra could only describe as a leer in Sir Derek's direction, but a very genteel one, befitting her purple turban and large diamonds. "But you know what girls are, Sir Derek," she went on, generously admitting Allegra into a category from which she had outspokenly excluded her for almost the past half dozen years. "They *will* hang back and behave in this missish way, when if we only knew the truth, they're most wishful to step forward!"

And with a smart tap of her fan upon Sir Derek's arm she marched off to join another group of her guests, leaving no doubt whatever in Allegra's mind that, if Sir Derek had previously been unaware of the fact that his intentions towards her were known to others, he must certainly be apprised of it now.

She could not now avoid, however, allowing him to lead her into the set, and accompanied him silently across the floor. He was silent, too, until, as they took their places, he unexpectedly enquired if she had rather not dance.

"Because in that case," he said, looking down at her with his glinting smile, "I shall have the opportunity of discovering whether your resolution to converse with me only in monosyllables at dinner was due to a burning desire to hear more of Mr. Brownridge's exploits on the hunting field or had some more personal bias behind it. Speaking for myself, I find him a bit overenthusiastic on the subject of his own merits—and those of his horses— but there is no accounting for tastes, I believe."

Allegra was betrayed into a gurgle of laughter. "Yes, isn't he *dreadful!*" she agreed; and was at once taken up by Sir Derek, who said firmly, "That settles it, then. It *is* personal. Would you care to sit down with me on that very uncomfortable-looking sofa and explain to me exactly why you find conversation with me so much to be avoided?"

Allegra said with quite unnecessary emphasis that she would not. "I mean," she added hastily, "I should much prefer dancing. I really am very fond if it—only I have been out of the way of it, you see, since I have been in mourning."

She then heard with relief the first notes of the music sounding, and devoted herself to her performance of the steps with all the zeal of a young lady attending her first evening party.

She was not surprised to find Sir Derek an excellent dancer, and if it had not been for the self-consciousness caused by her awareness that she and he were again the object of the most unblushing interest on the part of the other guests she would have enjoyed herself very well during the ensuing half hour. Sir Derek, evidently resigning himself to the impossibility of carrying on any more personal conversation with her during a country dance, talked cheerful commonplaces to her during the

set, and when it came to an end went off, as in duty
bound, to solicit Charlotte's hand for the next, while Allegra thankfully accepted the offer of a youth in awe-inspir-
ingly high shirt-points, who—as youths frequently did—
thought her directness dashing and said daring things to
her. At any rate, he thought they were daring, and as Allegra, who was thinking about Sir Derek, answered him
somewhat absentmindedly instead of laughing at him, as
she usually did at young gentlemen who seemed disposed
to make cakes of themselves over her, he was quite
pleased with himself and retired at the end of the set with
the determination to ask her to stand up with him again
and to cut out Sir Derek.

As it happened, however, cutting out Sir Derek turned
out to present no particular problems. Apparently that
observant gentleman had no more desire than had Allegra
to pander to the ungentlemanly curiosity of the rest of the
company—if such an adjective can be used to describe an
emotion evinced chiefly by the ladies—and so retired
from the dancing lists after standing up with Charlotte
Colbridge to devote himself to cards in the small drawing
room, much to the disappointment of all the censorious
dowagers and romantic young ladies who wanted to see
him paying violent court to Miss Herington so that they
could talk about it later.

Even Allegra was a little disapointed, though she would
have died rather than admit it, and found herself growing
angry at Sir Derek all over again for going off in that cool
masculine fashion and leaving her to face the barely
concealed satisfaction of her cousin Charlotte as she
flaunted her own conquests to her between sets.

"I *told* Mama that it was all a hum and Sir Derek
hadn't the least intention of offering for you," said Charlotte, who was examining her blonde curls, threaded with
a silver ribbon, in a pier glass while awaiting the return of
one of her own swains from the dining room, whither he
had gone to procure a glass of orgeat for her. "And

Lizzie Morford's aunt," she added unkindly, "who lives in London, told her that old Lady Eastham told *her* that Sir Derek had a perfectly scandalous creature—but of course perfectly stunning as well—in keeping when he was in Lisbon, and everyone *knows* about the tons of beautiful women there are in Brazil, where he was last."

She then walked off with her swain and her glass of or-geat, while Allegra looked at her own flushed and lovely—but to her at the moment highly unsatisfactory—reflection in the glass, wondering why in the world a man like Sir Derek would ever wish to marry a female who looked like that, and then told herself that it did not matter to her in the least if he did not.

So when Sir Derek emerged from the card room presently, just as the musicians were preparing to play a waltz, and came up to request the pleasure of leading her on to the floor, she gave him no immediate response but only flirted her fan instead, despising herself for adopting once more the brittle mannerisms of their first encounter, but quite unable at the moment to find any more satisfactory way of dealing with the situation.

To her surprise, however, Sir Derek neither persisted in his solicitations nor took offence and walked off. Instead, he stood regarding her with a slight, thoughtful frown for a moment, and then, his brow clearing suddenly, pronounced enigmatically but with an air of complete satisfaction: "Lady Hatherill."

"I beg your pardon?" said Allegra blankly.

"Not at all," said Sir Derek politely. "Shall we waltz?"

She found her hand in his, his arm about her waist, and before she could gather her wits to protest had been swept off to the centre of the floor. She looked up at him, gasping a little, but prepared to do battle.

"I don't believe I said I should care to waltz with you, Sir Derek!" she said.

"Didn't you?" Sir Derek glanced down at her, his eyes glinting under lazy lids. "And yet here we are, waltzing together after all. Life is full of surprises—is it not, Miss Herington?"

"Some of them," said Allegra with much meaning, "very disagreeable ones! And I should like very much to know what you meant by saying, 'Lady Hatherill!' in that particular way!"

"In what particular way?" enquired Sir Derek, whirling her in expert circles down the room. "You dance very well," he added approvingly. "I don't know why, but one expects a tall girl to ride well, but not to dance well—"

"Thank you!" said Allegra crushingly. "But you have *not* answered my question, you know!"

"Well, you haven't answered mine, either," Sir Derek said reasonably. "I said, 'In what particular way?' and you didn't tell me."

"In a very *smug* way, then," Allegra said, grudgingly acknowledging his point, and would have gone on, but he interrupted her to say, "No—was it? That's odd. As a matter of fact, it ought to have sounded triumphant."

"Triumphant?" Allegra's feet almost missed a step.

"Why, yes," said Sir Derek. "Do watch yourself, my dear girl, or we shall disappoint all these nice people who are displaying such a generous interest in our performance. Isn't *triumphant* what one feels when one has solved a riddle?"

"*What* riddle?" asked Allegra, goaded into expressing her baffled curiosity when she would much have preferred taking exception to his admonition on her dancing.

"The riddle of how a refreshingly natural girl is turned into a mannered young woman, quite against her own better judgement, I should believe," Sir Derek said, with amiable frankness. "And now, you see, I have hit upon the answer—therefore the triumph. Do you know, when you flirted your fan at me just now in that irritatingly affected way that I had thought up to that time was the exclusive property of middle-aged former belles, I suddenly seemed to see Lady Hatherill quite clearly before me? She *was,* I take it, once an Accredited Beauty? But you really shouldn't allow your own very satisfactory manners to be corrupted by hers, you know."

Allegra listened to this quite outrageous speech—which was uttered, moreover, in such a perfectly *dégagé* way as to make it even more outrageous—with the feeling that it was actually possible that she might explode. At the same time she was conscious of a bitter wish that Lady Warring, who had been so high in her praise of Sir Derek's manners, were present to hear what that much admired gentleman was capable of saying to a perfectly innocent female whom he had dragooned into waltzing with him—and the upshot of the matter was that she discovered she was either going to hit Sir Derek or begin to laugh. Much to her own disapproval, she found herself doing the latter.

"That is much better," said Sir Derek, looking at her with a cordiality that made her regret exceedingly that she had not given way to her alternate impulse. "As far as I know, I am not particularly cowardly, but if I did not quail before the look you directed at me just now it was only because I am persuaded that you would not so far forget Lady Hatherill's training as to attack me in the midst of your aunt's party, with quite twenty people looking on with their eyes starting out their heads the better to see us. And at any rate," he added with some satisfaction, "now I know that I was mistaken."

"About what?" Allegra could not prevent herself from asking, though she wished very much that she were not the sort of person who lets curiosity get the better of her.

"You," said Sir Derek. "When I first saw you at Questers the other day, I was quite sure you could not be the same girl I remembered from my visit to Rolveston, and that a wicked fairy had probably—as I understand their practice is—substituted a changeling for you at a rather late date. Now I know how mistaken I was."

"But you—you scarcely noticed me when you were at Rolveston!" Allegra protested, feeling oddly breathless and hoping that it was merely the rapid movement of the waltz that was giving her this peculiar sensation.

"Oh, no!" Sir Derek contradicted her calmly. "I daresay I gave that appearance, for I believe I was quite an insufferable young puppy at that age, and would have considered it much beneath my dignity to betray an interest in anything but the cut of my coat or the set of my neckcloth. But I assure you that I have never been unobservant. And now," he added, as the music showed signs of winding to a close, "since I may have no further opportunity for a private word with you this evening, I shall ask you now if I may call upon you tomorrow, when perhaps we can do something about satisfying the very evident expectations that we appear to be rousing in the minds of all these good people."

Allegra thought in the utmost indignation, "If this is his way of making me an offer—!" and, looking up to see Sir Derek's dark eyes amusedly and very comprehendingly gazing down at her, flushed vividly.

"Yes—that is—if you *truly* wish to," she found herself saying disjointedly, and then thought despisingly that even Susan Warring would have managed the matter with more aplomb and waited for Sir Derek to say that he didn't care to after all.

But he only thanked her gravely, and the music ended and he went off, leaving her with the feeling of having been through a cyclone or some equally exotic storm.

Not long afterwards the guests began to depart, and as soon as the last of them had gone she fled upstairs, feeling that to be obliged to hear her aunt's comments on her dinner party and Sir Derek, after everything else she had borne that evening, was really too much to ask of her. Unfortunately, she could not so easily escape Hilary, who came upstairs directly on her heels, perched herself on the foot of her bed, and demanded to be told what had occurred between her and Sir Derek.

"I was glad he asked you to stand up with him the second time," she said, "because Charlotte was being horrid about it and said he wouldn't. Do you like him any better now?" she concluded, looking hopefully into Allegra's face.

Allegra said she didn't know but he had asked permission to call on the following day—upon which Hilary's eyes widened.

"Oh, Allie!" she said in an awed voice. "That means he really is going to ask you, doesn't it?"

"I don't know. I expect so," said Allegra in a gruff, offhand voice, and then wondered to her own astonishment and horror if she was going to begin to cry.

But she resolutely quelled this missish impulse and said instead that it was late and they had better go to bed—an opinion reinforced by the great yawn which, in spite of her intense interest, escaped her young sister at that moment.

Chapter Five

IF IT HAD been Allegra's intention to remain at Chatt Park all the following day in expectation of Sir Derek's visit, Mrs. Colbridge—who of course knew nothing of that gentleman's plans—soon put an end to this determination by informing her that she wished her to go into the village that morning and make several purchases for her. Hilary, who was in the room when this request—or rather command—was conveyed to her sister, at once offered to go herself, and, when told that she would be required to look after Master Humphrey and Miss Cecelia Colbridge, showed signs of mulishness, to the extent that Allegra feared she might even blurt out to her aunt the reason why it was imperative for her elder sister to remain at home that day.

Allegra gave her a warning frown. "No, no, I shall be glad to go," she said, and told her sister later, in a hurried conference at the head of the stairs, "It not at all likely that Sir Derek will come here so early in the day, goose! I believe a Tulip of the Ton considers it a dreadful solecism to be seen out of his bedchamber before noon. And, at any rate, if I am obliged to sit for one more half hour listening to Aunt congratulating herself upon the success of her dinner party and asking leading questions about Sir Derek's intentions, I shall undoubtedly go stark raving mad, in which case I shan't be able to marry him anyway."

Which made Hilary laugh and agree to allow Allegra to go without lodging any further protests with their aunt, although she was still doubtful, it seemed, of the wisdom of this course.

Allegra accordingly set off towards the village a few minutes later. To say the truth, she was glad to be able to get off by herself for a while, and enjoyed her brisk walk in the fine spring air, which seemed to brush some of the cobwebs out of her head that had accumulated there during a rather wakeful night. In the morning sunlight, the fancies that had disturbed her half-waking dreams seemed quite absurd, and she told herself practically that nothing could be more suitable than for Miss Allegra Herington, spinster, aged five-and-twenty, to accept the unexpected good fortune that was to be offered her and agree to become Lady Herington. As for Sir Derek himself, he was undoubtedly a most personable man, of excellent understanding and apparently amiable disposition, and if there was no attachment on either side, they were both, after all, beyond the age of youthful ardours and would no doubt come to a quite satisfactory arrangement with each other once the knot had been tied.

So lost was she in this agreeable sense of euphoria that she quite failed to note a middle-aged groom who strolled out from the stables of the Rolveston Arms as she passed that respectable hostelry and touched his forelock to her, until he spoke her name.

"Miss Allegra!"

She turned. "Oh—it's you, Pember," she said, recognising her father's head groom for many years, and smiling at him. "Well, I am very glad to see you! My uncle told me you were working at the Arms now. How do you go on here?"

"Tolerable well," said Pember, who was a stolid, rather lugubrious-looking man, but had endeared himself to the late Sir Thomas by understanding horses—or so Sir Thomas had maintained—better than anyone else in the county. "And much better for seeing you, miss," he went on, with an unwonted approach to warmth. "I heard tell as how you was back at home again—not to say as it's *home,*" he added darkly, "when there's a stranger at Rolveston and you and Miss Hilary at Chatt Park, where there's never a horse in the stables fit for you to ride and what Sir Thomas would say to it I don't know!"

"Sir Thomas would say that it's the luck of the game, and there is no use crying over what can't be helped," said Allegra, smiling. She added encouragingly, "Come, it is not so bad, Pember! You have a good place here, and as for my sister and me—we shall come about, never fear!"

"Ay!" said Pember, but in such a dubious tone that he might have been saying the reverse. "I've no doubt of *that,* Miss Allegra, for you was always one to lay hold o' things and sort them out till they went the way you wanted them to go. But you're young still—"

"And *you* are not so very old," Allegra retorted, mischief in her eyes. "I am sure I have been told you have been walking out with one of my aunt's housemaids—Emily, isn't it?"

Pember coloured beetroot-red and was heard to mutter somewhat unintelligibly that that was his own affair and good girls were hard to come by these days and that Emily was as flighty as a rabbit.

"But there's others not so well off as me, Miss Allegra," he went on, returning to his original direly forboding manner. "Happen you've not heard the news about Mr. Rudwick, now?"

"About Mr. Rudwick? What about Mr. Rudwick?" asked Allegra, immediately on the alert, and chiding herself because she had not been able, in the press of events since her return to Cambridgeshire, to visit the old agent.

"Only that he's to be turned off," Pember said, with gloomy relish.

Allegra stared at him. "Impossible!" she exclaimed. "I heard only the other day that Sir Derek had no intention—at least, I understood—"

"A-ah!" said Pember. "Intentions is one thing and doing's another, Miss Allegra. There's a jumped-up fellow came down from London with Sir Derek only yesterday, and with my own ears I heard Sir Derek say that he was his new agent and would be stopping here at the Arms till Mr. Rudwick's house was ready for him."

He broke off, observing with satisfaction the flush of indignation that had arisen in Allegra's face.

"If that is true—" she began impetuously.

"Oh, it's true, right enough, Miss Allegra," Pember assured her. "And it will break Mr. Rudwick's heart, so it will, to have to leave Rolveston at his age. Many's the time I've heard him say myself that it was the only home he'd known for forty years, and he hoped to lay his bones there when his time came—"

"Yes. I know all that, Pember," Allegra said, and she cut the conversation short and went away, in such a flame of anger at Sir Derek and pity for Mr. Rudwick that she walked straight past the Honourable Mrs. Brownridge, who was sitting in her carriage outside the draper's, as if she didn't exist.

Her anger was still high when she returned to Chatt Park, and the sight of Sir Derek's phaeton standing before the front door merely added fuel to the fire. She entered the house and consigned the parcels she had brought from the village into the hands of the butler, untied the strings of her bonnet and cast it upon a Buhl table beside the drawing-room door, and walked without hesitation into that apartment, where she found her aunt in conversation with Sir Derek.

"Oh, Allegra—here you are at last!" said Mrs. Colbridge, nicely divided between unjustified irritation at Allegra for not being at home to receive Sir Derek's call and the desire to appear amiable before her guest, which made her behave in an even more foolish way than usual. She rose, giving a knowing smile to Sir Derek, who had also risen on Allegra's entrance. "And now," she said, to him, "I'll be bound you and Allegra have a great deal to say to each other, Sir Derek, so I'll just run off and see that she's matched my embroidery silks properly. *Not*," she added with dignity, suddenly struck by the thought that Sir Derek might consider she was shirking her duty in leaving her niece alone with him, "that I should do so if it was Charlotte, you understand, for after all *she* is not out yet and I believe I know a mother's place as well as any woman alive. But Allegra is her own mistress. though a guest in my house and my niece, so that in a way I stand to her in the place of her mama, but still it is all quite different from Charlotte's case—"

Sir Derek, looking fatigued, for he had been enduring his hostess's conversation for a full quarter hour, said he quite understood and on no account was she to allow such scruples to detain her.

"Such a delightful man!" said Mrs. Colbridge, who had once heard a marchioness say this and had been saving it up for use upon the proper occasion, and she thereupon bustled out of the room.

Sir Derek stood regarding Allegra, observing with an appearance of approval the particular radiance that excitement of any kind always gave to her, for, as she had not yet spoken a word, he had no way of knowing to what ominous cause the flush on her cheeks and the brilliance of her eyes were due.

"Shall we sit down?" he enquired after a moment, as she made no move to seat herself or to indicate that he should do so. "I imagine that your aunt's rather direct tactics may have discomposed you, but I assure you that they need not. After last night neither of us can have the slightest doubt as to what is expected of us—which I cannot say that I am entirely sorry for, as it makes my task the easier. I have not, you see, been much in the way of making offers of marriage up to this time—"

He broke off, looking at her with an expression of slight enquiry as she continued to stand regarding him without speaking or moving. If she had been in less of a blind rage she would have realised with some gratitude that he was doing his best to relieve, by his light tone, what he felt must be her embarrassment over her aunt's mortifyingly obvious manoeuvre in leaving them alone together; but she was in no mood to notice such fine distinctions, and immediately decided to take offence at his words and to add the levity of his manner to the sum of his other iniquities.

With her usual directness, she would have liked to lunge at once into the matter of Mr. Rudwick, but this turned out to be impossible as Sir Derek—continuing, it appeared, to interpret her silence as embarrassment—approached and took her hands, saying in a somewhat gentler tone, "Forgive me; I seem to be going about this very clumsily. But I believe there is no need for either of us to feel constrained. Lady Warring, I hope, has acquainted you with my feelings. Your father's death has placed both of us in a situation in which marriage seems advisable, and marriage to each other eminently suitable. What you would look for in such a marriage I cannot tell, but let me assure you that I shall strive to give you no cause to regret your decision if you will consent to have me—"

"Well, I *won't* have you," said Allegra, finding her voice at last and snatching her hands from Sir Derek's. She rushed on, goaded by the expression of complete astonishment that had appeared upon his face, "I *couldn't* marry a man who has behaved in such an *unfeeling* way to poor Mr. Rudwick, and—and if you wish to know the truth I have held you in dislike from the start! I suspected what you were when you turned the Binters off, only I never thought that *anyone* could be so cruel as to send that old man away from Rolveston. Not," she went on even more incoherently, and backing away from Sir Derek as if she were afraid he was about to try to take her hands again, "that he would be happy living there now in any case, with you turning everything upside down and probably furniture with Egyptian crocodiles on it in the drawing room—"

"One moment!" Sir Derek's voice, with an unfamiliarly stern note in it, suddenly cut across this tirade. Allegra, startled in her turn, broke off and Sir Derek went on, "Your having taken me in dislike is something I may regret, but cannot quarrel with, Miss Herington. But it appears that you are laying other matters at my door—"

"Yes!" said Allegra, recovering from this momentary check and going on as impetuously as before. "I have just learned that you brought a new agent with you from London yesterday, Sir Derek, and that Mr. Rudwick is to be put out of his place. But I daresay that is quite what I should have expected, for I believe it is far beneath the dignity of a Tulip of Fashion to trouble himself with the feelings of the people who serve him—"

"Not quite!" said Sir Derek, who, though he appeared

to have recovered from his initial astonishment, seemed to be restraining his own temper now only with some difficulty. "Acquit me, Miss Herington: I may not have been bred up at Rolveston, but, believe me, I have every intention of honouring my obligations to those who have served it."

"Rolveston! What do you know of Rolveston?" Allegra flung at him.

"Not much, I admit, but enough to know what it needs in the way of management and when a man is past his work. Rudwick himself—"

"Oh, yes! I know what you are going to say! He offered himself to resign his post. Of course he did! But if you had the least thought for anything but your own convenience, you must have known that it would break his heart to be turned off! But of course you do not care for that! All you care for is making Rolveston into some odious sort of showplace to add to your consequence, and—and getting yourself a comfortable wife, who will not interfere with you in any way—"

"If by 'a conformable wife' you mean yourself, Miss Herington," said Sir Derek acidly, "let me assure you that you have strangely mistaken your own character! However, on that head I shall say nothing! It was my own folly to think of offering marriage to a woman with whom I was barely acquainted—"

"Yes!" Allegra interrupted, in a shaking voice, "it *was* folly, Sir Derek! *And* intolerable arrogance, to believe that you had merely to throw your handkerchief and I should be overjoyed to accept your offer. Perhaps in *your* world this is the way such matters are arranged, but let me assure you that nothing would be more repugnant to me than to enter into a marriage with a man for whom I have neither the slightest regard nor—nor respect," she concluded, surprised and a little impressed by the quite sensible flow of her own words, for inside she was a seething turmoil of disagreeable emotions.

At the same time, however, she felt a certain exhilaration in venting her pent-up feelings upon Sir Derek's head, and in the knowledge that she had discomposed him quite as much as he had discomposed her. It even disappointed her a little that at this stage in the conversation he regained control of himself and said to her in a very even tone, "Then I have only to apologise to you, ma'am, for inflicting attentions upon you that are so obviously unwelcome. Pray accept those apologies and be assured that you will never again be troubled by further conversation from me on this matter!"

"Good!" said Allegra, and then, feeling that she was not living up to the lofty tone the interview was suddenly taking on, said in a voice that she tried to make as remote and cool as the one her opponent had used, "I am very sorry to have been obliged to give you pain, Sir Derek—"

"Well, you haven't!" retorted Sir Derek, rapidly descending from his own self-imposed high level of conduct and regarding her with what she could only feel was unmitigated dislike. "As a matter of fact, I am very grateful to you, Miss Herington. The idea of going through life with an unreasonable female doesn't precisely charm, you know!"

"I am *not* unreasonable!" said Allegra hotly.

"No?" said Sir Derek, with what she immediately characterised as a most ungentlemanly bluntness. "Have a talk with Rudwick, pray, and then be so good as to tell me what you think of *that* statement!"

And he gave her a very curt bow and walked unceremoniously out of the room.

For a moment Allegra, left on the field of victory, stood feeling much as the Duke of Wellington must have felt when he saw the French retreating at Vitoria. But then the appalling realisation of what she had done fell upon her. She had refused Sir Derek; she had given up Rolveston forever; she had condemned Hilary—no doubt awaiting in innocent expectation abovestairs the happy outcome of her interview with Sir Derek—to a lifetime of penury and obscurity.

"Oh, good God!" she said, aghast, and both her hands flew to her burning cheeks. "What a *widgeon* I have been!"

She had no time in which to engage in self-recrimination, however, for at that very moment her aunt entered the room.

"Well?" she said eagerly. "Well, my dear? Is it settled then? I saw Sir Derek go off; really, he *should* have stopped to speak to me, or to your uncle—not that Mr. Colbridge is at home just now, for he is gone to Huntingdon—"

"For heaven's sake, ma'am," said Allegra, quite distracted by her aunt's obvious assumption that the match had been made up between herself and Sir Derek, "pray do not be jumping to conclusions. There could be no reason for Sir Derek to feel he must speak to my uncle—"

"No reason!" Mrs. Colbridge looked at her incredulously. "Why, whatever do you mean, my dear? Has he not made you an offer, then?"

As Allegra, unwilling to betray either herself or Sir Derek, remained silent, trying to hit upon some reply to her aunt's questions that would satisfy her curiosity without informing her as to what had actually occurred, Hilary came into the room, looking enquiring and mischievous.

"Well?" she demanded, echoing Mrs. Colbridge's words. *"Did* he—"

"Yes—no!" said Allegra, wondering if it might not be simpler to drown herself than to be obliged to answer any further questions. "That is—oh, do go away, both of you, and leave me alone!" she begged, in a voice that in spite of herself she could not keep quite steady.

Hilary and Mrs. Colbridge looked at each other. The latter was the first to speak.

"Well!" she said indignantly. "If that isn't the shabbiest

thing that ever I heard of! To raise all your hopes and then not speak out, after all—well, all I can say is that my poor papa may have been a wool-merchant, but he would have scorned to act so scaly to a female!"

"But he didn't—I mean he *did* ask me!" said Allegra, obliged in spite of herself to come to Sir Derek's defense.

"He did?" Mrs. Colbridge's bosom seemed suddenly to swell to a good deal more than its natural size. "He *did* ask you? Allegra Herington, and You Refused Him?"

Allegra, feeling like a criminal in the dock, looking imploringly at Hilary, but Hilary only stared at her in an awed way and said, "Allie—you *didn't!*"

"Yes, I did!" said Allegra defiantly, driven to the wall. "He has turned Mr. Rudwick off and brought a new agent from London—and he thinks I am an unreasonable female, and—and we shouldn't suit in the least, I am quite sure!"

"Merciful heavens!" said Mrs. Colbridge, sinking down into a chair and beginning to fan herself frantically with her handkerchief. "What has *that* to say to anything, you unnatural girl! I am sure Mr. Colbridge was the last man in the world I should have looked to marry if he hadn't been the most eligible gentleman of my acquaintance, and only see how well the match has turned out, for I am sure we do not have words above once in a sennight, and then it is never over anything of the least consequence! Hilary, I am sure I feel one of my spasms coming on! Run upstairs at once and fetch my vinaigrette, and, Allegra, you must contrive some way to convey to Sir Derek that you did not mean a word of what you said. I shall send Mr. Colbridge to Rolveston the moment he returns—that is it—and he shall say that you are quite overset by your folly in refusing him and did not mean it in the least."

But upon this point Allegra was firm. Not all her aunt's representations of the irreparable damage being done to her nerves by her niece's hen-witted refusal of a man who could give her all the elegancies of life, to say nothing of taking her and her sister off her relations' hands forever, could induce Allegra to make the attempt to retrieve the consequences of her own folly. As a result, there was a very disagreeable scene between aunt and niece, to which Mr. Colbridge, arriving home in the middle of it, added his own mite by informing Allegra of the precise amount in pounds, shillings, and pence that the maintenance of her and her sister in his household was likely to oblige him to lay out each year.

The upshot of all this was that Allegra, her temper already in a highly uncertain state, lost it again and told her uncle in pithy terms that he could stop calculating his losses because she and Hilary were going to Brussels, and she thereupon dragged her younger sister out of the room, ordered a highly interested footman who had been eavesdropping in the hall to fetch their portmanteaux from the box-room, and went off upstairs to begin to pack.

"But you haven't written Cherry that we are coming!" protested Hilary, who, though quite an incensed as was her sister by her relations' cheese-paring ways, yet felt that it behooved someone to maintain some sanity about the whole affair. "And—and we have made no travel arrangements—"

"I don't care!" said Allegra. "We shall take the night-mail to London, and stop at an hotel there—but I won't stay in this house another hour, or eat another morsel of food in it—" She broke off remorsefully, seeing her sister's troubled face. "Oh, Hilary darling, I'm a *beast!*" she said. "I've made the most dreadful mull of it—and now I'm dragging you off to Brussels as if I were *quite* demented—"

"You're not demented in the least," said Hilary loyally. "And it's Aunt Colbridge who is the beast—yes, and Uncle too! Only I can't quite help wishing," she added somewhat wistfully, "that we were going to Rolveston instead of Brussels. Was Sir Derek *very* horrid to you?"

"Yes!" said Allegra, her cheeks flushing anew as she

remembered some of the very uncomplimentary phrases that gentleman had used. "But I expect *I* was horrid too—only I had a reason, because I met Pember in the village and he told me that Sir Derek had turned Mr. Rudwick off and brought in a new agent for Rolveston."

Hilary agreed that that had been a very good reason for being horrid to Sir Derek, but went on looking so unhappy that Allegra felt impelled to go over and give her a hug.

"Don't worry!" she said, with a confidence she was far from feeling. "We shall come about; I am sure of it! Perhaps I shan't have to go schoolmistressing forever, you know, because there are scores of English in Brussels just now, and who knows but that I shall make a conquest of an elderly peer who will come to visit his granddaughter at the Pensionnat and marry me out of hand, and then take us off to live in a castle with a hundred and twenty servants indoors and out? Or, better still, you will meet the handsome son of a duke in a Guard's uniform who will fall madly in love with you—"

Hilary, tracing the pattern of the much-worn quilt upon her bed with her forefinger, said that would be nice but she didn't think she was good-looking enough, as her nose was a snub; but this Allegra refused to allow. In her eyes her young sister—who was certainly a very attractive girl, though not in the least of a classical turn of countenance—was worthy of the attentions of a nonpareil among men, and even in the hurry of her preparations for departure she began to make new plans for Hilary, vowing to herself that she would not allow her own bungling of the affair of Sir Derek to sink her sister's future as well as her own.

Chapter Six

THREE DAYS LATER Allegra and Hilary arrived in Brussels, having been fortunate enough, upon reaching London, to book passage immediately on a packet leaving for Ostend.

Their arrival—although they were quite unaware of this fact—almost coincided with that of the celebrated *cantatrice,* Catalani, who had consented, at an enormous fee, to appear at several select parties to be given there during the ensuing weeks. Brussels, in fact, did not in the least present the appearance of a city trembling before the threat of the Corsican ogre who had escaped from Elba two months before, and on the contrary seemed to be endeavouring to capture from Vienna, where the great Congress had been going on all winter to the tune of innumerable balls, concerts, *petits soupers,* enormous dinner parties, and fêtes of every description, the reputation of being the gayest capital in Europe.

And if the streets were thronged with the smart blue of Dutch uniforms and the rifle-green of Belgian dragoons, with British scarlet growing more prominent each day as the Duke of Wellington assembled the army he was to lead against Napoleon, this merely added colour to the festivities and in no way dampened the spirits of the English visitors still bent on flocking abroad after their long confinement to their own island during the late wars.

"In fact, *ma chère,*" said Mlle. Jusseau when, on the evening of the Misses Herington's arrival, a yawning Hilary had been sent off to bed and she and Allegra sat together in her snug sitting room in the tall, narrow house off the Place Royale that she had converted into the Pensionnat Jusseau, "I have seven English among my girls already, and more are arriving every week. It seems that Bonaparte holds no terrors for *vous autres,* for all the English here express every confidence in the Duke and, with him in Brussels, appear to feel quite as safe as if they were in London."

Allegra, whose affectionate feelings towards her old preceptress had been made even warmer by the cordiality with which her unexpected arrival had been greeted by Mlle. Jusseau, said that one of the arguments Lady Warring had used in endeavouring to dissuade her from coming to Brussels had been her fear that the city might fall into the hands of the Bonapartist forces.

"And what were the other reasons?" enquired Mlle. Jusseau, sitting very upright in a *bergère* armchair beside the fireplace and regarding her former pupil with a slight smile upon her small, wrinkled, intelligent face.

Allegra said, rather uncomfortably, "Well you know, of course—about getting married and that sort of thing."

"Ah," said Mademoiselle calmly. "And whom were you to marry, *ma chère?*"—which caused Allegre to wonder, as she often had in her childhood, whether Mademoiselle's eyes, so small and black in her ugly but somehow fascinatingly alive face, were possessed of some penetrating magic power that let her see exactly what was transpiring in other people's minds.

She had had time, during her journey to Brussels, to reflect a good deal on the scene that had taken place between herself and Sir Derek at Chatt Park, and had an uneasy feeling—especially in view of Sir Derek's parting recommendation that she talk to Mr. Rudwick himself about his dismissal—that she was very likely to find herself quite in the wrong on that matter when all the facts were in her possession. But feeling that one is in the

wrong does not make one any more anxious to confide
this disagreeable state of mind to others, so she said mendaciously to Mlle. Jusseau that she didn't know that there
was any gentleman in particular.

"That," said Mademoiselle equably, "is quite untrue.
You are a very poor liar, Allegra; you always were. But
of course if you do not care to tell me, I should not
dream of pressing you."

Upon this Allegra naturally felt herself to be an exem-
plar of the basest ingratitude and said that she would be
glad to tell her, except that it seemed rather hard on the
gentleman concerned to have other people know that his
suit had been rejected.

"If you will persist in rejecting the suits of perfectly eligible gentlemen because of a young man who has been
dead for half a dozen years, *ma fille,* you will end your
days *comme moi,*" said Mlle. Jusseau, with a slight gesture at her modest sitting room, "only not so prosperous,
I think, for you have not the patience for drudgery that I
have."

"How do you know that he was perfectly eligible?"
parried Allegra.

"Because I know Lady Warring. She is a woman who
thinks always of what is *comme il faut,* and she is sincerely attached to you." Mlle. Jusseau's small dark eyes
blinked rapidly once or twice, in a disconcertingly reptilian manner. "Sir Derek Herington," she pronounced after a moment's pause, with what Allegra could only think
of as a Delphic oracle's knowledge of events. "Is it
possible that he has made you an offer?"

Allegra gave it up. "Well, I don't know how you
know," she said, "but he did."

"And you refused him?"

"Yes!" said Allegra, looking dangerous.

"Very well, very well! You need not look at me as if
you wish to snap my nose off," said Mlle. Jusseau. "I
daresay you know quite well what you are doing, and will

much prefer a useful life spent in instructing the young to being the wife of a man who I understand is not only rich, but amiable and personable as well."

"He may be rich and personable, but he is certainly *not* amiable," said Allegra rebelliously. "And I don't in the least care to talk about it, Cherry. What's done is done, and we are here now, and since you have said that you will give me a position, I daresay we shall not starve. Only I *am* unhappy about Hilary," she went on, a slight, worried frown suddenly creasing her brow. "Of course I was obliged to bring her with me, as leaving her with Aunt Colbridge would not have served at all, since she had no intention of doing anything but making a household drudge of her. But I cannot bear her to be buried here with me, without the least chance to meet *any* eligible gentlemen or enjoy the sort of things girls of her age do enjoy—parties and balls and picnics—oh, *you* know, Cherry!"

Mlle. Jusseau, looking thoughtful, said she did indeed know.

"And she is *très jolie, très gaie,* the little Hilary," she said after a moment, "of a type to make a great success in Society, one sees. A pretty gown, a coiffure *toute à la mode,* the opportunity to be seen and admired, and *voilà!—la petite* becomes a countess, or at least the wife of one of your dull English *Sirs* who wishes a charming wife to look at when he comes home fatigued from his everlasting sports and horses. It is a pity."

"Yes," said Allegra disconsolately. "But what am I to *do?* I can't send her to Aunt Hatherill; she can't endure Hilary, and even if she would have her, it would be almost as bad for her there as it is here, for Aunt would not exert herself in the least to take her into Society."

Mlle. Jusseau, the sibylline look still upon her face, continued to ponder. Presently she said, in her calm, precise way, "There are—as you are aware—many English in Brussels just now. I do not speak of the military alone;

there are also ladies of fashion—the Duchess of Richmond, Lady John Somerset, for example—who have
hired houses here and entertain on a lavish scale. Some
have even brought their young daughters, whom I may
boast of having received into my establishment. Only last
week, I may tell you, Lady Milgrom brought to me her
daughter, Miss Chloe Milgrom, a young lady of much the
same age as your Hilary. Now I have no doubt that the
two young ladies, given the proper opportunity, will find
much in common upon which to build the sort of violent
friendship that young ladies are so frequently inclined to
form. *Eh bien*—let us go a step further. Lady Milgrom,
visiting her daugher at my establishment, is introduced by
her to her friend, Miss Hilary Herington, the daugher of
Sir Thomas Herington, who has come, like Miss Chloe,
for a few months of study to the Pensionnat Jusseau, and
who is about to make her come-out in Society. What is
more likely than that Lady Milgrom invites her to one of
her small evening parties? And after that—"

"After that, having made her entrée into Brussels Society, she may be invited anywhere!" Allegra finished it
with enthusiasm. "Cherry, you are a genius! Only," she
added, a slight frown again appearing upon her face as a
new thought entered her mind, "if Lady Milgrom
learns—as she must, from her daughter—that Hilary's sister is employed as a teacher here, it will ruin everything—"

"Yes, I am thinking of that," said Mlle. Jusseau, her
manner as unruffled as before. "You are quite right; it
will not do. But if you were introduced to her as merely a
distant relation, an impoverished connexion of the Herington family, reduced by circumstances to earning your
own living—"

She looked a trifle enquiringly at Allegra as she spoke,
as if not quite certain—even as well as she knew her former pupil—that any English young lady of quality would
be willing to see her consequence diminished in such a

style. But Allegra seemed quite undaunted by the prospect.

"Famous!" she said immediately. "The impoverished gentlewoman—well I *am* one now, most assuredly, so the part should certainly not come amiss to me. All the same, I shall take good care to remain in the background, so that it is unlikely that Lady Milgrom will ever see me—"

"But she must see you, *ma chère,*" Mlle. Jusseau contradicted her. *"Naturellement,* Hilary will sometimes require a chaperon, for it is not to be expected that Lady Milgrom or any other English lady with whom she becomes acquainted will wish to trouble herself always to take her about. The only difficulty I foresee over your being accepted in such a role is the chance that you may meet some person who knows you as Hilary's sister—"

"Not very likely!" Allegra said confidently. "For once I am happy that, while I was with Aunt Hatherill in Bath, I went about so little. My circle of acquaintance there was confined exclusively to a set of old fogies who would not dream of going anywhere near Brussels while it is in this unsettled state; and as for the people I met in London during my one season there, it is scarcely likely, I think, that they would remember or recognise me any longer. Our Cambridgeshire neighbors, you know; tell me if you think any of *them* haunt fashionable circles in foreign capitals!"

Mlle. Jusseau said that she was aware they did not, but that awkward incidents, in her experience, were apt to occur exactly when one did not expect them. And what, she asked, about the gentleman—if they were so fortunate as to see one appear—who would wish to offer Hilary his hand and fortune?

"Oh, if it comes to that," Allegra said, brushing aside this obstacle, "he will be so much in love with her by that time that he won't care a rush that she has a sister who is a beggarly schoolmistress and will no doubt think it a very good joke. Hilary would never take the fancy of a prig, you know! But you must know as well as I do,

Cherry, that if Lady Milgrom or any other of your tonnish English ladies is told that Hilary is merely the sister of one of your teachers, and not a young lady sent by her family for a few months' 'finishing' to Brussels, she will never think of inviting her to her home."

Mlle. Jusseau acknowledged that this was so, adding a few rather brutally candid observations on the peculiar manners and mores of *vous Anglais* that made Allegra remember rather uncomfortably what she had forgotten over the years that had elapsed since she had last seen her old governness Mlle. Jusseau's French sense of superiority over her English patronesses.

Now was not the time, however—with Mlle. Jusseau's kindness towards her and Hilary fresh in her mind—for Allegra to dwell on such memories, and if it occurred to her later that night, as she lay awake in her very French *en bateau* bed in the small bedchamber she shared with Hilary, that there had been something perhaps overprompt in the readiness with which Mademoiselle had formulated her plan for launching Hilary into the society of the English colony in Brussels, this too she felt obliged to gloss over in her mind. After all, governesses, especially those who never married, frequently did become and remained excessively attached to their pupils. And even Mademoiselle's generosity in offering to supplement Hilary's wardrobe—which was certainly quite inadequate to any extensive social life—by having Marthe, one of the maids employed at the Pensionnat and a very clever needlewoman, make several frocks for her from a store of materials that had been presented to her over the years by various employers seemed not too unusual in the light of this fact.

"*Quite* unsuitable for a governess," Mademoiselle had said disparagingly, with a glance at her own spare little figure clad, as always, in impeccable black. "I have never been able to think what to do with them, so that I shall be positively grateful to you for taking them off my hands.

And perhaps a gown or two for you as well, *ma chère,*"
she had added, "since you will be obliged to go into
company and I am sure have bought nothing but mourning clothes since your father's death."

But to this Allegra had endeavoured to protest—only
to find that protests were quite unavailing when Mademoiselle's mind was made up. Indeed, on the very next
morning Marthe, a tall, competent-looking middle-aged
woman, appeared in the small bedchamber bearing pins
and measures and lengths of crapes and cambrics and
muslins wrapped in silver paper. She had orders from
Mlle. la Directrice, she said: the blue cambric, the pale
puce, the orange-blossom muslin for Mlle. Hilary, but the
green Italian silk for Mlle. Allegra. Only look at this
gown pictured in the latest number of *La Belle Assemblée,* with rows of thread lace trimming the flounces
about the hem of the narrow skirt: it would become Mlle.
Allegra *à ravir.*

Hilary, to whom Allegra and Mlle. Jusseau had agreed
that it would be unwise to confide immediately all the details of the benevolent plot for her future that had been
concocted between them, surveyed the rolls of fabrics
spilling over her bed in astonishment, and evinced a good
deal more interest in the small white kitten which had
followed Marthe into the room, and which, she explained,
she had brought back with her from a visit to her home in
Ghent with a view towards the eventual replacement of
Mlle. Jusseau's old mouser, which was getting past its
work.

But she submitted docilely enough to having Marthe
take her measurements, and only when that industrious
female had left the room remarked candidly to her sister,
"Good gracious, Allie, I did not like to say it before that
woman, but it appears to me that poor Cherry must have
windmills in her head! Whatever am I to do with all those
dresses? *I* am not like that odious Milgrom girl I met this
morning, who is to make her come-out this Season and

can talk of nothing but the balls and parties she is to attend and the frocks she will wear to them."

"That—odious Milgrom girl?" Allegra repeated a trifle falteringly, watching Hilary encourage the white kitten, which had remained behind, evidently preferring her company to Marthe's, to enter into mortal combat with the claw feet of the mahogany washstand. "But how can you have met her?—I mean, how can you have met anyone here yet?"—for the two sisters had breakfasted with Mlle. Jusseau in the directress's own apartments on this first morning.

"Oh, it was while you and Cherry were talking about what you were to teach," Hilary said, picking up the kitten which had just despatched one of the mahogany feet to its own great satisfaction, and cradling it in her arms, where it purred enthusiastically for several moments and then fell asleep. "I went off downstairs and there was a girl going by and she said she was Chloe Milgrom and I said I was Hilary Herington and then she told me about her come-out."

"Did you tell her," Allegra asked rather anxiously, "that I was your sister?"

"I didn't tell her anything. *She* did all the talking," Hilary said disparagingly. She then added, "Why?" with some slight interest seeing the relieved expression upon her sister's face.

"Well, the fact is," said Allegra, endeavouring to speak in a casual voice, "that we thought—Cherry and I, that is—that it might be best if you and I weren't sisters here. I mean, if the other girls were to think you have been sent here, like them, to complete your education, and that I am only a distant relation who has come down in the world and has accepted a position here, you might receive invitations—"

"Well, *I* shan't tell them such a clanker; you may depend upon that!" Hilary said with instant indignation. "As if I were ashamed of being your sister!"

"Not ashamed—only sensible, love!" urged Allegra. She drew Hilary down beside her upon the bed. "Look at it this way, my dear," she advised her. "It doesn't in the least matter what people here think about *me*, because I have had my chance—a whole Season in London—and if I hadn't fallen in love with Neil I should probably be Lady Macdougal today, which is a very lowering thought, I assure you, for a sillier man I have never met! But I can't give you a London Season, and Aunt Hatherill won't, nor will Aunt Colbridge, so it is only right that you should have the next best thing—a chance to go to parties and fêtes and picnics here, and to meet eligible gentlemen while you are still young and pretty and—oh, Hilary, can't you see that I made such a mull of it with Sir Derek, losing my temper in that perfectly cockle-brained way instead of being meek and comfortable like the sort of female he wants for a wife, that I *must* do something for you now?"

Hilary, looking into her sister's troubled face, said stoutly that she did not see it in the least; but it was plain that the prospect of picnics and parties, after she had been schooling herself to the thought of spending her days quietly within the rather grim portals of the Pensionnat Jusseau, was alluring. Allegra, who knew her young sister very well, saw the tables turning in her favour, and by dint of making a joke of the matter and encouraging Hilary's natural love of the mischief involved in taking people in with such a hoax, soon succeeded in gaining her consent to the mild deception involved.

Of her more serious purpose—that Hilary might find a husband in one of the well-born young Englishmen in the Duke's army who were now flocking, as Mlle. Jusseau had assured her, to the balls and other entertainments being given in Brussels by their countrywomen, or among the less military-minded young gentlemen of good family who had come to share in the present excitements and gaieties of the city—she said nothing at all. There would

be time enough to think of that, she felt, when she saw
how Hilary got on in Brussels Society.

Which was all satisfactory enough to Hilary, at any
rate, for she had just thought of a name for the kitten
(unchristened as yet, Marthe had said, owing to having
been rescued at the last moment from the sack in which it
and six of its equally nameless brothers and sisters were
to be conveyed to the Scheldt) and had waked it up to inform it that it was to be called Bluebell—though why
Bluebell when its coat was pure white she might have
found it difficult to explain.

Chapter Seven

ON THE MONDAY following, Allegra took up her duties as
instructress at the Pensionnat Jusseau. As these were confined exclusively to the French-speaking pupils of that in-
stitution, they gave her little opportunity to observe how
Hilary was progressing in her relations with Miss Milgrom
and the other English young ladies in Mlle. Jusseau's select academy; but on this head she soon found that there
was no need for her to worry. Hilary, who made friends
quite as rapidly and almost as indiscriminately as did
Bluebell, was within a week at the centre of every activity,
condoned and not condoned by the mistresses, at the Pensionnat, and, having earned the gratitude of the English
boarders by smuggling a pot of hot chocolate and an
enormous cherry tart into their dormitory when they were
all thought to be fast asleep, had quickly taken on the
role of ringleader. She was, in fact, enthusiastically intro-

duced to one visiting mama (not Lady Milgrom) by her sporting-minded daughter as "my very best friend, Hilary Herington, a regular out-and-outer!"—which caused her mama severely to deplore such language and to wonder whether Mlle. Jusseau was quite as particular as might have been desired in monitoring the conduct of her pupils.

Upon this occasion Hilary, regarded as A Bad Influence, received no invitation, but Mlle. Jusseau's predictions turned out to be more accurate in regard to Lady Milgrom. Miss Chloe Milgrom's mama was a stout, foolish, and very effusive lady of some forty years, whose sole interest in life lay in insinuating herself into circles to which nothing but her husband's wealth enabled her to aspire. Having dragged that long-suffering gentleman off to Brussels, merely because she had heard that all the *ton* was flocking there, she had recently managed the triumph of securing one of the elegant gilt-edged cards of invitation entitling them to attend the concert, ball, and supper given by the Duke of Wellington for the King and Queen of the Netherlands at the Salle du Grand Concert, and had consequently been taken with the ambition to give a ball herself. And, as she had told her husband with some pride, though she could not offer her guests the Catalani, as the Duke had done, or Royal Highnesses of any nationality, she *did* count upon having as many Guardsmen, Hussars, and Dragoons as her rooms would hold, for young officers would always be bound to come where the best champagne in Brussels was to be had.

It was not to be expected that Miss Chloe Milgrom, even though she had not yet made her formal come-out, would be denied by her mama the splendid opportunity to meet young men of title and family that the ball would afford. And, exactly as Mlle. Jusseau had foretold, Hilary's credentials as the daughter of a baronet caused her to be welcomed to the guest list with open arms, Lady Milgrom even going so far as to condescend to her coming in the company of her relation, Miss Allegra Herington—"who takes me about everywhere," Hilary had confided to her with a great show of artlessness, "for my aunt, Lady Hatherill, would not at all like it if I went alone."

Lady Hatherill, disclosed by an avid search of Debrett's to be the relict of an earl, with a title the creation of which went back to Charles II, clinched the matter; Miss Allegra Herington was to be admitted to the ball *en chaperon,* and Hilary in great glee informed her sister of the coup she had brought off, only to find Allegra not at all appreciative of the trouble she had taken.

"For it will be much better if I go about with you as little as possible," she warned her. "Cherry is right; awkward coincidences *can* occur, and though the chances of my meeting someone who knows me are quite remote, one really never knows."

And, indeed, as she found to her sorrow on the next afternoon, one really never did.

The day was a Sunday, and she and Hilary had taken advantage of their freedom to explore the Parc De Bruxelles, situated only a short distance away from the Pensionnat. Here Hilary, having admired the lake and enjoyed the colorful kaleidoscope of uniforms passing by, interspersed with the occasional black mantilla of a Bruxelloise and the fashionable wispy muslins and cambrics just venturing forth for the first time on this mild spring day, was seized with a desire to feed the swans on the lake, and went off to the pavilion to see if she might purchase some bread for that purpose there. Allegra, left alone, sat down on a rustic bench, and was meditating with satisfaction upon the charming picture Hilary had presented that morning as she had tried on the pale puce muslin she was to wear to the Milgrom ball when a masculine voice pronouncing her name suddenly made her jump.

"Allie Herington, by all that's wonderful!" said the voice, and the next moment she was looking up into a ruddy, bony face rising above a colonel's silver lace and scarlet.

"Oh—Hep!" she gasped. "How you startled me! What in the world are you doing here in Brussels?"

There were several other military gentlemen in Colonel Hepworth's company, which was all that saved her, she was quite sure, from being swept into an exceedingly public embrace, for though she had once refused an offer of marriage from the Colonel, made under the influence of brandy and his admiration of the skill and stamina she had displayed during a long day in the hunting field, he had never held this against her.

As it was, he was content to give both her hands a bone-crushing squeeze, and appeared about to present her with pride to his interested companions when she forestalled him by saying hastily, with the inventiveness born of necessity, "Oh, Colonel Hepworth, now that you are here, I wonder if I might have a little talk with you on— on a matter of great importance."

Upon which the other military gentlemen, taking their cue, walked on together, albeit a trifle regretfully, while Colonel Hepworth sat down beside her upon the bench.

"Now, what's this 'Colonel Hepworth' business?" he demanded. "And what are you doing in Brussels, my girl? The last I heard of you, you were living with that she-devil of an aunt of yours in Bath. Couldn't stick it, eh? Could have told you so, if you'd ever taken the trouble to ask me."

"Well, I *couldn't* stick it," said Allegra with some asperity, "though how I could have asked you when you were in America I quite fail to see. Why aren't you there now?" she added accusingly.

"More action here," said the Colonel promptly. "That is, there isn't yet, but there's bound to be soon."

"Oh, do you think so?" asked Allegra, a trifle startled, for, like most of the other English in Brussels, she had been lulled into a sense of security by the sight of the city going placidly about its ordinary business and of the Duke taking the time not only to attend balls and concerts but even to give some of his own. "But—but we are quite safe here, aren't we?"

"Well, you're safe now," Colonel Hepworth said judiciously. "Shouldn't care to lay any wagers, though, that Boney won't be heading in this direction soon, once he has this Champ de Mai affair out of the way. If I was you, I'd be thinking of getting back to England."

"But I can't!" said Allegra, in some slight discomposure. "I mean—not unless there's any *real* danger, Hep. You see, I am employed here."

"Employed? *You?*"

"Yes. I am the English mistress at a school here—well, I really couldn't help it, you know," she defended herself, seeing the Colonel's eyebrows go up. "I told you I couldn't get on with Aunt Hatherill, and it was quite as bad with the Colbridges, so I have taken a position here and brought Hilary with me—"

"Well, I might have known it," said Colonel Hepworth resignedly. "Out of the skillet and into the fire; that's you all over, my girl. If you had to go schoolmistressing, why couldn't you do it in England? Or better still," he added reflectively, "marry me. The offer's still open, if you care to take it."

"Well, I don't—thank you very much all the same, Hep," Allegra said, a mischievous smile appearing upon her face, in spite of her concern. "And you know you will be glad I said so before the next quarter hour is past, for what you would do with a wife I can't think—and no more can you!"

"Well, you may be right about that," the Colonel equably agreed. "Cork-brained thing to do, to go about proposing to females. You never know when they might accept you. All the same, we might go on like winking, you and I, you know. Two of a kind."

"I am *not*," said Allegra indignantly, well aware that

the Colonel's rash and even foolhardy attachment to dangerous exploits of every description had given him a reputation almost equalling that of the celebrated Colonel Dan MacKinnon who had once gone completely around the auditorium at Convent Garden by running along the ledges of the boxes. "I mean I'm not in the least like you. And I daresay we should fight like cats."

"Still wearing the willow for young Alland—that's it, I expect," said the Colonel, who could be disconcertingly perceptive when it suited him. "I'll tell you what, my girl, if you don't take care you'll end up on the shelf. Alland was a good lad, but nothing brings a good man back, you know. Look at your father. And life goes on—that sort of thing."

"Yes, I know," Allegra said, her fine eyes growing dim for a moment. "And it seems such a long time ago now—about Neil, that is. Sometimes I can't believe it ever really happened."

"Then marry some other good fellow and put it all in the past where it belongs," the Colonel recommended. "Much the wisest thing to do, old girl, instead of jauntering about the Continent pretending to be a schoolmistress."

Allegra shook her head. "I don't think so," she said. "Papa always said I had a *curst independent streak* and I believe I have. No, it's Hilary I want to see well and safely married now—and I may be in the way to make that possible, for she is beginning to be acquainted with some of the other girls at the Pensionnat who will be making their come-outs this year, and to receive invitations—" She went on, turning a suddenly rather anxious face on her companion, "Only—I daresay I must tell you —I have thought it best to give it out that I am merely a distant relation of hers who has come down in the world, and not her sister, for it wouldn't do at all for people to know the truth."

"Yes, I can see that," said the Colonel unexpectedly—

or it might have been unexpected if Allegra had not known him well enough to realise that he had never been one to blink at facts. "Set of damned self-righteous tabbies, sorry, Allie, our countrywomen. Still there's something to be said for it, you know. Keeping up the standards and all that. There's this fellow Milgrom—looks as if he ought to be mucking out stables and' probably his grandfather did, but he'll nabble half the smarts in town to dine with him because he knows where the best wine in Brussels lives. Wouldn't miss one of his dinners myself on any account, which goes to show you."

Allegra laughed and said that she was glad to hear it, because the Milgrom girl was at the Pensionnat and Lady Milgrom had invited Hilary to one of her parties.

"I expect she will meet eligible gentlemen there?" she said hopefully, and the Colonel said as sure as check, only she couldn't count on seeing the real cream of the *ton* there, the Duke or the Somersets or the Lennoxes, or any of the diplomatic Johnnies.

"Including that cousin of yours, Derek Herington," he concluded, adding that, strictly speaking, of course, Derek was not diplomatic any longer, but had only come over to Brussels, he understood, as a favour to the Duke, who thought he might be useful in dealing with the Prussians because somewhere along the line in his very active career he had managed to win the confidence of both the Prussian Chief-of-Staff, General Count von Gneisenau, and the Commissioner, General von Röder, whose irritability was a byword at the Duke's Headquarters.

At this point Allegra, upon whom this speech had fallen like a bombshell, managed to say in an appalled voice, "Derek Herington? But—but, good God, *he* isn't here! Is he?"

"If he isn't, there's someone doing a deuced good job of it going about impersonating him," said the Colonel. "Look here, what's the matter? You look like someone with a pain in his pudding-house."

"Oh, I *am!* I mean I have!" wailed Allegra. "Oh dear, was there ever anything so unfortunate! He is certain to throw a rub in our way!"

"Shouldn't think he would if he knew what it was you didn't want him to do," said the Colonel kindly. "Very good sort of fellow, Derek, once you get to know him. Didn't realise you did. Remember asking him once if he'd met you—Lisbon, it must have been, or was it Madrid?—at any rate, there was some good Malaga and we made a night of it, and he said only once, when you were a chit of a girl with your hair all down your back and as wild as be-damned."

"Well, we have met since then and—and didn't get on in the least," Allegta said, a harassed look on her face, though through all her concern she was conscious of feeling distinct surprise that Sir Derek Herington, the man of fashion and ornament of diplomatic circles was considered by the Colonel as a very good sort of fellow. "And—oh dear, I know he will be *quite* irritated if he learns I am a schoolmistress here, and it will spoil all Hilary's chances if he discloses our true situation!"

The Colonel said soothingly that, setting the hare's head against the goose giblets, he considered it highly unlikely that Derek would cry rope on her, and then pointed out to her, with some justification, for at that very moment Hilary came towards them from the pavilion accompanied by no fewer than three young gentlemen in scarlet coats, that it would take more than Derek Herington to spoil *that* chit's chances, because she seemed to have turned into a deuced fetching piece.

"Yes, she has—hasn't she?" said Allegra proudly. "Only she really must *not* go about making friends with unknown young men—"

"That's all right. *I* know them," said the Colonel, rising as the little group came up and bestowing an avuncular kiss upon Hilary, much to the envy of her three companions. "Well, you naughty puss, what have you been up to now?" he enquired benevolently. "Grown up—have you?—while my back was turned and set to play havoc with all the young fellows."

Hilary, very pink and pretty with the excitement of conquest, said she had only gone off to the pavilion to try to buy some bread to feed the swans, only there wasn't any, and so these very kind gentlemen—with a glance at them from under her long lashes that made Allegra wish in amused disapproval to shake her, and all the young military gentlemen determine to die, if necessary or even feasible, for her sake—had insisted upon buying cakes instead.

"Which seems *quite* extravagant," she said, with more provocative play of those extraordinary lashes, so that Colonel Hepworth told her to stop acting like a baggage or he would turn her over his knee.

"All right now," he said. "I'm going to make a respectable woman of you by introducing these three codlings to you properly, but, mind!—don't go and do it again. May I present Ensign Lord Roderick Buccan, Ensign Sir Francis Pelton, Cornet Playsted—Miss Hilary Herington and her—er, *cousin*, Miss Allegra Herington!"

The three young gentlemen, who instantly became inarticulate, bowed very civilly to each of the ladies and then stood looking guilty but stubbornly determined not to give ground. Cornet Playsted, a fresh-faced young gentleman who appeared to be not very much older than Hilary herself, was the first to take courage to address Allegra under Colonel Hepworth's watching eyes, and enquired earnestly if it would be all right, since they had bought the cakes, to give them to Miss Hilary so that she could feed the swans.

"Yes, certainly," said Allegra; but, determined not to let Hilary out of her sight again, she rose and prepared to accompany them. Colonel Hepworth then said he must get back to his friends and took his leave of her, advising her by the way not to worry about that little matter, as

Derek was all right. Ensign Lord Roderick Buccan, a wiry young gentleman with a bony, attractive face and eager eyes, who, as he had been standing just beside the Colonel, could not help overhearing these words, looked interestedly at Allegra as the Colonel went off.

"Oh, I say," he said, "are you *those* Heringtons? I mean, are you related to Derek? I'm his cousin, you know," and then he fell into blushful silence, apparently self-convicted of putting himself forward in an unseemly way.

Allegra, somewhat discomposed by this revelation, said faintly that Hilary's father had been Sir Thomas Herington, and wondered how much Lord Roderick knew of the ramifications of his family. But apparently, like most young men, he knew very little, for he only said he dared say that was the man Derek had inherited the title from and it must have been deuced hard on Miss Herington to have her father die and someone else come into the estate.

"My mother always says you can't have too many sons in the family," he said to Allegra with engaging candour. "I mean to say, then there's always someone to inherit. But I'm number five and even if Father is a duke it means I shall have to make a do of it in the Army if I'm to get on, what with all the girls to be dowered, too. There's six of *them* and none of 'em beauties: at least that's what my mother says, and she ought to know because *she* was."

Allegra, who had been rapidly endeavouring to determine from this freely but somewhat sketchily provided information exactly who Lord Roderick was, at this point, recollected that Sir Derek Herington's mother had been the sister of the present Duchess of Wyon, who was apparently Lord Roderick's mother. Allegra herself had a slight hunting-field acquaintance with the Duke and the Duchess, as one of their country seats lay not far distant from Rolveston in Suffolk, and had even been asked as a girl to one or two balls at Hadfield. Of these she now remembered little, except for a memorable occasion when one of the Duchess's King Charles spaniels—for she kept almost as many dogs as the Duchess of York had at Oatlands—had got into the ballroom and caused a middle-aged peer, absorbed in performing the *pas d'été* in the quadrille, to fall over it and break his leg. But she had never heard of Lord Roderick, who must have been at Eton at that time, and could only hope devoutly that he had never heard of her.

Meanwhile, they had reached the sheet of water where the swans sailed, and Lord Roderick, basely deserting her, went to try to cut Cornet Playsted out with Hilary, in which endeavour he appeared to succeed very well. Allegra, watching Hilary's laughing, happy face as she coaxed the swans to feed from her fingers while her three admirers vied jealously for the honour of breaking the cakes into crumbs and placing them in her hand, could not help remembering the prediction she had made at Chatt Park about her young sister's meeting the handsome son of a duke who would fall madly in love with her and marry her, and thought that Lord Roderick, though perhaps not quite handsome and certainly, with his eager diffidence, not in the least what one expected a duke's son to be, might fit the part ver ell if Hilary liked him. Only, of course, considering his revelations about his worldly prospects, it would be even nicer if it were someone who was rich as well.

As all three of the young gentlemen insisted upon escorting Hilary back to the Pensionnat, she had no opportunity to learn her sister's views on the matter until they were inside the house, where Mlle. Jusseau at once appeared and invited them to come upstairs to her sitting room and tell them how they had enjoyed their visit to the Park.

"Oh, it was beyond anything great!" said Hilary, and she launched at once into an account of the incident of the cakes, in which Mademoiselle appeared to take a very satisfactory interest.

"And they are *all* going to Lady Milgrom's ball on Saturday," Hilary concluded happily, "or at least they have not got invitations yet but they are quite sure they can manage to. And Lord Roderick says he will bring Bluebell a ribbon with a bell on it that I may tie around his neck so he doesn't catch birds—not that I expect he is *quite* old enough yet for that. And he says that everyone calls him Roddy."

But to this last broad hint Mlle. Jusseau immediately took exception, and told Hilary, exactly as she had been used to when she was nine years old, not to be forward and to say Lord Roderick.

When Hilary had run off to share her afternoon's adventure with the English boarders (who took a very satisfactory interest in it, and accepted quite literally a description of Lord Roderick in which he was lavishly invested with every virtue possessed by the hero of the latest French romance that had been smuggled into the Pensionnat), Mademoiselle said rather dryly to Allegra that it appeared their schemes for *la petite* might almost be unnecessary, as she seemed quite capable of finding her own way into the society of eligible young men without their aid. To this Allegra, who was secretly very proud of her sister's conquests though conscious that they had come about in an unorthodox manner, agreed, and then told Mademoiselle about her meeting with Colonel Hepworth and the disquieting news he had given her about Sir Derek Herington's presence in Brussels.

"I thought I might call upon him—much as I should dislike to, for we are *not* upon terms—and ask him not to give it away that I am Hilary's sister," she said, "only I stupidly forgot to ask Colonel Hepworth where he was staying."

"*Eh bien,* I can find *that* out easily enough," said Mlle. Jusseau, who had taught in Brussels for many years before coming to England and apparently had lost none of her connexions there. "And I think it a very good idea for

you to see him, for as a gentleman of the first consequence he might do much to ease your way in Society—"

"Ease *my* way?" Allegra interrupted, her colour rising.
"Indeed I shall desire him to do no such thing!"

"That is as you wish," Mademoiselle said calmly. "But
the little Hilary is another matter—*hein?* He might do
much for her, also; indeed, since he can scarcely avoid acknowledging her as his relation, he is in a way bound to
do so for his own sake." She rose. "You are making a
bêtise because of false pride, *ma chère*," she said. "But of
course if that is what you wish—"

Allegra, feeling that she had been put in the wrong,
said that naturally she didn't wish it at all, and that she
would go see Sir Derek if Cherry could find out where
lived. But she thought rebelliously that not even for
Hilary could she bring herself to ask anything of Sir
Derek, and privately considered it to be highly unlikely
that he would accede to any request made by her, even
if she could bring herself to make it.

Chapter Eight

THE NECESSITY of approaching Sir Derek on the subject
of the mild deception she was practising on Brussels Society gave Allegra a rare night of broken sleep. After wak-
ening twice from disagreeable dreams in which Sir Derek
had, with great hauteur, put her in her place as a foolish
schemer and assured her of his intention of exposing her
as such to the world, she finally gave up the struggle and
got out of bed, where she slipped on a dressing gown and

sat down beside one of the two small *oeil-de-boeuf* windows that the little bedchamber possessed.

She would dearly have loved to light a candle and forget her troubles in a book, but refrained from doing so for fear of waking Hilary, and instead sat looking out at the tall pointed gables of the houses beyond the small garden behind the Pensionnat, which by day had bright yellow walls and blue-tinted roofs but now only glimmered palely under the calm night sky. The house was perfectly still, for the girls and the other mistresses, who slept on the floor below, had long since gone to their beds, as no doubt had Mlle. Jusseau, whose private apartments occupied the remainder of the top storey of the house.

Suddenly, however, a slight sound roused her attention; someone, she was sure, had just passed the door of her room. A board creaked softly; whoever the nocturnal prowler was, he—or she—was evidently taking some pains not to be heard. Allegra, half-uneasy, half-intrigued, could not restrain her curiosity; she went to the door, opened it cautiously, and peered out. She could hear the soft sound of footsteps now descending the stairs below her, and a faint gleam of candlelight moved steadily down the stairwell.

The thought that someone might be ill or some accident have happened then occurred to her. Only Marthe, she knew, besides herself, Hilary, and Mlle. Jusseau, slept on the top floor of the house, and if Cherry were ill she might have sent her maid to fetch a doctor, while she remained alone. Upon impulse, Allegra lit her candle and went down the hall to the door leading to Mlle. Jusseau's bedchamber. It stood open, and in the light of the candle she could see that the bed had not been slept in.

More puzzled than ever, she turned again and went quietly down the stairs to the first storey. Nothing but darkness and silence met her there. As she stood irresolute, however, the sound of low voices coming from below reached her ears; she recognised Mlle. Jusseau's voice and then a man's deeper tones. Almost without considering what she was doing, she approached the stairhead and saw in the centre of the shadowy ground-floor hall below, clearly visible in the light of the candle Mlle. Jusseau held in her hand, a burly, dark-faced man in a bottle-green coat, in the act of bestowing something in one of his inner pockets. Mlle. Jusseau herself was fully dressed, her grey hair arranged in its neat daytime fashion, and she was speaking rapidly to her nocturnal visitor.

What the reason for this odd behaviour on her old governess's part could be Allegra had not the least guess, but, suddenly acutely embarrassed to find herself eavesdropping, she was turning hastily away towards the stairs leading to the second storey when she heard the sound of a ⌐ ⌐r closing softly below. Almost at the same moment Mademoiselle's voice came to her ears.

"Allegra! *Qu'est-ce que tu fais?*"

Allegra, feeling as uncomfortable as if she were six years old with guilty jam on her face, turned around again.

"Oh, I am so sorry!" she said rather incoherently. "I heard footsteps and of course I didn't know what it was, only I thought somone might be ill and I came to see—"

"Quite natural," said Mlle. Jusseau, ascending the stairs calmly but looking at her, Allegra thought, rather searchingly. "But, as you see, no one is ill, *ma chère*. It was only an indigent and—I regret to say—not quite respectable relation of mine, who prefers to make his calls upon me for assistance at rather unusual hours. I am sorry if we wakened you."

"Oh, you didn't!" said Allegra, made still more uncomfortable by these disclosures. "I mean, I already was—"

"Worrying over your interview with Sir Derek?" Mademoiselle said indulgently. "Foolish child! You had best have it over with and go tomorrow. I shall manage very well without you here."

And she said good night and went on to her own bed-

chamber without pausing, leaving Allegra with an odd
and not quite agreeable feeling that there was something
more to the matter than Mlle. Jusseau had seen fit to
disclose to her. But what it could be she had not the least
idea, and Mlle. Jusseau's manner had not invited
enquiries. Allegra, feeling acutely for the first time that
she was quite as dependant upon her old governess's good
will here as she had been upon the Colbridges' at Chatt
Park, knew that it would not be wise for her to refer
again in the morning to the eccentric relation who preferred to make his calls in the middle of the night, and in
fact she was not even prepared to ask Mademoiselle how
she had found out so quickly where Sir Derek was staying
in Brussels—as it appeared that she must have done, or
she would not have proposed that Allegra go to see him
on the following dày.

In the morning, as soon as breakfast was over, Mademoiselle, looking so calm and respectable that it was impossible to believe that any relation of hers would dare to
be anything but respectable as well, informed Allegra that
she would find Sir Derek at the Hôtel de Belle Vue in the
street of the same name, and told her that Jules, the manservant who served as porter and general factotum at the
Pensionnat, would drive her there as soon as she had put
on her bonnet and gloves.

"Yes, but—ought I to go so early?" Allegra objected,
feeling her heart sinking in a most cowardly fashion at the
thought of the interview before her. "Sir Derek will certainly not be up at this hour."

"Then he must get up," said Mlle. Jusseau coolly. "Do
not be a goose, Allegra! If you wait, he will have gone
out, or be engaged, and you are in such a state of nerves
that you will scarcely venture a second visit if you do not
succeed in seeing him on the first."

Allegra, putting on a *dégagé* air, said that she was not
nervous in the least, and then, being too sensible not to
realise the importance of alerting Sir Derek to her new

position as Hilary's distant cousin, went upstairs to put on her sage-green bonnet. Happily, Marthe's clever fingers had succeeded in quite disguising the unbecomingness of this article of apparel by stripping it of its thread net trimming and audaciously curtailing the poke to reveal, instead of totally eclipsing, its wearer's face, and the sage-green dress she was wearing, too, was almost unrecognisable now as the rather dowdy garment Hilary had so deplored: with its sleeves cunningly slashed and puffed and its skirt narrowed to display the elegant lines of its wearer's figure, it might have stepped directly from the pages of *La Belle Assemblée*—where, indeed, its exact prototype was to be found.

Thus attired, Allegra was able to contemplate her appearance in the glass with something more akin to satisfaction than had been possible on the occasion of her first meeting with Sir Derek, and had descended the stairs and gone outside to seat herself in Mademoiselle's neat gig, already drawn up before the door in readiness for her appearance, before another disquieting thought occurred to her. Why was Mlle. Jusseau—the highest of sticklers where the proprieties were concerned—sending her alone to see Sir Derek at his hotel? Allegra herself, who considered that she had long outgrown the age at which it was necessary for her to be accompanied by a maid or some other female companion when she went out, had been accustomed for several years—much to Lady Warring's disapproval—to conducting herself quite as freely as if she had been of Lady Warring's own age, so that it had scarcely occurred to her until this moment that for her to call upon Sir Derek alone at his hotel might appear distinctly odd and even improper to him.

But that the same thought had not occurred to Mlle. Jusseau was incredible, and Allegra, sitting very upright against the squabs as the gig moved sedately down the street, was obliged to consider the possibility that that perspicacious female had allowed her to undertake her er-

rand with the cynical but practical thought in mind that if
Sir Derek might be made to feel that she had been
compromised he might be persuaded again to offer marriage to her.

If Mademoiselle had been present at that moment, Allegra, in spite of the regard in which she held her, would
assuredly have taxed her with this Machiavellian intention; but she was not, and Allegra found herself obliged
to decide whether to proceed to the Hôtel de Belle Vue as
she had planned or to return to the Pensionnat Jusseau
and give Mademoiselle a large piece of her mind. It was
not a difficult decision: Sir Derek *must* be informed of her
new status as instructress at the Pensionnat and distant
relation of Hilary before he inadvertently betrayed her.
And if he should take any ridiculous fancies into his head
as to the impropriety of her visiting him at his hotel, she
would take good care to disabuse him of the notion.

So she allowed Jules to drive her on to the Rue de
Belle Vue and to set her down at the Hôtel, where she
sent up her card and was soon shown into an elegantly
furnished saloon upon the first floor. Here she was received by a very superior manservant, who informed her
woodenly that his master would see her as soon as
possible and then left the room, his very back suggesting
outrage at the notion of anyone's presuming to call upon
a gentleman at an hour when only tradesmen and servants
should be up and about.

Allegra, feeling that his intention, as surrogate for his
master, had been to put her in her place, at once decided
not to be put there and occupied the ten minutes that
elapsed before Sir Derek appeared very pleasurably in
thinking up several telling remarks to make to him on the
subject of town beaux, until she recollected that, after all,
as she had a favour to ask of him, it would be better not
to set his back up. She had just time to put on a more
amiable face before Sir Derek appeared, wearing a hand-

some brocade dressing gown and with a slight frown upon his own countenance.

"May I enquire, Miss Herington, what has induced you to make this singularly ill-judged call?" he asked curtly, after casting a quick glance at her which seemed to reassure him as to the fact that she appeared to be suffering from no immediate personal distress. "Even if some accident has occurred, it would have been more advisable for you to send a message rather than come here yourself."

This was not an auspicious beginning. Allegra felt her hackles rising, and with some difficulty kept the amiable look pinned upon her face.

"I must offer you my apologies, of course, Sir Derek, for disturbing you at so early an hour," she said, with an airiness that she was made infuriatingly conscious was not in the least convincing. Indeed, remembering Sir Derek's devastatingly frank comments to her at the dinner party at Chatt Park, she was quite sure that he was setting it down as her Lady Hatherill manner. "But the matter is somewhat urgent—"

She paused, suddenly becoming conscious that Sir Derek with a rather grim frown upon his face was a far more formidable figure than she could have imagined from her previous acquaintance with him, even after her experience with his hasty anger when she had rejected him.

"Yes?" he said unencouragingly. "And what is this somewhat urgent matter, Miss Herington?"

Allegra, who had been walking about the saloon while waiting for Sir Derek's appearance and who observed that she was pointedly *not* being asked now to sit down, said rather heatedly that if he was in such a hurry she would tell him.

"Do," said Sir Derek with more brevity than civility.

"Very *well!*" said Allegra. "I daresay you have heard from Lady Warring or—or *some*one what I am doing here in Brussels, for you don't seem at all surprised to see me—I mean, that I am here."

"I am not," said Sir Derek, as briefly as before. "Go on."

"And—and Hilary is with me, of course," Allegra continued, but finding it more and more difficult to proceed with her explanation under Sir Derek's unsympathetic gaze, "and Mlle. Jusseau and I thought it might be better, since she might receive invitations to go into Society from the mothers of some of the other girls at the Pensionnat, and in fact has already done so from Lady Milgrom, if I—that is, if people thought that I was merely a distant connexion of hers and not her sister—because I *am* employed as a schoolmistress—"

She broke off. Sir Derek was looking more unsympathetic than ever.

"I see," he said.

"But I don't think you do," Allegra said in a rather harried voice, for she was conscious that her explanation had been a remarkably foolish and disjointed one for a young woman who prided herself upon her cool intelligence. "I mean—well, you *must* understand," she went on, "that if Hilary has not the opportunity to go into Society here she will have not the least chance of making a suitable marriage, and people simply will not invite her anywhere if she is known only as the sister of a schoolmistress—"

"I imagine that her chances to marry respectably would be considerably less impeded by her being known to be the sister of a schoolmistress than by her being exposed as the sister of what some people would not hesitate to call an adventuress!" said Sir Derek scathingly. "Do you tell me that this remarkably shatter-brained scheme has Mlle. Jusseau's approval? I cannot think so!"

"Well, it has!" said Allegra, her colour heightening. "And what is more, Colonel Hepworth—I believe you know him, for he says he knows *you*—who is a very old friend, does not find it so very reprehensible, either!"

A sudden smile gleamed for a moment in Sir Derek's dark eyes.

"Oh, if you are quoting Hep to me as an authority on the proprieties, your choice is excessively ill-advised," he said, upon which Allegra, with more heat than logic, said that *he* was a gentleman, at any rate, thus seeming to imply—if anyone wished to take it in that spirit—that present company was not. The smile disappeared from Sir Derek's eyes, and he said dryly, "In spite of that, Miss Herington, I shall not apologise to you for my lack of hospitality. You have no business to be here, and the sooner you leave the better pleased I shall be. I gather that you have come to request me not to betray my knowledge that you are Hilary's sister to any of my acquaintance here in Brussels. If you will take my advice—"

"Well, I shan't!" Allegra muttered mutinously, under her breath.

"—you will put an end to this charade before it has gone any further," said Sir Derek, who was looking as exasperated as a gentleman can who is doing his best to keep his temper in the face of increasing provocation. "You have already, it seems, come across at least one person here who knows you to be Hilary's sister—Colonel Hepworth—"

"Yes, I have!" said Allegra. "And he has introduced me to several other gentlemen as Hilary's cousin—and I may say that *all* of them displayed an excessive interest in Hilary, and that one of them was your cousin, Lord Roderick Buccan—"

"If you think," said Sir Derek, his exasperation now bursting its bonds at this flaunting of young Lord Roderick before his face, "that Roddy cares a rush whether the next pretty girl he falls top-over-tail in love with has relations any more disgraceful than the last—who I may tell you boasted a cent-per-center for an uncle and a mother

who could have passed for an abbess if she wasn't one—
you are fair and far out, Miss Herington! And if you have
any idea of looking in *that* direction for a husband for
your sister, you had best drop it at once. Roddy is nineteen—far too young to be thinking of marriage, especially
with a girl who has not a penny to bless herself with!"

Allegra's chin went up. "I daresay," she said, "that you
do not think Hilary good enough for a duke's son! Let me
tell you that the Heringtons—"

"I know all about the Heringtons," Sir Derek said
acidly. "I am one myself, if you will remember. And your
sister may marry as many duke's sons as she likes, as long
as they have the means to support her in a style befitting
their station—which Roddy has not! But that is neither
here nor there," he added after a moment, obviously controlling his temper and speaking in a decisive voice. "If
you are determined upon going into Society here, I shall
see to it that you receive the proper invitations—provided, of course, that you drop this childish and entirely unsuitable pretence that you are not Hilary's sister—"

He got no farther, for Allegra, dumbfounded, had uttered an exclamation of disbelief.

"You will do that! But—but why should you—?"

"Because I have not the least wish to see a pair of females who must be known by their very name as my relations exposed to ridicule and censure!" Sir Derek said
blightingly, thus instantly absolving Allegra of any obligation to be grateful to him and causing her to be quite satisfactorily angry with him again, for which she was very
glad, for she had had a horrid feeling for a moment that
perhaps his character was not so entirely black as she had
been thinking it. "And now," he added, in a tone that
suggested the complete impossibility of her doing anything
but what she was told, "I shall ask you to leave, Miss
Herington. How did you come here?"

Allegra, in a tone suggesting that she would do entirely

as it suited her to do, said in Mlle. Jusseau's gig, which was waiting for her below.

"Very well," said Sir Derek. "Go back to the Pensionnat and you will hear from me. I think my aunt Lady Spinley's evening party on Thursday will do for a beginning. I shall call for you and your sister at nine."

Allegra, feeling that events were moving rather too rapidly for her to keep up with, and finding herself impelled towards the door by Sir Derek's hand under her elbow, said rather breathlessly, "But what about Lady Milgrom and—and Lord Roderick and his friends?"

"As far as Roddy and his friends are concerned," said Sir Derek, improvising masterfully, "Colonel Hepworth is well known to be an incurable jokesmith, and in introducing you to them as your sister's cousin he was merely pitching one of his Banbury tales. About Lady Milgrom you need not concern yourself. She is universally recognised as a hen-witted female, besides being no one at all in Society. Had you and your sister the intention of attending her ball?"

"We *have* the intention," Allegra corrected him, with ominous sweetness.

"Have you? Then you must change it," Sir Derek said imperturbably. "You may be my guests at the Opera on that evening instead. Do you like Gluck?"

Allegra said with emphasis that she detested Gluck, upon which Sir Derek said with unimpaired calm that he dared say she would have a very dull evening of it then but it couldn't be helped, and firmly escorted her to the door.

"Odious, overbearing, detestable man!" Allegra fumed, as she descended the stairs. "As if all Hilary and I needed to ensure our success in Society were *his* sponsorship!"

But Mlle. Jusseau, when Allegra had smoulderingly confided to her the results of her visit to the Hôtel de Belle Vue upon her return to the Pensionnat, showed herself only too willing to believe in Sir Derek's high opinion

of the influence his taking up the Misses Herington would
have upon their being accepted in Brussels Society.

"Mon Dieu, this is beyond anything that I had hoped,"
she declared, an expression of the greatest satisfaction
upon her small, ugly face, "knowing the terms on which
you stood with him!" Allegra opened her mouth to protest, but Mademoiselle went on, speaking quite as severely
as she might have done to a thirteen-year-old Allegra a
dozen years before. "You will be foolish beyond permission, *ma chère,* if you show yourself ungrateful for Sir
Derek's actions in your behalf! Of course you will accept
his kind offer to procure cards to his aunt's evening party
for you and Hilary, and his invitation to the Opera as
well. To Lady Milgrom you may send your regrets. She is
all very well if one can hope for nothing better; but under
Sir Derek's sponsorship you will be accepted at once into
the First Circles in Brussels, and without the necessity of
carrying out this unseemly deception with regard to your
own consequence."

"Is his social credit so high, then," asked Allegra, incredulously and still a little rebelliously, "as to make even
my schoolmistressing acceptable?"

"Je le crois bien!" Mademoiselle said unhesitatingly.
"Why, you foolish child, are you not aware that the Wel-
lesleys—both the Duke and his brother the Marquis—are
long-standing friends and sponsors of his, and that he is
related through his mother to many of the first families
in England?—besides being looked up to by all the younger men as being what you English call 'top-of-the-trees,'
a nonpareil among gentlemen addicted to your sports?"

Allegra, with an odd, uncomfortable feeling that she
had somehow been put in the wrong by Sir Derek by his
never boasting to her of all these heroic attributes, said
that of course she knew about his family but not the other
things, and then felt a little as the beggar-maid might
have done if she had refused King Cophetua and had to
go on living in her mud hovel. But there was no use now

in regretting what was past, which indeed she could not really regret after her latest experience that morning with Sir Derek's utter lack of good manners in dealing with her visit to his hotel; but she was glad, all the same, when Hillary came into the room with the white kitten and the talk turned to the dresses they would wear to Lady Spinley's evening party on Thursday.

Chapter Nine

HILARY, OF COURSE, was delighted to learn that there was no longer any necessity for her to disown Allegra as a sister, and was so much in charity with Sir Derek for making this possible that she greeted him, when he arrived at the Pensionnat Jusseau on Thursday evening to escort her and Allegra to the Spinleys', with all the cordiality of an old friend. She was looking particularly fetching that evening in the pale puce gown that Marthe's clever fingers had produced from Mlle. Jusseau's muslin, with her dark hair charmingly arranged *à l'anglaise* by that same useful female, who had transferred some of the devotion she lavished upon Mademoiselle to the younger Miss Herington—a fact that did not surprise Allegra, for her sister had been notorious since her nursery days for enslaving servants of all ages and both sexes, whom she treated as valued equals and confidants.

It was more of a triumph to see the light of approval that evening in Sir Derek's eyes as he surveyed the two young ladies whom he was to introduce into Brussels Society that evening. Allegra, always quite unself-conscious as to any claims she herself had to beauty, was inclined to give all the credit for that approval to Hilary, but her own appearance, in Italian silk of a ravishing almond-green-colour, with an opera comb set behind the heavy knot of coppery hair on the crown of her head, was such as to cause Sir Derek to realise for the first time how captivating a picture she could present when attired in a becoming gown in the first style of elegance.

Hilary, peacocking with great satisfaction under his admiration, did most of the talking as they settled themselves in the carriage and drove the short distance to the house the Spinleys had taken in the Rue Ducale, plying Sir Derek with questions as to the people they might expect to meet there that evening. The Duke? Very probably. The Prince of Orange? Oh, undoubtedly. What was he like? A very amiable young man, with engaging manners. Handsome? No, he could scarcely be called so.

"That," said Hilary wisely, "is no doubt why the Princess Charlotte cried off from her engagement to him," and, upon being informed by Sir Derek that that was the reasoning of a very young lady, said buoyantly that the Princess was a very young lady herself, and that was why she was sure she was right.

She then expressed a desire to meet the scandalous Lady Caro Lamb, who had come to Brussels, she had heard, to escape the disappointment of seeing Lord Byron married to Miss Milbanke, and when Sir Derek stated emphatically that he would certainly *not* introduce her to that lady even if she were present at the Spinleys' that evening, said oh, very well, then he might present her to Lady Frances Webster, who she understood to be the Duke's latest inamorata.

"Where do you learn all this gossip?" Sir Derek enquired, amused but slightly puzzled by Hilary's artlessly knowledgeable airs. "I should have thought a girls' school the last place in the world for the latest crim. con. stories to be circulated."

"Well, *there* you are quite mistaken," Hilary said seriously, "for there is nothing the girls like to talk of more. And Cherry—Mlle. Jusseau, that is—knows absolutely *everything* there is to know about Brussels Society, and I hear her talking to Allie sometimes. I can't think where she picks it all up, for she never goes anywhere herself, but of course she *did* do governessing for some very tonnish families here before she came to England, and I expect she keeps up connexions with some of her old pupils."

Sir Derek said firmly that that was all very well, but he had no intention of starting off her career in Brussels Society by making her acquainted with all the most gossipped-about females in town, and then added, with a gravity belied by the gleam in his dark eyes, that he knew several very respectable elderly ladies with whom she might pass an improving hour or two that evening.

Hilary looked at him suspiciously. "I think you are funning," she said, "and if you are not, it will be the horridest take-in that ever was, to ask us to a party and then make me sit talking to old ladies! I want to dance!"

Sir Derek, relenting, said that dance she should, and then, looking at Allegra, so should her sister. But Allegra at once said certainly not, she was there only *en chaperon* and people would think it very odd indeed to see a schoolmistress dancing.

"Not if the schoolmistress is Sir Thomas Herington's daughter and my cousin," Sir Derek said, and, with his usual cool disregard for her objections, said that he would claim the second set and the third with Hilary.

"What will you do for the first?" Hilary demanded, between curiosity and mischief.

Sir Derek said not to ask so many questions or she would frighten prospective suitors away, which made Hilary giggle.

"No, but what *will* you?" she persisted. "I think you are trying to fob me off."

"I am," said Sir Derek resignedly, "but as it seems to

be doing no good I shall tell you. I am engaged for the first set to Miss Hardison."

"Who is Miss Hardison?"

"She is Lord Balmforth's daughter and that is the last question that I shall answer," said Sir Derek. "You have scarcely given your sister the opportunity to speak a word."

But Allegra was so much overcome by sensations having to do with the strangeness of going to an evening party escorted by a gentleman whose suit she had refused less than a month before, to say nothing of the sudden and unaccountable dislike she had taken to the unknown Miss Hardison, that she had very little conversation and was excessively glad when the carriage drew up before the Spinleys' house in the Rue Ducale.

Within the house, which was a very elegant and commodious one, with a pair of saloons decorated in the Empire style—all mahogany and bronze, and hung with gold-embroidered draperies of crimson brocade—Sir Derek made his two protégées known to Lord and Lady Spinley. The latter was one of the three beautiful Elsbree sisters—the other two being, or having been, as the case might be, the Present Duchess of Wyon and Sir Derek's mother, Lady Maria Herington—and like all the Elsbrees had large dark eyes and great simplicity of manner, so that she was universally known as a lovely widgeon. This, however, was not quite correct, for she had married off three daughters very creditably.

At sight of more marriage-fodder in the person of two motherless young females whose connexion with her, although exceedingly slight, was sufficient to allow her to dip her fingers into the matchmaking pie, her face brightened and she said dear Derek had done exactly right to bring them. She then said she was sure there would be any number of unattached young men in her saloons that evening, which made Allegra realise that she had found a valuable ally, and as she passed on into the rooms that had been set aside for dancing she made a grudging mental acknowledgement that Sir Derek, in enlisting his aunt's interest in their favour, had accomplished a master stroke.

The first person to come up to them when they entered the saloon was young Lord Roderick Buccan, looking very smart in his scarlet regimentals, who had been standing talking to another young officer but concluded his conversation without ceremony as soon as his eyes fell upon the new arrivals.

"Oh, I say," he said eagerly to Hilary, "this is beyond anything great, Miss Hilary! I didn't know you were acquainted with my aunt. Miss Herington—your servant," he added, blushing slightly as he recollected himself and bowed belatedly to Allegra.

Allegra laughed. "No, no, never mind about me," she said. "I am here only to chaperon my sister and shall now retire in good form and allow you young people to enjoy yourselves." She cast a glance at Sir Derek, a half-defiant look of mischief in her eyes. "I daresay Sir Derek has already informed you that I *am* her sister, and that Colonel Hepworth was *cutting a wheedle,* as I believe you young men put it, the other day?"

"Yes. He is the most complete hand, isn't he?" said Lord Roderick, who appeared to accept the Colonel's eccentric sense of humour with unquestioning enthusiasm. "One never knows what sort of rig he will be running next! Miss Hilary, you *will* stand up with me for this set, won't you?" he went on, again transferring his attention to Hilary, who indeed had never lost it entirely and appeared to be reciprocating with equal fervour. "If you don't, it will spoil everything!"—which struck Allegra as such a very youthful thing to say that she laughed again and said of course Hilary would stand up with him, for it would be too dreadful to think of such a catastrophe occurring.

"I thought," said Sir Derek to Allegra in a tone of considerable asperity as Hilary and Lord Roderick walked off together, "that I had made it particularly clear to you, Miss Herington, that you would do well not to encourage Roddy to imagine that he is falling in love with your sister."

"I don't think he needs any encouragement," said Allegra, who was looking reflectively after the departing pair. "Besides, I like him. Is he really so purse-pinched as you say?"

"Yes! The Duchess unfortunately is quite eighteenth-century in her addiction to gaming; I could not begin to tell you what she has cost my uncle over the past thirty-odd years."

"But she has so many children!" Allegra said, fascinated by these revelations of misconduct in High Life. "Eleven, I believe Lord Roderick said. Surely that should have—?" She paused delicately.

"Well, it didn't!" Sir Derek said roundly, taking her meaning. "One of them—not Roddy; Cecil I think it was—was almost born in the carriage as she was returning home from a polite gaming-hell in Curzon Street. The coachman gave in his notice the next day."

Upon which he and Allegra both laughed and then Sir Derek, recollecting himself, said that all the same he meant what he had said about Lord Roderick and if she had to be matchmaking she might encourage Hilary to look kindly upon young Robin Playsted, who, owing to the recent death of an elder brother, would come in for a very nice place in Kent one day and was already, according to Lord Roderick, so *épris* with Hilary that he had written a poem in honour of her eyes.

"He hasn't!" said Allegra, awed. "That nice boy? I should never have believed it of him!"

"Well, there is nothing so reprehensible about writing poetry!" Sir Derek said, looking rather stung. "I have done it myself in my grasstime."

"Now that," declared Allegra, "I do *not* believe. A

gentleman who approaches the idea of matrimony with so much rationality and cool detachment—"

"Unfortunately—or perhaps I should say fortunately—there was no thought of matrimony in my mind when I wrote it," Sir Derek said, with a pleasurably reminiscent air that Allegra for some reason found particularly irritating; and then, having thus neatly turned the tables on her, which her gentlemanly reference to his ill-fated matrimonial schemes concerning her perhaps deserved, went on to say calmly, "And now, shall we see about finding a partner for you?"

Allegra, taking refuge in hauteur, said she had told him once before, and would repeat it, that she would not dance.

"Nonsense!" said Sir Derek, quite as impervious as usual to objections. "In that gown it is manifestly impossible for you to pretend to be nothing but a chaperon. What is your preference? An Hussar? A Lifeguardsman? Or perhaps one of our gallant Belgian allies? I am afraid my aunt has a penchant for military men; we seem to be quite overrun with them this evening."

"Thank you," said Allegra in a tone strongly intimating that she was not thankful in the least, "but I do not require a partner, Sir Derek! If you will see that Hilary is provided for, that is all that is necessary."

And she was turning away, with every indication to Sir Derek that their conversation was at an end, when she almost ran against a dark, very handsome gentleman in the blue uniform with a scarlet-and-white collar that she had learned to recognise as that of the National Militia. The gentleman uttered hasty apologies in French; at the same moment his eyes made a swift survey of the almond-green gown and the vivid face with its flawless complexion beneath the high knot of flaming hair, and an expression of deep appreciation, such as no English gentleman would have dreamed of allowing himself upon a first encounter, crossed his aquiline features. Almost simultaneously he took in Sir Derek's presence and immediately laid his hand upon his arm.

"Tiens!" he said. "What fortune! You will make known to me this lady, Derek, upon whose train I have most rudely almost trodden, so that I may offer properly my apologies?"

"With the greatest pleasure," said Sir Derek promptly. "How do you go on, Gilles? I haven't seen you since Lisbon." He turned to Allegra. "Miss Herington, *may I* present Captain the Baron de Lempriere?"

The gentleman bowed, a look of some slight surprise crossing his face.

"Miss *Herington?*" he repeated. "But you are then perhaps—Derek's sister?"

"Oh, no! Only a distant connexion," said Allegra hastily, at the very moment that Sir Derek said, almost equally hastily, "No! My cousin!"

The Baron observed with a smile that there seemed to be some difference of opinion here, and said that if Miss Herington would do him the honour of standing up with him for the set that was just then forming he would be happy to explore with her the ramifications of the Herington family tree.

"But I am not dancing—" Allegra began, only to find her hand taken by Sir Derek and given into the Baron's with, as she later expressed it to Hilary, "the most odiously *paternal* air!"

"Nonsense!" said Sir Derek kindly. "Lempriere is an excellent dancer; I am sure you will enjoy excessively standing up with him."

And he strolled off to find his own partner, leaving Allegra fuming, but obliged to conceal her feelings out of civility to the Baron, who had become serious the moment her hand had touched his and said something very Gallic about Romeo and Juliet and palm to palm being holy palmers' kiss.

"You see I am acquainted with your Shakespeare," he

said, with a meaning smile to which Allegra did not quite know how to respond, so she merely said the first thing that came into her head, which was that she was very fond of Shakespeare.

The Baron, however, appeared to find this quite satisfactory, and led her into the set as the musicians struck up a country dance. Here she was able to see at once that Sir Derek had been correct in indicating that her partner was an excellent dancer, and she was soon made aware as well that he was adept in yet another art—that of polite flirtation. Almost every word he spoke to her was in one way or another a delicately turned compliment, and Allegra, whose social experience—except for her single Season in London, when Lady Hatherill's vigilance had protected her from the attentions of blunt country squires and their callow offspring was at a loss as to how to stem this flood of elegant dalliance.

Even a retreat to what Sir Derek had called her "Lady Hatherill manner" did not noticeably dampen the Baron's ardour, and she was beginning to feel excessively uncomfortable when, going down the dance, she saw Sir Derek looking at her with a glint of amusement in his eyes. At the same moment she became aware that he and his partner, a tall, very handsome, dark-haired young woman clad in a robe of celestial blue satin trimmed with blond lace, were also carrying on what appeared to be a very agreeable flirtation, and for some quite unknown reason her chin went up. She gave Sir Derek the blandest stare of which she was capable at the moment, and, upon Baron de Lempriere's observing meaningly to her the next moment that Titian had always been his favourite painter, said with great aplomb that if he meant her he was quite out, for her hair was common garden-variety red.

"I should not call it so!" said the Baron fervently. "No! *Couleur de flamme,* rather!"

"What a lovely thing to say!" said Allegra with equal fervour, and then looked down the set defiantly at Sir

Derek while the Baron, satisfied that he was making progress, embarked upon yet another compliment.

During all this time, involved as she was in her own amorous difficulties, she had not ceased to keep an eye upon Hilary and Lord Roderick, and did not know whether to be elated or disturbed to see that they appeared to be getting on together as splendidly as two young people of different sexes and equally high spirits usually do when they have taken an instant liking to each other. She was quite conscious that Sir Derek's opposition to any romantic involvement between Hilary and his young cousin would most probably be echoed by Lord Roderick's family, who could scarcely be expected to be overjoyed at the idea of his bringing home a penniless bride; but still it pleased her to see her young sister enjoying herself. So she told herself that probably when Hilary danced with young Cornet Playsted, whom she could see now standing against the wall with the forlorn look upon his face of a very nice puppy whose bone has been taken away from it, she would look just as happy, and that there was therefore nothing to worry about, and went back to coping with the Baron.

At the end of the set Sir Derek came up to claim her hand for the next dance.

"Oh, I must see about Hilary," said Allegra, pretending to have forgotten all about Sir Derek's promise to stand up with her.

"You need do nothing of the kind," said Sir Derek firmly. "Young Playsted and Francis Pelton, as you may observe for yourself, are at this moment disputing each other's claims to the honour of leading her on to the floor, and as you do not know which of them to favour—not being acquainted with their respective worldly prospects—you would best leave her to make the decision herself."

"I am not so mercenary!" Allegra said, rather warmly. "But when one has nothing—owing *entirely,* I may say, to one's misfortune in not having been born a boy—"

"If that is to my address," said Sir Derek reasonably, "kindly recollect that I could not help being born a boy any more than you could being born a girl. Besides, you will remember that I tried to give Rolveston back to you in my own no doubt very arrogant—I believe you did say arrogant?—way."

"Yes, I did!" said Allegra. "And you were! Exactly as if you were hiring a kitchen-maid!"

"No, no, I should leave *that* to my housekeeper," Sir Derek murmured soothingly, which made Allegra long, not for the first time, to hit him. Fortunately, she recollected in time how very odd Lady Spinley's guests would think it if she did, and therefore meekly allowed herself to be led out on to the floor instead.

"I see you have made a conquest of Lempriere," Sir Derek continued the conversation with what Allegra considered his usual lack of tact, or even good manners, once the music had begun. "I think it only fair to warn you, though, that it will not do to give him too much encouragement, for he is much more likely to offer you a *carte blanche* than lawful matrimony. He is something of a connoisseur, you see, where female beauty is concerned, and I believe considers you a species of rare exotic. You are not in the least in the common style, you know."

"Thank you!" said Allegra with some asperity, for she was not at all certain whether she was to consider this a compliment or not. "But it was you yourself who presented him to me, remember!—and if you wish to preserve my virtue from his attentions, no doubt it will be sufficient for you to inform him that I am merely a lowly schoolmistress to cause him to lose all interest in me!"

"Not at all! He is not so faint-hearted as that!" protested Sir Derek imperturbably. "And I have no fears whatever for your virtue, Miss Herington. You seem to me in many respects a very sensible girl, and certainly quite capable of putting Lempriere in his place if you should desire to do so."

"I am not a girl!" said Allegra smoulderingly. "And as for my virtue—that, Sir Derek, is no affair of yours!"

"It would have been if you had married me," Sir Derek said, to which all Allegra could think of to say in reply was a very ungracious and unsatisfactory, "Well, I didn't!"

"No, and a very good thing," said Sir Derek approvingly, at which rejoinder—so mortifying from a gentleman one had rejected!—Allegra lapsed into outraged silence.

Chapter Ten

JUST AS THE set was ending, something of a stir was caused by the entrance of the Duke of Wellington, who had brought with him the Prince of Orange and several members of his Staff. Allegra had the honour of an introduction to both these august gentlemen by Sir Derek, who seemed not at all disconcerted by the coolness with which she had behaved towards him during the set; and she was obliged to admit that what Mlle. Jusseau had told her regarding his relations with the hero of the hour was quite true. The Duke was exceedingly affable to her, almost embarrassing her by calling the attention of those surrounding him to the very pretty contrast afforded by her vivid colouring and the stately dark beauty of the Honourable Miss Hardison, who chanced, in the crush about the distinguished guests, to find herself beside her; but Allegra could not help thinking that the greater part of the attention he paid to her was due rather to his regard for Sir Derek than to his admiration for her charms.

In this, however, she was not quite correct, for the Duke, who had always an eye for a charming face and figure, would have been disposed to admire her whether she had been Sir Derek's kinswoman or not.

She could not fail to note as well the deference with which the younger members of the Duke's Staff hung upon Sir Derek's words when his opinion was solicited on the merits of a horse one of them had recently purchased, or the easy camaraderie with which the young Prince of Orange behaved towards him, and was even conscious of a slight and quite unaccountable feeling of pride when she observed that all the splendour of the military gentlemen's scarlet and silver lace, their white net pantaloons and furred pelisses, could not cast into the shade the superior elegance of Sir Derek's tall figure in its black coat, white waistcoat, and satin knee-breeches.

But why this fact should please her, unless it were family pride at work, she could not imagine, and it vanished immediately when, as the musicians struck up a waltz, she observed him approach Miss Hardison once more and solicit her hand for the dance.

Allegra herself had had no intention of waltzing, feeling that it was far too dashing a dance for a schoolmistress to engage in, and also that it was her duty to see to it that Hilary did not allow herself to be led out on to the floor by one of her young admirers; for though her own come-out had occurred some years before the waltz craze had swept London, she was aware of the convention that had grown up prohibiting a young girl from performing this dance in public before she had been approved by the Patronesses of Almack's, that most exclusive of London clubs.

Unfortunately Hilary, although cautioned not to waltz, appeared to have thrown prudence to the winds, for before Allegra could disentangle herself from Royalty and Staff she was engaged, with Lord Roderick, in showing everyone else in the room how waltzing should properly be done. So Allegra, seeing the manifest impossibility of preserving her from the displeasure of the august Patronesses of Almack's, the sacred precincts of which it seemed highly unlikely that she would ever enter, at any rate, yielded to the importunities of plump, agreeable Sir Alexander Gordon of the Duke's Staff and whirled off into the dance with him.

Some time later, quite dizzy with waltzing, compliments, and a champagne supper, the latter of which she had enjoyed in the company of Captain the Baron de Lempriere, she had sat down to catch her breath on a high-backed, crimson-upholstered mahogany *canapé* standing against the wall when she was joined by Lady Spinley, who said she had been wishing to talk with her all the evening, only at one's own parties it was always so boring, what with young men who would not dance and young ladies who were dying to, and trying to do one's duty by everyone.

"But I was happy to see, my dear, that you and your sister have never lacked for partners," she said, "only really *not* Roddy Buccan, I think I should warn you, for he *must* marry where there is a fortune even if only a modest one, and young Robin Playsted seems *so* attentive."

Allegra, who realised that her ladyship's intentions were of the kindest, said with a smile that it was early days to be thinking of marriage, and that Hilary had only just met the two young men.

"Yes, I know, my dear, but there is a *something,* you know, about the way Roddy looks at her—and she at him," said Lady Spinley, her head on one side, considering the young couple, who were, most improperly, dancing together for the fourth time that evening. "I don't mean romantic, because neither of them is, in that upsetting way so many young people have taken to being these days and I do think it is all Lord Byron's fault, only now he is married perhaps he will stop being romantic and we can all go back to being sensible again. But they seem to enjoy being with each other so much—and that can be very dangerous, you know."

"Yes, I do know," Allegra admitted, a tiny frown creasing her brow. "And I shall really do my best to see to it that she does not fall in love with him, Lady Spinley—though I daresay you will not think it, with my permitting her to dance with him so often this evening. I am quite to blame, I know. If I had not been dancing myself—"

"But it is quite natural for you to be dancing, my dear child," Lady Spinley said, with the warm, soft tolerance that caused her to be so universally liked.

Allegra shook her head. "Oh, no!" she said firmly. "I am twenty-five, you know—*and* a schoolmistress, as I expect Sir Derek has told you."

"Yes—*so* unsuitable!" said Lady Spinley. "But we shall not think about that, for I am quite sure there are half a dozen gentlemen I can call to mind whom you would suit very well, in spite of your lack of fortune. There is poor Sir Arthur Huddleston, for example, who lost his wife last year—"

"But I do not wish for a husband for myself, ma'am!" Allegra said, laughing in spite of herself at her ladyship's assumption that everyone in her acquaintance would be better off in the married state.

But Lady Spinley only said with mild obstinacy that of course she did, exactly as she might have told one of her own daughters when they were small that they really did wish to practice on the pianoforte.

"The only difficulty is," she confided, her thoughts turning in another direction as her eyes fell upon Sir Derek, who was dancing at the moment with one of the Duchess of Richmond's daughters, Lady Georgiana Lennox, "in persuading gentlemen who really *should* be married to take the step. There is dear Derek, for example, who has had more caps set at him than I could count, and still unmarried! But I *think*," she went on, "from something he let fall the other day, that he has all but decided now to offer for Dianeme Hardison, which I must say I am excessively glad of, for she is exactly the sort of wife he should have. Such an elegant figure, and so accomplished that she makes one quite ashamed of oneself! I know it will be a comfort to you, my dear, to think that Rolveston will have such a suitable mistress. Derek has been telling me of the improvements he is making there; I quite long to see it!"

During this speech—which was not, after all, of very great length—such a variety of emotions had made their way pell-mell through Allegra's breast that she would not have been surprised to find that half an hour had elapsed since Lady Spinley had begun to speak. Astonishment, anger, mortification, jostled one another for supremacy in her mind, and she had, in addition, the very unpleasant sensation that her heart had suddenly taken up permanent residence in her pretty Denmark satin sandals. It was one thing to have rejected Sir Derek's addresses; it was quite another to find him apparently forming the intention of offering for another young lady before so much as a decent month had elapsed. And yet why, after all, should she be surprised by this? His intention had been to marry, and he had never pretended that his offer to her had been prompted by any warmer feelings than a conviction of the eligibility of the match.

No, it was not *that* that had discomposed her, she told herself. It was the notion of Dianeme Hardison—odious, pretentious name!—as mistress of Rolveston that galled. Looking at her now as she waltzed with Sir Derek, Allegra thought she had never seen such an unbecoming air of possessiveness in an unmarried female, such gay triumph in every movement of her undeniably graceful and well-formed figure. And Sir Derek, with besotted male stupidity, seemed to be actually enjoying it. It occurred to Allegra suddenly that what she would really like to do more than anything in the world would be to scratch the

Honourable Miss Dianeme Hardison's eyes out and then
retire to some comfortable coal cellar where she could cry
to her heart's content. Not that she was jealous of Miss
Hardison—certainly not! It was merely the thought of her
queening it at Rolveston that was so upsetting.

The sound of Baron de Lempriere's voice at her elbow
brought her abruptly out of these disagreeable thoughts.

"Miss Herington—we have not waltzed, and the evening for me will not be complete until I do. You per-
mit—?"

Miss Allegra Herington, schoolmistress, was well aware
that she had already drawn quite enough attention to herself that evening by standing up twice with the dashing
Captain and then allowing him to take her in to supper,
and that she ought to respond to his present application
by saying demurely, "Pray hold me excused, sir; I have
already danced a great deal more than I had intended."

But what she actually did was to smile up at the Baron
quite as cordially as Miss Hardison was smiling at Sir
Derek and, excusing herself to Lady Spinley, to say to
him, "Of course! I adore waltzing!"

The next moment she was out on the floor with him,
circling in his arms just as Miss Hardison was circling in
Sir Derek's, and when the two couples came close to each
other she gave Sir Derek the smile of a young lady who is
so blissfully happy to be where she is that she is scarcely
conscious of other people's being around, and took a
great deal of satisfaction in seeing the disapproving frown
that abruptly erased the smile upon *his* face.

Baron de Lempriere's voice in her ear was asking in
low, urgent tones if he might call upon her on the following day.

"Certainly not," said Allegra. "It would be most improper."

"Improper?" The Baron's face expressed his bewilder-
ment at this new instance of the madness of English
mores, which could discover cause for disapproval in a

gentleman's paying a perfectly conventional morning-call upon a lady. "But I do not understand—"

"I am a schoolmistress, you see," Allegra explained, primming her mouth slightly in a way that the Baron found entrancing. "Oh yes, quite beneath your touch, M. le Baron—although I *have* the honour of being a connexion of Sir Derek's. At midnight—or I daresay in these modern times a little later, as I am sure it is far past that hour already—I shall turn into Cinderella again and my so beautiful gown, as you have been kind enough to call it, into rags."

The Baron said gallantly that he was sure she would look enchanting in any dress, but she saw the gleam that leapt into his eyes at this disclosure and was able to interpret it very accurately. Inexperienced she might be, but she was not wholly unversed in the subtleties of the male mind, and she realised that the Baron—who, if he had had matrimonial intentions, might have found her lack of consequence dismaying—was undoubtedly pluming himself upon the new possibilities for successful romance that this knowledge of her worldly condition had opened up. To storm the citadel of an unmarried English young lady of birth and fortune, protected as she must certainly be by her careful family, was one thing; it was quite another when this same lady was discovered in the role of a penniless schoolmistress, unshielded by residence with relations of consequence and no doubt amenable to the lure of expensive presents.

"If I may not call," he said, his hand clasping hers a little more tightly, his arm encircling her waist a little more boldly, "then perhaps a small excursion into the country? The weather has turned so fine—has it not?—and there are friends of mine who are planning a charming fête, a moonlight picnic near Hal, on the banks of the Senne—"

"My dear Baron," said Allegra, making play with her fine eyes and beginning to feel quite intoxicated by this suddenly discovered talent for light flirtation, "is it your intention to ruin my reputation completely? I have heard of these moonlight picnics, where one— or should I say two?—can so conveniently contrive to become lost in a secluded coppice, and so, I am sure, have the mamas of my pupils."

The Baron sighed, and said that if she must be so bound by tiresome propriety he would then suggest a more prosaic daylight excursion, to which scheme Allegra, who had just obtained a full view of Miss Hardison's cameo-pure profile as she smiled up into Sir Derek's eyes, immediately and cordially assented. The music soon afterward came to an end, and Allegra, finding herself standing near Sir Derek, who had remained in conversation with Miss Hardison at the conclusion of the waltz, had what can only be described as a highly reprehensible impulse to make mischief between them—solely, of course, because it would never do to have Miss Hardison as mistress of Rolveston!—and trod up to him to enquire sweetly if it would be possible for her and Hilary to be taken home.

"I cannot sleep the morning through as if I had nothing to do, as you others can, Sir Derek," she said, looking at Miss Hardison as she did so with such an expression of virtuous humility upon her face that it might have deceived almost anyone but a young lady who wished to marry Sir Derek. To any young lady coming under that category it must have been at once apparent that a spoke was being thrust in her wheel, and Miss Hardison accordingly turned to Sir Derek and said with a sweetness quite as overpowering as Allegra's that of course she knew Miss Herington was a connexion of his, but would it really not be better if he were to introduce them to each other properly?

This Sir Derek proceeded to do, and why he should have felt reluctant to comply with this request when it had been his chief object, in bringing Allegra to Lady

Spinley's ball that evening, to introduce her into the English colony in Brussels, of which Miss Hardison was one of the chief ornaments, he would have found it difficult to say.

But at any rate he did make the introduction, and both ladies expressed a pleasure they did not in the least feel, after which Miss Hardison, taking up the gauntlet that had been cast down to her, said to Sir Derek that she hoped he would at least not leave the ball until the quadrille had been danced.

"I daresay it was very foolish of me, but I *had* expected—since we seem to have stood up for it together every time we have been in company at a ball since you arrived in Brussels—" she said, refraining from finishing her sentence but glancing up at Sir Derek with such an expectant air that he could not fail to take her meaning.

That she had made a mistake, however, was immediately apparent. Sir Derek, averse, like most gentlemen, to having his life arranged for him, or perhaps merely acknowledging the superior reasonableness of Allegra's request, shrugged and said that he was very flattered, but he was sure she would have no difficulty in finding another partner.

"In fact, I shall find one for you before I go," he said—which unfortunate words immediately put Miss Hardison upon her mettle, and she smiled with such devastating effect upon Sir Alexander Gordon, who was walking by at the moment, that he at once halted and enquired if she had a dance for him.

"How very nice of you to ask!" said Miss Hardison. "I believe the set is just forming for the quadrille, Sir Alexander," upon which, although she did not go so far as to put out her tongue at Sir Derek as a young lady of lower station might have done, she gave him a look that expressed much the same sentiment and walked off with Sir Alexander.

In the carriage, driving back to the Pensionnat, Allegra

was in such high fettle that Sir Derek could not help observing it, and he remarked presently, in a rather damping tone, that he was glad to see her in such spirits, but hoped it was not the particularity of Lempriere's attentions that had put her in alt.

"His making you the object of his gallantry will do you no good, as I have warned you," he said, "and may lead to positive harm if you are imprudent."

Hilary, who had been yawning prodigiously in her corner of the carriage, though she would have died rather than admit that she was sleepy, said not to be stuffy and Allie was never prudent.

"And the Baron is ve-ry handsome," she went on beatifically, almost falling asleep in the middle of a word, "and I danced ev-er-y dance—"

Allegra gave a gurgle of laughter, and Sir Derek asked her if she intended to see the Baron again.

"Yes, certainly," she said impenitently. "We are going for a drive on Sunday."

"I should prefer," said Sir Derek, improvising brilliantly, "that you come for a drive with me instead, Miss Herington. I have already asked Miss Hardison, and I am sure she would be delighted if you and Hilary would join us."

Allegra looked at him speculatively through the darkness.

"I daresay," she remarked after a moment, "that what really concerns you is that I may become involved in a scandal with the Baron, which will of course be disagreeable to you, as we bear the same name."

"Well—and may you not?"

"No, said Allegra composedly. "I cut my wisdoms a long while since, Sir Derek, and you yourself have said that I am quite capable of dealing with the Baron. Besides, I have come to the conclusion that, as I did not succumb to *your* well-known charm, I am immune to masculine persuasion."

Sir Derek, though looking vexed at her obstinacy, could not help grinning, and said "Jade!" appreciatively. "All the same," he went on, "you will come with me on Sunday."

"What, and disappoint the Baron, as well as ruin Miss Hardison's day? I think not!" Allegra retorted. "We go to the Opera with you on Saturday, you know, which will give you quite enough of our company."

Sir Derek looked a trifle grim, but did not pursue the matter further—which, far from pleasing Allegra as it should have done, for some reason rather depressed her.

The carriage drew up shortly afterwards before the Pensionnat Jusseau, and conversation was perforce suspended. Allegra, glancing out the windows as the wheels rumbled to a halt on the cobblestones, was suddenly aware of movement in the street beyond—a dark figure, which, it seemed, had just emerged from the door of the Pensionnat, darting across to the shelter of a doorway opposite and then, after a moment's pause, slipping swiftly out of sight around the corner.

Allegra sat up straighter. Surely, she thought, she had seen that figure before, that coat shining faintly bottle-green in the moonlight. Mlle. Jusseau's disreputable relation—but it had been less than a week, she recollected with some puzzlement, since she had seen him, at this same hour, in the hall of the Pensionnat talking to Cherry. It seemed highly improbable that he could have returned to apply to her so soon again; yet she could not be mistaken, she felt, in believing that it was indeed the same man whom she had seen on that occasion.

As she stepped from the carriage she recollected that Cherry had told her she had given instructions for Jules to wait up for their return; but it was Mlle. Jusseau herself who opened the front door to them. She was, as upon the first occasion when Allegra had surprised her with her nocturnal visitor, dressed in her usual daytime attire, and greeted Sir Derek with her customary imperturbability, enquiring as to the success of the evening's entertainment. He soon took his leave, and Mlle. Jusseau, observing that Hilary would fall asleep on her feet if she were left standing for another minute, sent her upstairs to bed at once.

"You are back rather early," she said to Allegra as the two more leisurely made their way upstairs after Hilary. "I had thought such fashionable parties went on for at least another hour or two."

"Well, they do," said Allegra, "but I made Sir Derek bring us home early. After all, I must get *some* sleep if I am to be of any use to you here."

She wondered if Mademoiselle would mention her visitor to her, but she did not. She only said calmly that Allegra was not to trouble herself over such things, as it was far more important to see Hilary suitably married than for her to settle down immediately to spending all her time in the schoolroom.

"You are coming along splendidly as an instructress, *ma chère,*" she said, "and there is no need for you to overdo. There will be plenty of time for that in a few months, when the Season will be over and you may devote yourself as rigorously as you like to your new profession."

Allegra said truthfully that she quite liked teaching and found the girls very willing to learn and well-conducted, upon which Mademoiselle observed with some *snobisme d'institutrice* that she of course accepted only young ladies *bien élevées* and of the best Belgian and English families, and then turned the conversation once more to Hilary.

"Was she much admired?" she asked, and Allegra said proudly that she had danced every dance and had been presented to the Duke of Wellington and the Prince of Orange.

"Ah, but the Duke is already married, and the Prince, I think, above her touch," Mlle. Jusseau said, with her dry humour. "But you will tell me all about it in the morning, at any rate—*hein?*"

"But not quite *all* about it," Allegra thought to herself as she went to her room; for she had no intention of telling anyone about her slight contretemps with Miss Hardison, or about the wholly unreasonable depression that had come over her when Sir Derek had not more strongly contested her decision to go for a drive with Baron de Lempriere on Sunday.

Chapter Eleven

ON THE FOLLOWING morning, however, Allegra found that, though she might keep *those* secrets from Mlle. Jusseau, there was very little else about the party at the Spinleys' that her old governess did not intend to learn from her. It was perhaps not surprising, she thought, but rather impatiently at last, that Cherry, having provided her and Hilary so generously with the opportunity to enter into Brussels Society, should take an interest in their progress there; but being expected to give a full account of everyone she had met on the previous evening, and of every word that had been said to her, seemed carrying things rather far.

Discussing the matter later that day with Hilary, whom she found describing to a rapt audience of all the English boarders her meeting with the Duke and the Prince of Orange, she discovered that her young sister, too, had had to endure a detailed inquisition from Mlle. Jusseau on the events of the previous evening.

"I think what it *really* is," said Hilary, "is that she is concerned—poor old thing!—about our safety here in

Brussels. She *would* hear every word that the Duke, and
Sir Alexander, and even Roddy let fall about what they
expect will happen next, and about what the Duke is doing to prepare for action against Boney. She goes in terror
of his marching straight into Brussels, I believe, and told
me this morning that if there is the least hint of such a
thing she will close the school and send the girls back to
their parents, and those who live too far away with the
mistresses to Antwerp, where she has a friend who keeps
another school. As if there were any chance of the Duke's
letting Boney come anywhere near here!"

"Yes," said Allegra slowly, "I daresay you may be
right—I mean about her being in dread of Bonaparte.
Only it seems odd, for you know Cherry is not of a nervous disposition; in fact, I should not have said she was
afraid of anything. I have seen her deal with everything
from mad bulls to housebreakers without so much as turning a hair."

"Oh, yes—but Boney is something quite different from
a housebreaker, at least to her, you know!" Hilary said
comfortably. "But I told her I should let her know everything I hear at once, so that she need not feel alarmed—
for going into company so much with military gentlemen,
one is bound to learn all that is going on."

She then lost interest in the matter and turned the subject, not very subtly, to Lord Roderick Buccan and the
extraordinary coincidence of his having spent so much of
his life within twenty miles of Rolveston without their
having met until they had both come to Brussels; and Allegra, in attempting to discourage her sister's obvious interest in that young gentleman, was obliged to give over
thinking of Mlle. Jusseau's rather unusual behaviour as
well.

But it did not entirely leave her mind, where it remained as a small nagging mystery, to be taken out at odd
moments and put in juxtaposition with the equally nag-

ging mystery of the indigent relation in the bottle-green coat who paid his calls in the middle of the night.

That neither of these problems was able to occupy more than odd moments of her time was not surprising, considering the way of life into which she and Hilary fell from that time forward. Apparently Mlle. Jusseau had been quite correct in stating that Sir Derek's patronage was all that was needed to launch them in Brussels Society, for from the day of his escorting them to the Spinleys' evening party—an event shortly followed by their appearance in his box at the Opera—invitations had flowed in upon them at a lavish rate. Lady Markland's breakfast, a small evening party given by Lady John Somerset, a picnic at the Ixelles lakes, a Review at Vilvorde—at all of these the Misses Herington were invited to put in an appearance, and soon gathered each her own corps of admirers. Allegra's was led by Captain the Baron de Lempriere and Colonel Hepworth, the latter of whom was so carried away by finding himself almost daily in her company that he proposed to her twice in a fortnight and each time the next day sincerely congratulated her on having had the good sense to refuse him.

"I'd make the devil of a husband, you know," he said frankly. "Matter of fact, I can't think why I go on proposing to you except you make a deuced fine figure on a horse and I never could resist a woman with a good seat. By the way, Derek mounts you very handsomely—that *was* his mare I saw you riding in the Allée Verte t'other day, wasn't it? You ought to get *him* to marry you, only he won't, I daresay. Going to offer for one of Balmforth's daughters, I hear—the good-looking one with the name nobody can pronounce."

Allegra replied with some asperity that she had not the slightest wish for Sir Derek to make her an offer, and that he had assured her that she was doing *him* a favour by exercising the mare.

"Now that," said the Colonel firmly, "is a clanker if

ever I heard one. It's deuced handsome of him to let you ride that mare, my girl, and if you're going to act like every other woman and see no good in a fellow just because he's casting out lures to some other female instead of to you, I'm glad you *wouldn't* marry me."

"You said that before," said Allegra with dignity. "And if you don't want to marry me, I *do* wish to goodness you wouldn't keep asking me, because it is *not* very agreeable for me to be obliged to refuse you."

Which made the Colonel laugh, and remark rather crudely that he dared say she enjoyed refusing fellows as well as the next woman, because they were all alike in that respect.

"You'll do it once too often, though," he warned her, which unaccountably made Allegra think of the day at Chatt Park when she had refused Sir Derek, and she said rather tartly to the Colonel that it wouldn't be too often as far as he was concerned.

But in spite of all this frank speaking they remained good friends, and if there was anyone to whom she could have poured out her present difficulties it would have been the Colonel. But even to him she was unable to put them into words, consisting as they did of a dashing Belgian Captain who was daily beseiging her with the most romantic of attentions and no doubt the most dishonourable of intentions, a much-loved but headstrong younger sister whose own romantic life was going in a direction exactly opposite what one would have wished it to, and the disagreeable sight of the Honourable Miss Dianeme Hardison making what appeared to be inevitable progress towards becoming the mistress of Rolveston.

Some of these difficulties came to a head on a bright day near the end of May when Baron de Lempriere drove her and Hilary out to one of the Reviews that in these times were the contstant entertainment of the fashionable world. Open barouches, phaetons, and curricles brought ladies in muslins and gauzes and Villager hats, and gentlemen in long-tailed coats and gleaming Hessians, to. view the martial splendor of the various components of the Allied armies, with hampers of cold chicken and champagne on the box containing all the ingredients for a picnic luncheon to be enjoyed when the military spectacle had been concluded.

On this particular occasion—the Review by the Duke of the British Calvalry on the banks of the Dender, not far from Grammont—Allegra had intended to cry off from a half promise to the Baron to accompany him, for she had been suffering some severe qualms of conscience over the neglect of her duties at the Pensionnat Jusseau. But Mlle. Jusseau, informed of this self-sacrificial intention, would have none of it.

"Ma chère," she said, with a shrug of her narrow shoulders, "let us be frank. As I have told you before, you have an opportunity now—you and the little Hilary—which it is entirely unlikely you will be offered again. *Enfin,* if it will make you easier, I will tell you that I too have an opportunity—which is to acquire an affluent patroness who may be of great use to me in the future. But yes!" she added tranquilly, as Allegra looked at her in sudden surprise. "I too have something to gain in this, *ma fille.* And I assure you that I shall not be above expecting my reward if either you or *la petite* makes a brilliant match and becomes a person to reckon with in Society. You may repay me very well then by recommending the Pensionnat Jusseau to all your friends in the higher nobility who have daughters to educate. I have not yet, you see, had the honour of receiving the daughter of an earl or of a duke!"

Allegra smiled, and said that if she were to marry an earl or duke she would certainly see to it that all her fellow countesses and duchesses were well acquainted with the merits of the Pensionnat Jusseau; but, looking into Mademoiselle's small shrewd black eyes, she thought that after all it was not quite a joke, for Cherry would certainly have every right to expect both her and Hilary to do everything in their power to help her if either of them were to marry well, and the benefits she would obtain from such a connexion would be cheap at the price of a few months' scamped work in the schoolroom.

So she very sensibly thanked Cherry and said she and Hilary would go to Grammont with the Baron, and when he arrived to escort them there they were accordingly ready to receive him, attired in very becoming figured muslins, Hilary in a chip-hat tied under her chin with cherry ribbons and Allegra in a wide-brimmed confection of satin-straw.

"You will find it perhaps *ennuyant*," he said to them as he handed them up into the very dashing high-perch pha-eton he was driving, "for it is excessively warm today and one soldier, after all, looks very much like another."

But Hilary, giving a little bounce on the seat to express her complete inability to be bored by anything that partook of the nature of an outing, said oh no, for Roddy had said he would be there, and there would be Colonel Hepworth and Robin Playsted for her to pick out, to say nothing of the Duke and Marshal Blücher and any number of other notables.

Allegra sometimes wondered what Hilary made of the Baron and the Baron of her, but Lempriere, for his part, appeared to have accepted with praiseworthy resignation the fact that his squiring of Allegra inevitably meant the squiring of Hilary as well (though on more than one occasion he had shown himself extremely adept at providing that artless young lady with an alternative gallant for the greater part of the evening, or afternoon, thus clearing the field for himself with her sister). As for Hilary, she had merely observed once to Allegra that the Baron seemed to be growing very particular in his attentions, and then had enquired rather offhandedly if Allegra thought he might make her an offer.

"No, I am quite sure that he will not," Allegra had replied, upon which Hilary had said with an air of some relief, "Oh, good! Because I like him a *little* for being so beautiful, but it would be much too wearing to have him about all the time looking romantic. And I never know what to *say* to him!"

For her own part, Allegra also suffered to some extent from this same disability; but since she had discovered that the Baron expected little more of a lady than to look charming and to listen to his soulful speeches, she had ceased to allow this to trouble her. And as she was aware that none of the several other gentlemen who had shown a particular interest in her since her introduction into Brussels Society was willing to commit himself to gallanting her day in and day out—with the inevitable matrimonial expectations that this would arouse—she allowed the Baron to take her and Hilary about, without giving much thought to the fact that this arrangement too had its drawbacks.

When they had arrived that afternoon at the natural amphitheatre on the banks of the Dender where the Review was to be held, a great number of carriages were already standing at convenient places for viewing the military spectacle to be provided for their occupants. Before them the troops, sweating under a blazing midday sun, were drawn up, six thousand strong, facing the temporary bridge that had been thrown across the Dender in expectation of the arrival of the Duke and his party from the village of Schendelbeke, on the other side of the river. The Baron, who was an excellent whip, manoeuvred his team skilfully through the throng, and brought it up beside a smart sporting phaeton with double perches of swan-neck pattern, in which a dark, elegant young lady wearing the most fashionable of yellow craped muslins and a ravishing flat-crowned hat of jonquil silk, with a coquettish little parasol on a long slender handle protecting her excellent complexion against the sun, sat with an equally fashionably attired gentleman. Allegra, though the

parasol half hid the lady's face from her, had not the least
difficulty in recognising Miss Dianeme Hardison and Sir
Derek Herington, and felt that Fate was amusing itself by
being spiteful that day, for it was obviously impossible for
her to enjoy the Review while she was obliged at the
same time to watch Miss Hardison simpering at Sir Derek
and no doubt gloating over the prospect of becoming
mistress of Rolveston.

But here she was doing an injustice to Miss Hardison,
who never simpered, being far too calmly self-assured to
engage in any such missish activity, and who cared so
little for Rolveston, having designs instead upon Sir
Derek's elegant town house in Berkeley Square, where she
intended to preside over a political and intellectual *salon*
in the Parisian style, that she would scarcely have minded
if it had disappeared from the face of the earth.

Greetings, of course, were exchanged between the two
carriages, and Allegra took a certain uncharitable
pleasure in observing that Miss Hardison appeared no
happier about the fact that they were to be neighbours
than she was herself. However, Miss Hardison said
graciously that it was very warm, and how much she pit-
ied the poor soldiers in their hot uniforms, to which Hilary replied seriously that there were much worse things
than that about being a soldier, and would have gone on
to present certain graphic details about living conditions,
including lice and rats in the Peninsula, all learned entirely at second hand from Lord Roderick, who had not
been there either, had not Allegra put a stop to it.

Meanwhile, Sir Derek was looking none too well
pleased to see her again in company with Baron de Lempriere, and was very brief with both her and the Baron
without being actually rude. Fortunately the Baron, like
most people obliged to operate in a foreign language,
failed to understand that he was being disapproved of,
and was so gay and talkative that he made everyone

uncomfortable except Hilary, who was oblivious to everything but her own enjoyment at being there.

That enjoyment was increased when, just as the Duke and his cortège of British and foreign notables appeared and rode across the bridge, Lord Roderick, dodging between carriages and under horses' hooves with the aplomb of a small boy half his age, came up to the Baron's phaeton and gave everyone in it his engaging smile.

"I say," he said, "I'm with Pelton and some other people but I saw you and I thought I'd come over. Do you mind?"

As there obviously was no room for him in the phaeton and conversation between him and its occupants was made difficult by the fact of their being perched some five feet above him, Allegra said they didn't but she rather thought he would.

"I mean, you can't see anything from down there and we can't take you up," she explained, raising her voice so as to be heard above the roar of applause that had greeted the Duke's appearance.

"Oh, that's all right," said Lord Roderick, who was looking at Hilary. "I'll just stand here. It's only a lot of fellows in scarlet coats, anyway."

As it was his obvious intention to remain there gazing up at Hilary, Allegra felt that it was her duty, especially with Sir Derek's eyes upon her, to make him go away; but unfortunately no method of accomplishing this, short of a direct order, presented itself to her mind, and since this was obviously ineligible she was obliged to content herself with drawing Hilary's attention away from her admirer by perseveringly calling upon her to note the various dignitaries accompanying the Duke as they rode slowly past the motionless line of mounted troops.

Hilary was quite willing to admire the Prussian Marshal Prince von Blücher, with his heavy white eyebrows and moustache, and Lord Uxbridge, the Cavalry commander, looking magnificent, as always, in his silver-encrusted

Hussar jacket and pelisse, but her eyes always turned back immediately to Lord Roderick standing below her, and almost all her conversation was bestowed upon him. As far as Allegra could make out, they appeared to be quarrelling over the merits of a literary effusion honouring Hilary's charms recently sent her by young Cornet Playsted, which Hilary, with a distressing lack of delicacy, had allowed Lord Roderick to peruse. Contrary to what might have been expected, it was Hilary who was criticising her admirer's tribute and Lord Roderick who persisted in defending it, which both amused Allegra and encouraged her to believe that perhaps the attachment that appeared to be forming between the two young people was not so serious as to require her concern.

She was therefore prepared to be complaisant when, the inspection finally having been completed and the troops having been marched past the saluting point by Lord Uxbridge, Hilary turned to her with an eager request.

"Roddy says that Francis Pelton has brought his sisters and they have cream cakes and *anguilles au vert,* and I've never eaten eels, so please may I go and have luncheon with them?" she begged.

Allegra said with a slight shudder that anyone who could mention cream cakes and eels in the same breath passed her comprehension, but she dared say Hilary might go if she promised not to be sick. Upon which Hilary, jumping up gleefully, was helped down from the phaeton by Lord Roderick and carried off, and Allegra, seeing Sir Derek's eyes fixed upon her in obvious disapproval, asked him rather defiantly, ignoring the presence of Miss Hardison and the Baron, what he thought she was to do about it.

"Obviously it is your intention to do nothing at all," said Sir Derek, which struck Allegra as such a totally unfair thing to say to a person who had already spent several wakeful nights worrying about her young sister's unsuitable attachment—though how Sir Derek was to be expected to know anything about her nights she did not trouble to ask herself—that she turned to the Baron and asked him very distinctly if they might move into the shade, for the sun was giving her the headache.

The Baron was only too willing to comply. He succeeded, in fact, with an ingenuity born of long experience in such matters, in finding a location so far removed not only from Sir Derek's carrige, but from any carriage at all, that their conversation, if conducted in decorously low tones, could not be overheard, and thereupon offered her a glass of champagne from the bottle he extracted from the picnic hamper.

Allegra accepted it, but she was already beginning to feel slightly dubious about the wisdom of having given the Baron the opportunity for what amounted to a tête-à-tête with her. It was one thing to parry his romantic speeches in a ballroom, with dozens of other people around, or in a carriage with Hilary beside them; but what was one to do with a gentleman who, taking advantage of the admittedly inadequate camouflage of the shifting, leafy shade in which they sat, dared in broad daylight to make love to her in the most outrageous terms.

"Je t'adore, je t'aime à corps perdu!" said the Baron's voice in her ear, his moustaches brushing her cheek while the champagne glass, drained of its contents, dropped unheeded to the grass below. "When will you cease this so English pose of ice-maiden and say to me what you feel, what you must feel, what I *will* you to feel with all my soul?"

The Baron's dark eyes burned into hers, but all Allegra, who had a lively sense of the ridiculous, could think of at this very dramatic and rather unnerving moment was that young Cornet Playsted's poetic effusions would gain a good deal if he could persuade the Baron to give him some lessons, and an involuntary choke of laughter escaped her.

"Eh bien! Cela t'amuse, donc?" the Baron said, looking so outraged that Allegra quickly composed her features and said of course not, only he really must not speak so to her, especially where people might hear him.

The Baron snapped his fingers. "That for *les autres*—that for *tout le monde!*" he said.

"Well, I don't say anything of the kind!" said Allegra prosaically. "I have a reputation to preserve, you will remember, and if you set every gabblemonger in Brussels to bibble-babbling about me I shall lose my position, so please *do* be more careful!"

Gloom overspread the Baron's face. "You wish to torture me," he said. "Yes! It pleases you to see my unhappiness."

"Nothing of the sort!" said Allegra encouragingly. "You have been *very* kind to both Hilary and me, which I *do* appreciate—only you really must get it out of your head that I shall accept a *carte blanche* from you, because I shan't, you know. I was much too properly brought up, and, besides, it would ruin all Hilary's chances to make a suitable marriage if it were known that I had decided to tread the primrose path."

The Baron, his gloom unappeased, muttered, "Hilary! Hilary! Always Hilary! She will marry that boy and go off and leave you—and you—you will have sacrificed a great love for *that!*"

"But it i*sn't* a great love, Gilles dear," Allegra said reasonably, beginning to feel that there was not so very much difference between a sulky small boy deprived of a treat and an ardent lover baulked of his desire. "Not on your part, and certainly not on mine. If I were out of your sight for a month, you would forget me—"

"Never!" declared the Baron; and then, his face brightening, he said triumphantly, "You called me 'Gilles dear'! Does not that prove—?"

"It proves that I like you very much," Allegra said firmly, "and that is all. But I shall not go on liking you if you make a scene here before all these people. Besides, I am very hungry. Is there anything in that hamper except champagne, or shall I be obliged to go and beg some eels of Francis Pelton?"

So the Baron reluctantly allowed her to explore the hamper, where she discovered excellent cold chicken and ham and some of the delicious pralines for which Brussels was famed, and as it was obviously impossible to make love satisfactorily while eating chicken the romantic moment passed, to Allegra's great relief.

Of course she and the Baron were obliged to go in search of Hilary when it was time to leave, for it was not to be expected that she would leave her young friends before she was dragged away. To Allegra's considerable annoyance, however, she was not discovered to be with the group she had joined, and one of the Pelton young ladies disclosed, after a *sotto voce* consultation with her sister that consisted chiefly of suppressed giggles, that she had gone off with Roddy Buccan quite a quarter of an hour before.

"The minx!" said Allegra to the Baron, looking really displeased. "She knows very well she ought not to do that. I shall comb her hair with a joint-stool when I find her"—which odd and slightly indecorous English expression so intrigued the Baron that she was obliged to explain to him that what she meant was that she would give her young sister a thundering scold.

To her relief, however, before she and the Baron could institute a search, Hilary and Lord Roderick appeared, the latter looking so sheepish and dazedly happy that Allegra had a sudden dire premonition that the worst had occurred.

And so, it appeared, it had. No sooner had they returned to the Pensionnat Jusseau and gone upstairs to their bedchamber than Hilary burst out with her news.

"Roddy and I have decided to be betrothed," she said.

"Of course he is not of age now, so he must have his papa's consent, but—"

"But!" interrupted Allegra, sitting down rather violently upon the bed, quite overcome by this abrupt confirmation of her fears. "Yes, I should think there are a great many *but*'s!" Hilary turned a surprised and enquiring face upon her. "Oh, don't look at me so innocently, you provoking girl!" said Allegra. "You know very well that it is quite out of the question for you to become betrothed to Roddy Buccan!"

"But, Allie," Hilary interrupted in turn, sitting down impetuously beside her, "you don't understand—"

"I understand very well," said Allegra with all the severity she could muster, for her heart smote her at the sight of her sister's eager, blissful face. "You think—both of you—that you have formed a lasting attachment, but—"

"It's not just a lasting attachment, Allie. We. Love. Each. Other," said Hilary, with the patient air of one explaining the alphabet to a backward child. "It is exactly like you and Neil, only Roddy isn't going to be killed. I won't let him be," she said, which modestly ferocious statement, spoken as a challenge to all comers, made Allegra want to cry, for she had never heard her young sister sound maternal before.

"But don't you see, love, that you *can't?*" she said rather helplessly, feeling that she was doing very poorly and wishing with all her heart that she could kiss Hilary and say, "Bless you, my darling!"—instead of being obliged to be the voice of Prudence and Worldy Wisdom and all the other cold virtues. "You have no fortune and neither has Roddy, and both Lady Spinley and Sir Derek have made it clear that he must marry prudently. And it is *quite* unlikely that his family will give their consent."

"No, I expect they won't," Hilary acknowledged reasonably, "so it simply means that we shall have to wait for a year and six days until he is of age. That is a very long time, but Roddy says if his father and mother meet me they may take a liking to me, because they mostly do like people—at least, the Duchess does if they like dogs, and she tells the Duke what he is to do, which he usually doesn't bother to think of for himself because he is only interested in books. And so then they might agree to our being married at once. Do you think it is at all possible, Allie, that I might go back to England and meet them soon?"

Allegra said firmly that there was not the least hope of such a thing, and thought of beginning at the beginning and trying all over again to make Hilary realise the impossibility of her dream of becoming Lady Roderick Buccan. But it seemed a hopeless task and for almost the first time in her competent, admittedly rather self-willed existence she felt the need of placing her dilemma in the hands of someone else, and determine to call upon Lady Spinley in the morning.

Chapter Twelve

A NOTE DESPATCHED to the Rue Ducale that evening brought the reply that Lady Spinley would be happy to see Miss Herington in the morning, and Allegra felt so much consoled at the thought of shifting at least a part of the burden of the responsibility she felt for Hilary's future on to someone else's shoulders that she confided the whole story of her sister's imprudence to Mlle. Jusseau, which she had not been able to bring herself to do previously.

Mlle. Jusseau, to her relief, took the affair very calmly and said that she was doing exactly right in consulting Lady Spinley.

"If the young man is not of age, there is nothing for you to concern yourself about immediately, *ma chère*," she said. "Many things may happen in a year."

"And six days," Allegra said with a faint smile. "Well, I hope you are right, Cherry, but I *do* feel dreadfully to blame in having allowed the matter to come to this pass. If I had taken more care of her—"

"My dear, neither you nor anyone else can prevent a child like Hilary from fancying herself in love with the first engaging young man she meets when she goes out into the world," said Mlle. Jusseau with her usual common sense. "It is how you manage the affair from this time out that is important."

And she thereupon proceeded to turn the conversation to the subject of what information Allegra had been able to pick up at the Review on the military situation in general and the security of Brussels in particular—a subject which she continued when Hilary entered the room. Allegra left Hillary explaining to her very kindly all that Lord Roderick had told her of the present disposition of the Allied armies, and went upstairs to think about her forthcoming interview with Lady Spinley.

When she arrived in the Rue Ducale a short time later, she was shown into a small sitting room furnished in the Empire style, where Lady Spinley was seated on an elegant *méridienne* with her tambour-frame before her. Upon Allegra's entering the room, however, she at once put her work aside and invited her in her usual kind manner to seat herself beside her.

"I know why you are come, of course," she said.

"You do?" Allegra looked a trifle startled. "But how can you? I mean, who can have told you?"

"Well, I saw Roddy last evening at the Marklands' rout-party," Lady Spinley said, raising her lovely dark eyes to Allegra's face with such a placid expression in them that Allegra had a sudden violently illogical notion that she was about to say that everything was quite all right after all, and Lord Roderick and Hilary could be married with his family's blessing. But this impression was immediately dispelled by her ladyship's next words. "He told me all about his wishing to be betrothed to your sister," she said, "and naturally I was obliged to tell him that it was quite unsuitable. Not, of course, that it did the slightest good—"

She cast a glance of mild enquiry at Allegra, who said ruefully, "Yes, that is exactly what I told Hilary—and, equally, it did no good there. And that is why I have come to you, ma'am—to see if together we may be able to think how to manage the matter."

"The sad thing is, you know," Lady Spinley said unexpectedly, "that there may really be nothing to manage, after all, because people—especially very young people—often fall out of love as quickly as they have fallen into it. And I do think that our children—only of course dear Hilary is not your child but your sister, so that you can't know *quite* what I mean—should be able to marry for love, except that there are horrid things like settlements and dowries that gentlemen always bring up. And I daresay they are right, because after all *someone* must be practical—which is why I have asked Derek to come here this morning. Spinley is really of no use whatever at this sort of thing."

Allegra, upon this mention of Sir Derek's name, felt her heart perform the sort of unpleasant gyrations that occur when one hears a sudden unforeseen noise in a dark room, and said with what she could only hope did not sound like dismay, "Oh, dear! I wish you had not done that!"

"Do you? But I can't think why not," Lady Spinley said, looking faintly surprised. "He is exactly the sort of person to tell one what to do when one is very uncomfortable about not knowing whether to do it or not. I expect it comes of his having been in the diplomatic service. And here he is now, I daresay," she added, as there was the sound of voices in the hall, and a moment later the butler entered to announce Sir Derek Herington.

Allegra, who vividly remembered Sir Derek's caustic words to her at the Review the day before, about her intending to do nothing whatever about Hilary and Lord Roderick, felt at once, as he entered the room, that she was being looked at accusingly, which was quite incorrect, for in point of fact Sir Derek at that moment was looking at Lady Spinley.

"Now what has put you into such high fidgets that you must needs send for me at this ungodly hour, ma'am?" he enquired, as he bowed over her hand. He then gave Allegra a cool glance and said, "Miss Herington—" to which she responded quite as coolly, "Good morning, Sir Derek. I fancy that I am the cause of your having been disturbed at such an early hour, but I can assure you that it was done quite without my knowledge. It was not *my* notion to involve you further in my affairs, and, if Lady Spinley will forgive me, I will suggest that you leave us to talk this matter over alone."

"Dear Miss Herington—!" began Lady Spinley, looking surprised by her tone; but Sir Derek cut her short staring at Allegra from under frowning brows in a manner that astonished her ladyship quite as much as had Allegra's odd incivility.

"*Your* affairs?" he said. "Pray enlighten me, Miss Herington. Have you fallen into some new scrape, then?"

"I was not aware, Sir Derek, that I had fallen into any old ones!" retorted Allegra, with considerable asperity. "And, at any rate, this is not a matter in which I consider that you are in the least concerned. In fact, if Lady Spinley had informed me that *you* were to be present here, I should never have come myself!"

"Miss Herington—Derek!" said Lady Spinley, looking

at them both reproachfully. "What *is* the matter? I am sure if I had thought you would come to dagger-drawing with each other I should never have asked you to come, Derek, but that, I must say, I could *not* foresee, for your manners are usually *quite* unexceptionable. And now *will* you stop standing there looking so thunderously at Miss Herington and sit down and tell me why you are angry with her?"

Sir Derek did sit down, but to his discredit showed himself immune to his aunt's soft charm and continued to look uncompromisingly at Allegra.

"You may as well cut line," he told her, with a bluntness that would have surprised his acquaintances in diplomatic circles, "because I have no intention of leaving here until I have discovered what this is about. Does it concern Lempriere?"

"Lempriere? No!" said Allegra, indignant colour flooding her face. "Of course it does not! How odious you are even to suggest such a thing!"

"Am I?" he said grimly. "Perhaps so—but you must forgive me for saying that your apparent astonishment at my coupling your name and his scarcely accords with your conduct! You have been seen in his company on more occasions than I could name—"

"And if *that*," interrupted Allegra, quite forgetting Lady Spinley's presence in her wrath, "is any of your concern, Sir Derek, I fail to understand how that came about! What right have you to censure my conduct? Oh, I know!" she went on disdainfully, as he opened his lips to speak. "We have the misfortune to bear the same name! Believe me, that is a circumstance that I regret quite as much as you do, and if I could change it, I assure you I should be only too happy to do so! As I cannot, however, I must beg you to believe that I consider it most important of you to presume upon it as an excuse to interfere in my life!"

"If I had not interfered, you would have found yourself

at Point Non-Plus long before this!" said Sir Derek undiplomatically.

"Derek—my dear!" said Lady Spinley. "*So* uncivil! Perhaps you have not breakfasted—is that it? If so, it will be no trouble at all to have Weddle bring you some ham and buttered eggs—"

"Thank you, Aunt, I have breakfasted!" said Sir Derek. "But if you, or Miss Herington, will be good enough to explain to me the reason why I have been summoned here—"

"Oh, dear!" said Lady Spinley, looking at him with an enchanting ruefulness. "Now you really are angry and it is all my fault! But how in the world was I to know that it would put you into such a disagreeable temper, dear boy?"

Sir Derek regarded her with much the same expression of goaded frustration upon his face that Othello must have had when he interrupted Desdemona's well-meant evasions about the handkerchief, and although he did not actually ejaculate, "The reason! The reason!" as Othello ejaculated, "The handkerchief!" it was plain that that was what he would have liked to do.

However, Allegra, seeing that he had no intention of going away, came to his rescue, and said in a very cold tone that, since he was so determined to know, she would tell him.

"It concerns Hilary and your cousin, Lord Roderick Buccan," she said. "They have taken it into their heads that they wish to be married."

"Oh, my God!" said Sir Derek, an expression of almost relieved exasperation abruptly replacing the grim look that had been upon his face. "Is that all? They are scarcely out of the nursery, either of them!"

"Now there, Derek," said Lady Spinley with dignity, "you are quite beside the bridge! You must remember that I myself was married at seventeen—and as for dear Roddy, I am very sure that General Maitland would not have taken him on his Staff if he had not considered him to be *quite* mature for his age."

"For his age—yes!" said Sir Derek. "But, for all that, nineteen is not an age to be married, ma'am! And if you knew as much of that halfling's petticoat-affairs as I do— not, understand me, that I am laying more at his door than the most revoltingly romantic of calf-loves—you would be aware that until a month ago he was dangling after a straw-damsel whom he met in a gaming-hell!"

"Oh yes, I know all about *that*," said Lady Spinley, dismissing this intelligence with the pitying tolerance of the lady of fashion for any news offered her by a mere male upon a subject upon which she is bound to be far more well-informed than he is. "But this is not at all the same sort of thing, you know. He is quite in earnest, and says very positively that if he cannot gain the Duke's consent to the match he is prepared to wait for a year—"

"Then let him do so!" said Sir Derek impatiently. "Good God, ma'am, you must know that long before a twelvemonth has passed he will have forgotten all about this hey-go-mad notion and be involved in quite another affair with another chit with whom he is convinced he is madly in love!"

Lady Spinley looked at him gently out of her lovely dark eyes.

"Of course, that is the sensible view to take of the matter," she said. "But, do you know, my dear, I think you are quite out in this case. Roddy is *truly* in love with her, you see—not the sort of thing so many gentlemen mean when they speak of being in love, which is quite an uncomfortable feeling, I imagine, and makes them do such ridiculous things that one often wishes to tell them that that is not at all the way to go about it; but what we females mean, which is caring for someone so much that you wish to be with them always, even when they have grown older and quite ordinary-looking and can't in any way be compared to goddesses or nymphs—"

Allegra, looking at Sir Derek, saw a skeptical expression still upon his face and said scornfully to Lady Spinley, "Oh, ma'am, I fear you are wasting your breath in trying to make Sir Derek understand such sentiments! *His* view of marriage is based wholly upon the practical; he has only contempt for those of us who believe that it should be otherwise!"

She had the satisfaction of seeing a slight flush darken in his face, and Lady Spinley, who could be very perceptive, felt that there was something here and looked interested.

"Well, I must say," she remarked fair-mindedly after a moment, "that I think you are right, my dear, for I do believe that if it were announced tomorrow that Dianeme Hardison was to marry Alding—which is not, after all, impossible, for he has been very attentive lately and he *is* a marquis—Derek would only look about for another young lady of quality who was as statuesque and handsome and well-born as Dianeme is and be quite as happy as he is now."

Sir Derek, whom sultans and tsars had never been known to discompose, appeared unable to bear these animadversions upon his character with the same praiseworthy equanimity, and said quite intemperately that he would remind both his aunt and Miss Herington that *his* affairs were not under discussion.

"No, but perhaps they should be," said Lady Spinley, looking speculatively from him to Allegra.

But Allegra said hastily that she had no desire whatever to intrude in Sir Derek's affairs if only he would be equally considerate and not intrude in hers, and what were they to do about Lord Roderick and Hilary?

"Take her back to England," said Sir Derek unsympathetically, and added, "And stay there. It was a skipbrained notion to bring her here in the first place! I can not conceive how you can have been so ill-advised as to believe that the Continent, and especially this part of it, was the proper place to establish yourself at this time."

"Well, if you can inform me what other alternative I had, I shall be obliged to you!" said Allegra, rising with considerable acerbity to this criticism; and then, remembering that he was quite aware that she had had the alternative of becoming his wife, coloured up so furiously that Lady Spinley regarded her with marked curiosity.

To add to her confusion, Sir Derek, raising an eyebrow at her, observed sardonically that he rather fancied he could answer that question, but naturally, since the alternative that had been offered her had been such a disagreeable one, it was perhaps understandable that she had preferred to come to Brussels.

"What on earth are you talking about?" Lady Spinley enquired.

Sir Derek most ungallantly made no reply and only looked at Allegra, who was now poppy-red and would have said "Devil!" to him if it had been at all socially permissible. As it was not, she said hurriedly to Lady Spinley, "N-nothing, ma'am! That is, nothing of importance. Sir Derek no doubt means that my—my situation with the aunt with whom I was staying before I came to Brussels was a very disagreeable one."

"Sir Derek means nothing of the kind—as you well know," murmured the gentleman, with such obvious intent to provoke that Allegra glared at him and said it was well for him that she had too much propriety to say more.

"For which I am truly grateful," said Sir Derek. "One's errors in judgement are so much better left in the dark—are they not?"

Lady Spinley said with an injured air that if they intended to talk in riddles she would go away and leave them alone, upon which both Allegra and Sir Derek suddenly became conscious that they had been behaving very oddly, and hastily resumed their ordinary manners. But Allegra, seething with indignation, was unable to bear her part in the conversation that followed with anything like her normal cool composure, and before she rose to leave had almost come to cuffs with Sir Derek once more over a caustic remark of his to the effect that he could well understand Hilary's refusal to hear reason in the matter of Roddy Buccan, considering the example set her by her elder sister.

"If you mean by *that*," said Allegra dangerously, "my friendship with Baron de Lempriere——"

"It is exactly what I mean," said Sir Derek. "Perhaps *she* would be more willing to attend to young Robin Playsted's suit if she saw you encouraging the attentions of a man like Sir Arthur Huddleston, who must and will marry again for the sake of his family, rather than bestowing your company upon a man who has obviously not the least notion of making you an offer of marriage."

"Has he told you so?" enquired Allegra, controlling her temper with a strong effort and speaking with such ominous sweetness that Lady Spinley looked quite alarmed.

"Told *me* so? Certainly not!"

"Then," said Allegra, "I should advise you not to make ill-considered statements about matters of which you know nothing whatever, Sir Derek!"

She had the satisfaction of seeing his eyes narrow incredulously.

"You do not mean to tell me that he *has* made you an offer?" he demanded.

Allegra rose. "Not as yet," she said, her hazel eyes meeting Sir Derek's hard dark ones with such open challenge in them that Lady Spinley, describing the scene later to her lord, said that she had almost expected to see a pair of rapiers appear in her guests' hands and the two of them spring to the salute. "But, after all, one never really knows—does one? What I mean to say is, one *has* received offers from even unlikelier quarters!"

She then thanked Lady Spinley and said good-bye to her, gave a frigid adieu to Sir Derek, and went off with the fixed determination of making the Baron offer marriage to her if it was the last thing she ever did in her life, only for the pleasure of being able to confront Sir Derek as the Baroness de Lempriere.

This laudable ambition had not vanished from her mind by the time she had arrived back at the Pensionnat Jusseau, but it was thrust into the background when, as she entered the hall, she was met by Marthe with the news that Ensign Lord Roderick Buccan had called to see her, and had been invited by Mlle. Jusseau to await her return in Mademoiselle's own sitting room.

"Oh, dear! Well, I shall go up at once," Allegra said, realising quite well what this portended; and she went upstairs to the sitting room to find Lord Roderick gazing with bemused attention at a Dagoty porcelain inkstand, its inkwell guarded by a belligerent-looking bronze eagle and a chastely draped Cupid, which had been presented to Mademoiselle by one of her former pupils.

"Oh, Miss Herington—" he said, spinning about with a guilty look on his face, as if he had been discovered purloining the inkstand instead of merely admiring it; and then was struck dumb.

"How do you do, Lord Roderick?" said Allegra, stepping forward and shaking hands with him. "I know exactly why you are here, so you need not trouble yourself to explain. But it will not do. I have told Hilary that, and I will say the same to you."

But she said it so kindly that Lord Roderick, whose temper was nothing if not buoyant, sat down in the chair to which she motioned him without appearing cast down, and even ventured to say hopefully that he knew he was not the sort of match she must have had in mind for Hilary, who was so pretty and lively and altogether enchanting that every fellow who clapped eyes on her fell head-over-ears in love with her.

"But I love her the most, Miss Herington," he said earnestly. "And, what's more, she says she loves me, and I give you my word that I'll do everything in my power as long as I live to make her happy, if only you will agree to our being married."

Allegra, whose mind was going back to just such another earnest young soldier who had sat in her father's bookroom at Rolveston some seven years before, saying almost these same words to Sir Thomas about herself, felt tears unexpectedly stinging her eyelids. How much in love she and Neil had been, how certain that their love must overcome all obstacles placed in the way of their happiness! But there had been no happiness, and now Neil was dead—as this boy too might soon be, if Fate were unkind, devoured by the same monster of war that had taken Neil.

She said in a rather shaken voice, "Oh, my dear, pray don't try to win me over. It will do no good, you know; there is your own family to consider."

"Yes, I do know, but *that's* only for a year," said Lord Roderick, "because I'm twenty, you know—or at least I shall be on Sunday," he added conscientiously and proudly. "But it will be almost four years before Hilary is of age, so we *must* have your permission, you see, ma'am."

Allegra admitted that she did quite see it, but added firmly that there was no point in going into that now.

"You are both far too young to be thinking of marriage," she said. "Or even of being betrothed, when there is no assurance at all that you will wish to be when you are a little older—"

"Oh, I shall wish to, right enough," Lord Roderick said confidently. "And so will Hilary. I mean to say, I know she is awfully young, ma'am, but she's true-blue. She's not like other girls."

"No, she is not," Allegra, conscious of the tenacity of her young sister's attachments, was obliged to agree. "But—oh dear, don't you see that, whatever *I* do, I can't make things come right for you? The very best thing you can both do is to forget about being betrothed until you are of age—and then, if you still wish to be, we can talk about it again."

Lord Roderick looked very much as if he would have liked to go on talking about it now, but he had very good manners and quite a sensible view of life for being not yet twenty, and so said instead that he dared say she was right but she would see that a year would make no difference.

"And I quite see that we couldn't be married just now, at any rate," he said, with the cheerfulness of the very young in contemplating their own demise—a cheerfulness that is understandable in view of their conviction that it will never occur, "because I may be killed if it comes to a battle with Boney, which it can't help but do now, everyone says. In fact," he added, with a sudden slight frown, "I'd feel a good deal easier, ma'am, if you could take Hilary back to England. Of course there's no question but that we shall beat Boney's army, for there is no one like the Duke, and we are all keen to be able to come to grips with the French. But if there should be a battle near here, it might not be at all comfortable, or even safe, for females for a time."

Allegra, who had so many private difficulties on her mind that the thought of coping with the French army seemed a mere bagatelle, said she appreciated his concern but as it would be rather difficult for her to leave Brussels at this time she thought she and Hilary must remain there unless matters looked like getting a great deal worse. She and Lord Roderick, both with the feeling of having brushed rather well through a situation fraught with all sorts of social and emotional perils, then made their adieux, Lord Roderick, as he was going out the door, adding an optimistic rider to their conversation in the form of a remark that he would write at once to his father, and that if the Duke did decide to give his consent to his and Hilary's being married soon he hoped that Miss Herington, for her part, would not thrust a spoke in their wheel.

Chapter Thirteen

DURING THE ENSUING fortnight it appeared that the fears Lord Roderick had expressed to Allegra concerning possible movement of the French army in the direction of Brussels had been as unfounded as all the other rumours and alarums that had been current in the city for more than a month, for life went on quite as it had done before, with fêtes and balls and rout-parties and Reviews filling each day.

In these diversions the Misses Herington continued to take part, but with a difference. For one thing, Hilary seriously considered herself as betrothed to Lord Roderick, in spite of the fact that his application for parental sanction of such an engagement had received in reply only a remarkably terse communication from the Duchess stating that Juno had had a splendid litter of seven and on no account was he to do anything foolish. She therefore took little interest now in functions at which his lordship was not to be present, and preferred staying at the Pensionnat, sharing the mild diversions of schoolgirl life there with the English boarders, to the most glittering of parties at which she knew she would not meet Lord Roderick— all on the off-chance that he might have the opportunity to look in at the Pensionnat between his military duties. Neither Allegra nor Mlle. Jusseau had thought it wise to forbid these visits, and as they always took place in Mlle. Jusseau's sitting room, with either that lady or Allegra in attendance, it was not felt that much harm could come of them.

As a matter of fact, Allegra, as her acquaintance with Lord Roderick ripened, began to have an increasing respect for that young gentleman's cheerful common sense, and to feel that he might be just the sort of person to guide Hilary through what was bound to be a tumultuous though interesting life—except, of course, that that was quite impossible.

So she perseveringly tried with no success whatever to interest her sister in other more suitable young gentlemen, and meanwhile made a praiseworthy effort to bring order out of the chaos of her own affairs of the heart.

In this latter attempt she was influenced—much against her will, for she was still very angry with him—by Sir Derek's plainspoken opinion that she was laying herself open to justifiable censure by seeing so much of Baron de Lempriere. It was all very well to go storming away from Lady Spinley's house with the fixed determination of bringing that dashing gentleman to her feet and causing him to offer her lawful matrimony, thus allowing her the beautiful satisfaction of being able to show Sir Derek how wrong he had been in saying she would not be able to; but Reason coldly informed her that there was little prospect of her accomplishing this, and that meanwhile she had her own future and Hilary's to think of. Hilary had been imprudent enough to become involved in a love affair that showed no signs of reaching a prosperous conclusion; and if Hilary was not to benefit by *her* opportunities in Brussels, it seemed that Allegra had best look to benefitting by *hers*.

And thinking of opportunities she was obliged to think of Sir Arthur Huddleston, whose suit Sir Derek had so strongly recommended to her. Sir Arthur was a middle-aged and rather dull baronet with a large and hopeful family for whom he was seeking a mother, following the death of his wife a year before, and he had shown a definite though (Hilary considered) somewhat fishlike interest in Allegra, consisting chiefly in regarding her speculatively out of his pale, protuberant eyes and taking her driving behind a pair of very slow-goers in his phaeton.

But he had a very nice property in Gloucestershire, Allegra was assured, and a placid and even agreeable disposition if one did not greatly mind being bored; so in despair over her own and Hilary's muddled futures she smiled at him and said civil things to him in the cool, entrancing voice that made even his dull pulses beat a little faster, and allowed him to cut Baron de Lempriere quite out of her life.

In all this she had had not the least notion of inflaming the Baron to heights of Gallic jealousy such as that gentleman had not experienced since his salad days; but no accomplished flirt deviously plotting conquest could have succeeded better in attaining this end. The Baron first satisfied himself with standing against the wall at parties with folded arms, following her every movement with the smouldering gaze of a Byronic hero; from this passive though dramatic mood he progressed to an active campaign of bombarding the Pensionnat with posies, books, bonbons, and even upon one occasion an exquisite and obviously very expensive ivory fan painted with delicate medallions, which Allegra promptly returned to him.

This caused him, upon the occasion of their next meeting at an evening party given by the Marquise d'Assche, to accuse her of cruelty, perfidy, and utter heartlessness; but Allegra, who was feeling more harassed that usual that evening, owing to having taken the terrifying notion into her head that Sir Arthur was about to offer for her before the night was out, only told him not to be silly, which so infuriated him that he ostentatiously left the party at once and spent the remainder of the evening cast-

ing gloom upon a convival party of Belgian Hussars and
English Dragoons at the Hôtel d'Angleterre.

Allegra's anticipations— or, more properly, her fears—
concerning Sir Arthur turned out to be unfounded, that
phlegmatic gentleman having been deterred from putting
into action what had indeed been his intention to make
her an offer that evening by the presence of Royalty,
which he so much revered that he spent all his time hov-
ering in attendance upon It instead of pursuing his own
interests.

But other and even more startling events fell upon her
the following day. She had been that afternoon, after a
day spent in the classroom, for a ride in the Park on the
handsome mare that Sir Derek, in spite of the ill feeling
between them, still sent to the Pensionnat several days a
week under the care of his middle-aged groom, John Holton, and had just dismounted from it at the Pensionnat
doorstep when a high-perch phaeton with a pair of splendid greys between shafts drew up beside her. Glancing up,
in the very act of gathering the skirts of her rather shabby
but well-cut blue habit to mount the steps, she saw that it
was Baron de Lempriere who was driving his dashing
equipage.

"Where *did* you find such a pair of prime 'uns in Brussels?" she demanded impulsively, joining Holton in a
knowledgeable and approving examination of the greys.
"Welsh-bred, surely?"

"Yes, I had them from a Captain of your English
Dragoons who was unfortunate enough to have had a bad
run of luck at the tables," said the Baron, flashing a smile
at her with no hint of the passionate gloom that had
marred their last meeting. "Do you like them? Come up
and I will show you what they can do."

Allegra hesitated, casting a glance at the door of the
Pensionnat; but inclination overcame duty and she said
she would come, but only for a few minutes. Holton assist-
ed her to mount into the phaeton, and then swung

himself up on his own horse and went off with the mare while the Baron, seeing Allegra settled comfortably beside him, gave the greys the office to start.

For a few minutes the conversation dealt only with the subject of the greys, which Allegra enthusiastically pronounced to be perfect steppers, with the small heads, broad chests, and powerful quarters of the true Welsh breed. The Baron, pleased with her approval, asked if he might not take her a little way beyond the cobblestoned streets of the town, so that he might better show their paces.

"Yes—very well," Allegra said, her father's daughter in her getting the better of her feeling that she really should return at once to the Pensionnat. "But only a *little* way," she stipulated.

"*Naturellement,*" agreed the Baron, and went on talking horses to her.

Allegra, except for a desire to be handling the ribbons herself, for she was quite as good a whip as was the Baron, was enjoying herself very much, for the day was fine and the scenery picturesque, and it was with some reluctance that she at length suggested that they had best be turning back. But to her considerable surprise, the Baron evinced not the slightest inclination to comply with her request.

"*Mais non,*" he said calmly. "You see, I am kidnaping you, *mignonne.*"

"Kidnaping me?" Allegra stared at him incredulously. "Oh, you are hoaxing me! *Do* be serious, Gilles! I really must return to the Pensionnat."

"But I am not at all hoaxing you," the Baron assured her seriously. "All the week you have been avoiding me, dancing with that stiff Englishman Huddleston and allowing *him* to escort you where you wish to go. *Enfin*—I now take matters into my own hands! Today you dine with me in the suburbs, at one of those little bourgeois cafés where we shall meet no one we know and I shall have you entirely to myself. There is something I wish to tell you," he went on, becoming somewhat flown with his own audacity and speaking more magniloquently by the moment, "and listen to me you shall, *ma mie!* I shall open my heart to you—"

"Oh no, pray *don't* do that!" Allegra begged, not knowing whether to be vexed or amused at this high-handed speech, but strongly inclining to the latter. "You know I have already told you that I shall not accept a *carte blanche* from you."

"Please—do not speak of such things! It is unbecoming!" said the Baron. "What I have to say to you is of a sacred nature!"

He spoke so severely that the thought flashed into Allegra's mind—*Good heavens, can it be that he intends making me an offer!*—and, quite shaken out of her amusement by this extraordinary idea, she said nothing at all for several minutes, while the Baron contemplated with satisfaction the brilliance of his strategy.

When she did speak, it was to try again to persuade him to turn back to the Pensionnat, but the Baron was adamant. Dine with him she should, at a little café he knew outside the Porte de Namur, and Allegra, after vainly representing to him that Hilary and Mlle. Jusseau would be cast into the greatest anxiety by her failure to return from the Park and inventing an entirely fictitious engagement that evening for which she was sure to be late, gave it up and allowed matters to take their course.

They arrived shortly afterwards at the café, where they found several Bruxellois burghers and their families already installed at the outdoor tables, drinking Faro, the ancient beer of the region, or sipping an excellent claret, which the Baron ordered. Allegra, quite unsure of what was in store for her in view of her companion's intimations of high romance, was relieved to find herself in such agreeably prosaic surroundings, and succeeded for a time, by dint of making persevering conversation on the rumours of military movements on the frontier that were disturbing Brussels, in drawing the Baron out by requesting his opinion as to the safety of her remaining in the city with Hilary.

The Baron, flattered to have his advice sought, said that in his opinion there was no danger.

"It is known," he said, "that Bonaparte was still in Paris on the tenth; impossible that he has reached the frontier by this time! Brussels is a nest of rumours, *ma chère,* not one in ten of which is based on fact. *Ma foi,* you see that your Duke does not disturb himself; he goes to the Duchess of Richmond's ball tomorrow night, and gives one himself later in the month!"

Allegra said yes, she knew that, but still she could not help being a little uneasy on Hilary's account.

"I should never forgive myself for bringing her here if there were any *real* danger," she said, upon which the Baron, getting quite above himself, what with the exhilaration of his own bold stroke of genius in getting her alone and her unusual deference to his ideas, undertook to explain to her very kindly the network of intelligence possessed by the Allied command, which made it impossible for them to be taken by surprise by anything Bonaparte chose to do.

"Naturellement," he admitted, "the same is true for the French as to *our* preparations, for there are Bonapartist agents everywhere, *vous savez.* Only last week a lady— you will not know her, as she does not move in the circles to which you are accustomed," he observed, with an air that informed Allegra quite plainly that the lady was, so to speak, no lady, "who has entertained quite widely military gentlemen, was taken up by the police when she was found to be in the pay of the French. A great deal of information, you understand, may be let fall carelessly at social gatherings, and these agents are like scavengers, picking up a bit here, a bit there, and sending it all on to be pieced together into a valuable whole."

"How very interesting!" said Allegra, who was not interested in the least but thought it best to pretend to be so for the sake of keeping the conversation in these safe channels.

But the Baron was not long to be diverted from his true purpose. When the *waterzooi* and *asperges à la flamande* he had ordered had been set before them and the waiter had retired, Allegra turned her attention to them with what she hoped was suitable enthusiasm. The Baron, however, after dipping a single stalk of asparagus in the delicious sauce of crushed boiled eggs and melted butter that had been prepared for it, set it aside with the air of a man to whom food is as nothing and said to her dramatically, "I can no longer contain myself! You must hear me now! I ask you to do me the honour of becoming my wife! Yes!"—as Allegra, who had just conveyed a portion of asparagus into her own mouth, stared at him, speechless, "my wife! Never had I thought to meet the woman who would cause me to say this before I considered it proper, in the due course of time, to settle myself and produce a family; but you—*you* have turned all my prudent planning, as you say, upside down. I wish to marry you now—at once!"

"For goodness' sake, Gilles," implored Allegra, who had by this time disposed of the asparagus and was able to speak again, "do remember where we are! You will have everyone staring at us!" She saw his face darkening and added hastily, "Indeed, I am *very* much obliged to you, and—and conscious of the honour you have done me—"

Good God, am I refusing him! a voice somewhere inside her said incredulously, and she stopped short and looked at the Baron rather helplessly. This at once caused him to feel masterful and he reached across the table, taking her hands and crushing them in his.

"Honour—obligation—what is all this to me?" he ejaculated, in a thickened voice. "Say you will have me—say you will be mine!"

Allegra, who was feeling all the embarrassment of a properly reared Englishwoman over being made the object of such a public display of Gallic emotion, blushed vividly and drew her hands hastily away, unfortunately overturning the sauce boat as she did so. This contretemps was sufficient both to put an abrupt end to the conversation and to bring the waiter down upon them, and by the time calm had been restored the atmosphere was charged more with frustration than with sentiment and the Baron was looking distinctly displeased.

"*Tiens! Quelle bêtise,* to serve food to one in a vessel that overturns!" he exclaimed.

"But it was all *quite* my fault!" Allegra said penitently, though feeling that she might have a fit of the giggles all the same. "I *am* so sorry! And it is such a *good* sauce!"

The Baron looked revolted. "Sauce! What do I care for sauces?" he ejaculated; but before he could go on with any further dramatic utterances Allegra cut him short.

"Oh dear, Gilles, pray don't begin all over again!" she begged. "I am very grateful to you, but I *don't* love you and I *can't* marry you—"

"Why can you not?" the Baron asked combatively. "What is to prevent you?" A look of jealous suspicion suddenly crossed his face. "There is someone else—*hein?*" he demanded.

"Yes," said Allegra. "There *is* someone else"—and knew as she said it that, for the first time since she had made Neil Alland's acquaintance, it was not of him that she was thinking, not of a bittersweet boy-and-girl love that had long vanished from the world of reality, but of a new love that was no less powerful for being, she was well aware, quite hopeless.

"Huddleston?" the Baron was demanding, fury at the thought of a successful rival overcoming gallantry. "I do not believe it!"

"Well, you are quite right not to, because he has nothing to do with it," Allegra said, suddenly feeling very tired and even a little cross with the Baron, which was rather unfair, for he could not help it that he was not the person she wished had carried her off and proposed marriage to her. "I shall probably never marry anyone," she said, "so now *please* can we stop talking about it and enjoy this delicious dinner that you have ordered? And then you must drive me back to town at once."

Baron de Lempriere, who had never visited England and so could not conceive of a young lady's feeling it possible to refuse an offer of marriage and then enjoy— *enjoy!*—eating her dinner in company with the gentleman whom she had rejected, was so much taken aback by this speech that he fell back upon his own dinner as the only resource left to him and for quite some time said nothing at all. He looked, in fact, so miserable and outraged that Allegra took pity on him presently and tried to coax him out of the sullens, but she succeeded very poorly in this, owing to his having worked himself around by this time to a conviction that she was totally lacking in any appreciation of his higher feelings and consoling his pride by looking very injured and superior. So Allegra finally gave over her attempts to induce a more friendly atmosphere, and saying, "Oh, very *well,* then!" internally to herself, turned her attention to the scene about her.

This was a very pleasant and comfortable one, with the tables around them crowded now with ruddy burghers and their buxom wives and families, waiters bustling about, and now and then a heavy waggon drawn by fat horses passing by on the road, its driver picturesque in a blue smock, striped stockings, and wooden shoes. She had been observing with some amusement the dexterity of one waiter who possessed the capacity to carry an apparently unlimited number of foaming tankards of beer, filled quite to the brim, without spilling a drop, when her attention was suddenly drawn by the unexpected sight of a familiar face. It was that of Mlle. Juseau's servant, Jules, who was in the act of alighting from a gig that had just driven up—a gig that she was able to identify as Cherry's own.

Feeling slightly surprised at his appearing here, outside the city, in Mlle. Jusseau's gig, she watched him as he glanced around for a moment and then approached a table at which a man sat alone, a tankard of beer set before him. The table was at some distance from her, and as the man was sitting with his back to her she could not see his face; but she realised suddenly, with a shock of recognition, that he was wearing a bottle-green coat. Cherry's nocturnal visitor, the indigent and importunate relation whom she had seen twice at the Pensionnat Jusseau? But why should he be meeting Jules here, quite obviously by appointment?

Still watching, she saw Jules sit down opposite him at the table and, drawing something from his pocket, slide it unobtrusively into the other's hand. He then said a few rapid words to him and, rising again, went quickly back to the gig and drove off at once. The man in the bottle-green coat continued to sit for a few minutes longer, sipping his beer; then, calling for the reckoning, he too rose and went off down the road. Allegra was able to see him clearly as he stood up, and there could be no doubt in her mind now, as she looked at that dark, heavy face, that it was the man whom she had seen talking to Mlle. Jusseau in the hall of the Pensionnat.

For a few moments after she had seen him depart from the café, puzzlement reigned in her mind—puzzlement over why Cherry had entrusted to a servant what she had apparently heretofore considered the rather delicate matter of providing her unfortunate relation with funds. And then suddenly, with such a sickening shock of enlightenment that for an instant the whole peaceful, commonplace scene seemed to reel about her, an idea came into her mind, and she heard again the Baron's voice saying, "A great deal of information, you understand, may be let fall carelessly at social gatherings, and these agents are like scavengers, picking up a bit here, a bit there, and sending it all on to be pieced together into a valuable whole."

Was *that,* she thought, why Cherry had been so insistent upon gleaning from her and Hilary every hint of military information that had been dropped by the officers of their acquaintance at the social events they had attended? Was that, too, why she had been so eager to see them enter the first rank of Brussels Society? And was the man in the bottle-green coat not an indigent, importunate relation but a courier, a Bonapartist agent, who could not risk being seen at the Pensionnat by day and to whom Jules had just passed the latest budget of information that his mistress had been able to gather?

Chapter Fourteen

ONCE THIS MONSTROUS suspicion had entered her mind, no other concern could remain there. She *must* return to the Pensionnat at once, she felt, see Cherry, and determine for herself if there were any grounds for the entirely incredible interpretation that it had suddenly occurred to her might be placed upon her old governess's behaviour.

How she was to go about making this determination she could not, in her present state of agitation, precisely decide, for if the incredible was indeed true and Mlle. Jusseau was acting as a Bonapartist agent, it was scarcely probable that she would admit as much to Allegra if the latter was so imprudent as to tax her with it. How fervently did she now wish that she were not on such bad terms with Sir Derek as to preclude her seeking his advice at once, before she even returned to the Pensionnat! But all her pride rose up to prevent her from confessing to him that she now appeared to be in a new difficulty, and one far worse than any into which she had previously fallen. Anything, she felt, would be preferable to being obliged to face renewed censure and exasperation from him over what he would no doubt consider as fresh evidence of her bird-witted propensity for finding herself in the briars.

Colonel Hepworth's name then occurred to her: she might consult him instead of Sir Derek—but she recollected that the Colnel was now stationed outside of Brussels, near Tournay, so that it was impossible for her to go to him with her story. Baron de Lempriere she dismissed as entirely unsuitable for the role of confidant and adviser: she knew him too well to think that he would manage such a business with either tact or sense. And at any rate he was so cross with her that no doubt he would only tell her it was all her own fault and go on sulking just as he was doing now.

She therefore said nothing to him of her suspicions but only hurried him into taking her back to the Pensionnat, which made him crosser than ever, and he left her at the front door without even pressing her to allow him to escort her to the Duchess of Richmond's ball on the following evening, which was perhaps just as well, for she had already promised Sir Arthur Huddleston that honour.

It was Jules who opened the door for her, his dark face looking quite as impassive as ever; but she had an odd feeling, as his eyes flickered over her riding habit—certainly a rather odd costume for her to be wearing at this time of the evening—that he had observed her at the café and was waiting to see if she would give any sign of having seen him there. This, however, she judged it to be unwise to do, and only walked past him into the hall, where she was at once met by Mlle. Jusseau.

"*Ma chère,* where in the world have you been?" Mademoiselle enquired, with a look of solicitude and some disapproval upon her face. "We have been quite worried about you, the little Hilary and I!"

Allegra, advancing farther into the hall and stripping off her gloves with what she hoped was a negligent air, said that it was all Baron de Lempriere's doing, for he had insisted upon taking her up in his phaeton to try the paces of his new horses, and then had positively bullocked her into dining with him at a little café outside the ramparts.

Mlle. Jusseau's wrinkled lids blinked once or twice, in their disconcertingly reptilian way, over her small black eyes.

"A café outside the ramparts," she repeated thoughtfully. "I see. I should not have thought it of the Baron, I confess. They are rather vulgar little places."

Allegra said somewhat incoherently that the one where they had been did an excellent *waterzooi* and that the *asperges à la flamande* had been delicious, and then was quite certain that she was looking so self-conscious that her old governess would immediately know that something was wrong and ask her what she had been up to, exactly as though she had been eight years old.

But Mlle. Jusseau merely asked calmly if it were to the Roi d'Angleterre that she had been, as she had been obliged to send Jules there on an errand and he had mentioned having seen her there with the Baron.

"It seemed so very unlikely that I thought he must have been mistaken," she said, "but I daresay, after all, that he was not, if it was indeed to the Roi d'Angleterre that the Baron took you."

Allegra, with what she could only hope was a convincing show of indifference, said she believed that had been how the café was called.

"*Eh bien,* you must then have seen him yourself," Mademoiselle said, her black eyes boring penetratingly into Allegra's hazel ones, and Allegra, forced into a corner, said oh yes, she had, and then wondered fatally if she had said just what Cherry had wished her to say, for she saw a sudden light, immediately veiled, flicker in the small black eyes.

But all Mademoiselle said was, "Did you, indeed?"—in a quite imperturbable voice, adding composedly that Allegra had best go straight upstairs now and reassure Hilary as to her safety, as her sister was quite certain she had eloped with Sir Arthur Huddleston or something equally dire.

So Allegra went upstairs, having accomplished nothing, she thought, in the way of discovering if Cherry really were a Bonapartist agent, but with an uncomfortable feeling that she herself had said all the wrong things to her in the brief conversation, though how she could convincingly have denied being at the Roi d'Angleterre or what harm Cherry's knowing of it could do did not immediately appear.

And so confused and torn by doubt was she by her suspicions—which seemed more wildly improbable than ever, now that she had just been talking to her old governess under (outwardly, at least) quite ordinary circumstances—that she poured the whole story out to Hilary the moment they were alone together in their bedchamber.

It was to Hilary's credit that she received an account in which Baron de Lempriere's offer of marriage, the activities of a mysterious relation of Mlle. Jusseau's, and Allegra's incredible suspicions concerning their respectable elderly benefactress were inextricably jumbled together without evincing either astonishment or confusion. In fact, when Allegra had concluded her narrative, she merely nodded and said, "Well, that explains it then," upon which Allegra enquired rather blankly, "Explains *what?*"

"I mean the way she has been with Roddy when he comes here, and insisting we tell her everything about military plans we hear and all that," Hilary said, abstractedly picking up the white kitten, which had been asleep on the hearth rug as if on purpose to emphasise the cosy tranquillity of the room, and tickling its whiskers, causing it to shake its head rather crossly and sneeze. "I was used to think it was because she was afraid of Bonaparte, but then you said she has never been afraid of anything and of course you are right, and it made me begin to think. If I had known about the man in the bottle-green coat, I should have been able to put two and two together long before this," she added, with a look of mild reproach at Allegra that made that harassed young lady enquire with some asperity why she had not told her of these suspicions if they had been in her mind.

"Well, I didn't want to worry you," Hilary said, allowing the white kitten to spring down from her lap and stalk offendedly back to its place on the hearth rug. "So I talked it over with Roddy instead, and he said we couldn't do anything because we hadn't any evidence, but that it might be just as well if we told her Banbury tales instead of the truth—about anything military, that is. We told her some splendid clankers," she said with modest pride, adding, with love's self-abnegation, "but it was mostly Roddy who thought them up, not me."

Allegra, who was beginning to feel that she must indeed have been dull-witted not to have been able to deduce that there had been something odd going on at the Pensionnat Jusseau when it had been apparent even to these two children, with some difficulty put her mortification aside and said that that was all very well, but what were they to do now?

Hilary considered this. "Well, there's Sir Derek," she said, after a moment. "He would know what to do, wouldn't he?"

Allegra flushed slightly. "I daresay he would," she said, "but I don't wish to trouble him any further with our affairs. If what we suspect of Cherry is true, we can't remain here, and he may think we are applying to him for assistance."

"Well, I can't think of anyone better to apply to," Hilary said frankly. "Roddy would help if he could, of course, but he rather thought he should be obliged to go to Ghent today, and, besides, he isn't rich like Sir Derek."

"If you think," said Allegra, firing up at once, "that I should take a groat from That Man—"

"Don't, then," said Hilary reasonably. "But at least he can tell you what to do about Cherry."

Allegra, her anger subsiding, looked at her rather distractedly. "Do you mean—turn her over to the authorities? Oh, but, Hilary, I couldn't! We've known her for such a long time, and she has been so kind to us here!"

"Because it suited her to be," Hilary said, with a ruthlessness quite foreign to her nature. Allegra looked at her in surprise. Hilary went on, her face kindling, "If anything she is doing makes it even a tiny bit more possible that Roddy—or Robin, or Francis Pelton, or *anyone*—might be killed, I don't care what happens to her. Don't you see, Allie, she *must* be stopped? It doesn't matter about *our* feelings."

"Yes, you are right, of course," Allegra said unhappily. "Only I still can't believe it—and we *may* be quite wrong, you know. We have so very little to go on—"

"Then tell it to Sir Derek and let *him* decide," Hilary said, rising and coming across the room to pull her from her chair. "I'll go with you, so that Sir Derek can't ring a peal over you for jauntering about the streets alone. Only you must get out of your riding dress first, or he *will* think you are mad!"

Allegra, thus adjured, hastily changed her habit for a walking dress of blue cambric, and the two young ladies, having tied on their bonnets, prepared to leave the room. Hilary, who was nearest the door, turned the knob and pulled, but the door did not open. She looked at it in surprise and pulled again.

"It must be locked!" she said, with an air of disbelief.

"Oh no, it can't be! Let me try it," said Allegra, coming over.

But the door would not yield, turn and pull as she would. The two sisters looked at each other in dismay.

"It is all my fault!" Allegra exclaimed bitterly, after a moment. "I admitted to Cherry that I had seen Jules at that café, and I expect I looked queer, and she must have guessed that I suspected the truth. But what can she mean by this?"

"She means to keep us here, *I* should say," said Hilary, wrinkling her brow. "But why I can't think. She *can't* hope—or even wish—to keep us locked up forever. People would be bound to notice if we simply disappeared!"

"Perhaps it is a mistake," Allegra said, rattling the doorknob once more. "Or an accident. Do you think anyone will come if we call?"

Hilary said that she didn't think so, as the walls were thick and no one ever came up to that floor but Cherry herself and Marthe; and just then any further speculation was made unnecessary by the sound of a key turning in the lock outside. The next moment Mlle. Jusseau herself walked into the room.

"*Eh bien,*" she said, calmly surveying two very flushed young ladies, each bonnetted and gloved for an excursion out of doors, "you are going somewhere, *mes petites?*"

"Yes!" said Allegra, scarcely knowing what sort of air to put on, and succeeding only in looking very determined. "We—we have an engagement."

Mlle. Jusseau's brows rose. "At this hour, and without an escort?" she enquired. "I do not think you are wise, *ma chère.*"

"That does not signify," Allegra said, still striving to keep everything on a very matter-of-fact level. "And—and we are rather in a hurry—"

She attempted to move past Mlle. Jusseau to the door, but Mlle. Jusseau did not stir to allow her to pass.

"Ma chère, I tell you, it is not wise," she repeated softly and, without raising her voice, added simply, "Jules."

There was a movement behind her and Jules, holding in his hand a large, wicked-looking pistol, appeared in the doorway.

"You see," said Mlle. Jusseau, almost apologetically. She looked indulgently at the two incredulous, startled faces before her. "You must not be frightened; *bien entendu,* Jules will not harm you if you do not try to leave this room," she said. "But I really cannot allow you to go to Sir Derek—it *was* to see Sir Derek that you were going, I daresay?—and make disagreeable accusations to him about me."

"I—I don't know what in the world you are talking of!" Allegra said, still desperately endeavouring to appear ignorant of the reason for these melodramatic happenings. "What *is* the matter with you, Cherry? I am beginning to feel that you must have taken leave of your senses!"

"No, no, I am quite in possession of my faculties, *ma chère,"* said Mlle. Jusseau, motioning to Jules to retire. He did so, closing the door behind him. "It is you who are all about in your head if you believe that I do not understand quite well that you have just put together several rather unimportant but significant incidents that have recently occurred to form an interesting whole that you would like very much to communicate to Sir Derek. You need not trouble yourself to deny it," she continued with unabated calm, as Allegra opened her mouth to speak again. "And I may tell you as well that it is quite true, what you are suspecting—only *so* unwise of you to wish to communicate it to anyone. You yourself, and the little Hilary, are so deeply involved in it as well, you see."

"We are involved in it?" Allegra said, unable to believe her own ears. "Why, what can you mean—?"

"I mean," said Mlle. Jusseau, in her precise voice, "exactly what I say, *ma chère.* If you will insist upon making your suspicions concerning my activities in the cause of the Emperor public, I will have something to say concerning yours as well."

"But we haven't done anything!" Hilary, unable to contain herself any longer, burst into the conversation at this point.

"Have you not, *ma petite?*" said Mlle. Jusseau, looking at her composedly. "Did not you and Allegra come here from England expressly for the purpose of entering Brussels Society, so that you might make yourselves useful to me by providing me with the bits of information that gentlemen of high military and diplomatic rank are often so imprudent as to let fall to pretty young women?"

"But—but we *didn't!*" Hilary protested vehemently. "You asked Allie to come here as English mistress!"

"And she has been spending such a great deal of her time since she arrived in Brussels in the schoolroom—*hein?*" said Mlle. Jusseau ironically. "Nor, I daresay, have you both allowed me to provide you with toilettes suitable for your roles!"

Hilary, struck dumb by the impossibility of refuting these statements, looked at Allegra, who said, with what she hoped was an air of decision, "Nonsense! No one would credit such an accusation made against us, Cherry! It would appear quite incredible."

"More incredible than that Mlle. Jusseau, who lived for so long in England, and who was known there always as a vehement partisan of the House of Bourbon, is now exposed as a Bonapartist agent?" Mlle. Jusseau asked. "I think not, *ma chère!* If the one accusation is believed, so will the other be. So you see that it is in your own interest that I keep you here in this room, where you can do neither me nor yourselves harm by foolish babbling of matters that do not concern you."

"But they *do* concern us!" said Hilary indignantly. "If anyone is killed because of something you do, it will concern us like anything! And, besides, you can't keep us locked up here for weeks and weeks! Someone will be bound to come looking for us."

"But it will not be for weeks, *ma petite!*" said Mlle. Jusseau, an odd triumphant light suddenly appearing in her black eyes. "No, no! In a very few days now the French army will be in Brussels; your Duke and *his* army will have fled, and you will then be free to go where you please and say what you please."

"He will *not* have fled!" said Hilary stoutly. "He never does!"

"Ah, but he has never faced *l'Empereur* before this!" said Mlle. Jusseau. "He will find this a rather different matter from the Peninsula, I fancy!"

Allegra, whose mind was going back to the dark days of her girlhood, when invasion had been in the air and Wellington's successes in the Peninsula were still to come, said incredulously to Mlle. Jusseau, "Then all the time you were at Rolveston you were hoping that Bonaparte would win! You were scheming—"

"No, no," said Mlle. Jusseau, "not scheming, *ma cherè*. What could I—one poor woman with her living to earn—have done to aid the Emperor at that time? But hoping—yes! That I have always done!"

And she gave the two Misses Herington a glance full of so much venom, as if she had saved it all up from the days when she had had to conceal her true sentiments while listening to them hero-worshipping Lord Nelson, that Hilary at once felt relieved of all necessity to like her any longer.

As for Allegra, she made up her mind then and there that if it was the last thing she ever did she would get out of that room, find Sir Derek, and return to foil her old governess's plans. In the event, however, she did not even succeed in keeping Mlle. Jusseau any longer in the room so that she might somehow induce or trick her into letting them go, for that astute female, being well acquainted with the resourcefulness of her former charges, went away almost at once, locking the door behind her.

"Well!" said Hilary with great determination, as soon as she and Allegra were alone. "We shall have to get out of here at once—*ça se voit,* as that odious Cherry would say! Have you any plans?"

Alegra looked at the windows. There were two of them, but both were small, of the oval kind called *oeil-de-boeuf,* and obviously not even Hilary could succeed in squeezing herself through one of them, even if they were not so far above the ground that she would kill herself if she did. Neither was it of any use to think of signalling from them, for they overlooked only a small, dank back-garden where no one but Jules and the other manservant, Joseph, was ever to be seen.

"Perhaps someone will hear us if we pound on the floor," Hilary said, but not very hopefully, for the house was so stoutly constructed that sounds scarcely penetrated from one floor to another, and she was aware that only a storeroom lay immediately below them.

Cudgel their brains as they might, they could think of no promising plan to free themselves from their enforced confinement, though they canvassed many, ranging from Hilary's scheme of tying a note around Bluebell's neck and putting him out one of the windows—an exploit that would assuredly have taken at least one of that adventurous feline's nine lives—to Allegra's more moderate hope that Sir Arthur Huddleston, calling at the Pensionnat on the following evening to escort them to the Duchess of Richmond's ball, would be moved to sound an alarm over their nonappearance.

But that this hope was a slender one she was well aware, for certainly Mlle. Jusseau would be clever enough to concoct some plausible tale of a minor indisposition that would successfully fob off the disappointed baronet.

So after several vain attempts to call someone's attention to their plight by pounding upon the floor and shouting from the windows—attempts which succeeded only in making them feel uncommonly silly—they gave it up and decided to wait until the morning, when Mlle. Jusseau would no doubt visit them again and they might try to persuade her or coerce her into letting them go.

In the morning, however, Mlle. Jusseau did not appear. Instead, it was Marthe who came in with a breakfast tray, with Jules just showing his dark face behind her in the doorway in case, it was obvious he was thinking, they were to try any tricks. Hilary, who had been concocting a fresh number of highly improbable schemes for their escape ever since she had waked up, was so disappointed when Marthe, with a scared look on her face, merely set the tray down on a table and then went out of the room again, that she refused for a time even to eat her breakfast.

But a healthy appetite finally gained the day, and after prophesying darkly that the chocolate was probably poisoned and that their bodies—when the poison had taken its effect—would be buried in unmarked graves in the back-garden, she consented to drink a cup of this delicious if doubtful beverage and to eat several fresh-baked rolls.

When breakfast had been consumed they decided to try pounding upon the floor again. But not the loudest din their joint efforts could produce brought anything in the way of a rescue party to their door, and at length Hilary, completely discouraged, gave up and, sitting down hard upon the bed, said it was plain they were going to have to stop there for the rest of their lives and if ever she got her hands on Cherry what she would do to her would curl her liver.

"Don't be vulgar," said Allegra automatically, feeling as discouraged as Hilary but making a valiant attempt to pretend that she did not.

"I shall be as vulgar as I like," announced Hilary pertinaciously. "What is the use in being a lady when you are locked up in a horrid, hot room with nothing to do and spies running rampant outside? If we do not succeed in getting out of here soon, I shall burst!"

Allegra said not to be silly, but to say the truth she was feeling much the same way herself. An inspired suggestion from Hilary that they set the house on fire having been sternly vetoed as being far too dangerous, that young damsel then fell into something perilously like the sulks, from which she did not emerge even when Marthe again put in an appearance early in the afternoon with another tray containing a cold luncheon.

Allegra, however, had made up her mind that persuasion might, in the end, turn out to be their best weapon and, knowing that Marthe was fond of Hilary—if that was the proper term for an awestruck devotion inspired apparently by a complete inability to predict what Hilary would next do or say—appealed to her for assistance before she could scuttle out of the room as she had in the morning.

"Stay just a moment!" she begged. "I know you do not wish us to come to harm. Is there not *some way* that you could help us to get out of this room? If we do not, God knows what will happen to us! You know Mademoiselle says that the French army will soon be in Brussels, and we are English!"

Marthe, without meeting her eyes, muttered that Mademoiselle said no harm would come to them, but Allegra saw her gaze go uneasily towards Hilary, who was sitting with her elbows on the table and a frown on her face, looking as if she fully intended to continue sitting there until the end of time.

"She is only a child!" Allegra urged, in a lower voice. "How can you be sure what the French will do? It will be upon *your* conscience, as well as Mademoiselle's, if anything happens to her!" She was able to see from the expression on Marthe's face that her words had had some effect, and, grasping her arm, went on quickly, "Perhaps if you could get the key—?"

Marthe shook her head violently. "*Non*! *Non*! Jules has it," she said. "I cannot—I must go now! All the young ladies are leaving and I am needed!"

She ran out of the room. Allegra looked blankly at Hilary.

"She says that all the young ladies are leaving!" she exclaimed. "Good God, is it possible that Cherry is right and there *is* to be a battle near here?"

She went quickly to one of the windows and looked out, but there was nothing to be seen but the same deserted garden and familiar rooftops, looking extraordinarily peaceful and uninteresting under a hot midsummer sky. Bluebell, having finished the saucer of milk that had been provided for his luncheon, came over and, jumping up into an armchair, began sharpening his small claws on it in a businesslike manner.

"Oh, *do* stop that, you provoking creature!" said Allegra, whose anxiety was beginning to make her cross, and she lifted the offending white kitten and dropped him upon the floor, from which Hilary indignantly retrieved him.

"It is Cherry's armchair, and I hope he *does* tear it all to flinders!" she said, cradling the reluctant Bluebell in her arms. "If only he were a prince disguised as a kitten, and I could turn him back into a prince by a kiss so that he could rescue us, I would," she said, implanting a kiss upon Bluebell's unresponsive nose and then looking at him critically, as though waiting for his fur and whiskers and tail to disappear. The next moment her eyes began to shine. "A disguise!" she gasped. "Oh, Allie! I have the most *famous* idea! You shall persuade Marthe to let you put on her cap and apron and stuff gown when she brings our dinner in to us, and then you can slip out of the house and find Sir Derek and bring him back to rescue me, too!"

"Don't be absurd!" said Allegra, who was still engaged in thinking of the horrid consequences that might occur if Marthe's words really portended what she thought they might.

"But I'm not!" protested Hilary. "Allie, *do* listen to me! It's a perfectly splendid plan—can't you see? You and Marthe are just of a height, and with the cap over your hair and her gown on, Jules will never think to look at you twice if you simply walk out of here carrying the tray and go off downstairs."

"And if I meet Cherry?" Allegra asked impatiently. "Do be sensible, Hilary! She would know me at once."

"Well, it will not make the least difference if she does," Hilary urged, quite undaunted, "for *she* will not be carrying a pistol and so she will not be able to stop you. And by the time she can call Jules, or Joseph, you will be outside in the street, where they will not dare to harm you." She clasped her hands together imploringly. "Oh, Allie, *do* say you will do it!" she begged. "I should love to myself, only I am too small and her dress would not fit me, and Jules would be bound to notice!"

Allegra, who had been at first inclined to dismiss the scheme as only another of her young sister's harebrained ideas, began to look thoughtful and sat down to consider. The chief drawback to the plan, she felt, would be the difficulty of persuading Marthe to agree to it; but on this point Hilary confidently asserted that there would be no difficulty at all.

"I can manage *that*," she said. "I shall tell her that it is a matter of life and death, or rather worse than death, because that *is* what happens to girls sometimes when enemy soldiers take over a city, you know. Roddy has told me some perfectly *ghastly* stories about the Peninsula—"

"Which was *quite* improper of him," Allegra said, a smile curving her lips in spite of herself, "to say nothing of the fact that *he* knows no more of what went on there than you do. But never mind! I daresay you believe that Marthe will take every word you say as Gospel——"

"Well, she will," said Hilary seriously. "She told me once that she liked hearing me talk because it was better than a play; she has seen only one of them but nothing will convince her that it didn't all really happen. And I shall tell her that if she will help us Sir Derek will give her a silk gown, because he will be so grateful to her for saving us."

Allegra was privately not very certain that gratitude would be the word to describe Sir Derek's feelings on learning that he was again to be called upon to rescue the Misses Herington from disaster; but it would not do, she felt, to cavil over trifles now, so she said she was sure Sir Derek would honour any promises made in his name and they had best get on with working out their plan.

By the time all the details of this had been refined to their satisfaction it was almost dinnertime, and they sat waiting impatiently for Marthe to appear so that they might put it into action. But, to their disappointment, when Marthe came in with the tray she had Mlle. Jusseau with her, which of course meant that there could now not be the least chance of their approaching her on the subject.

Mlle. Jusseau was looking very bright, her black eyes gleaming like obsidian in her small, wrinkled face. She enquired politely about their well-being, and when Hilary replied inventively that she had the headache and was certain she was coming down with something and must see a doctor, said tolerantly that she looked quite well to her.

"Patience, *ma petite*," she said. "It will not be long now, I assure you, until it will be safe for me to let you go."

"There is to be a battle, then? The French are indeed coming?" Allegra enquired anxiously; but Mlle. Jusseau only shook her head and smiled, and said that they should know everything in good time.

"Well, if you intend to keep us here, at least you need not starve us," said Hilary, looking with an aggrieved air at the dinner that had been brought to them. "Giblet pie and syllabub—ugh! I shan't eat a bite! Now if Marthe were to bring the tea tray later with cream cakes or macaroons, or perhaps some of those lovely pralines—"

"What a child it is!" Mlle. Jusseau said, looking at her indulgently. "Very well, *enfant;* you shall have your bonbons."

And she went out of the room, taking Marthe with her.

Hilary, pluming herself with an entire lack of modesty upon the success of this stratagem, executed an impromptu jig to celebrate her own cleverness, but Allegra, whose mind was already running on more practical lines, said that was all very well, but she was not likely to find Sir Derek at the Hôtel de Belle Vue if she were obliged to wait until perhaps ten o'clock to leave the house.

"Of course you won't find him there," Hilary agreed, her cheerfulness quite unabated. "He will be at the Duchess of Richmond's ball, which means that you will simply be obliged to go there instead of the the Hôtel."

"I shall be obliged—Good God, in a stuff gown and cap!" Allegra said, appalled. "But I can't! They would never allow me inside the door!"

"Gammon!" said Hilary, still undaunted. "You have your card of invitation, haven't you? And you know heaps of people who could identify you."

"But I *couldn't*—!"

"You needn't go into the ballroom, silly!" said Hilary impatiently. "Just ask for Sir Derek, and say it's a matter of life and death—"

"Or worse than death," emended Allegra, seized all at once by a helpless fit of the giggles at the thought of the butler's amazement at a servant-girl's demanding, in the middle of a ball, to have Sir Derek Herington brought out to her, and producing a bona fide card of invitation from the Duchess to support her claim.

But there was no help for it, if she was to manage to free Hilary without resorting to the unpleasant expedient of enlisting the aid of the Brussels *gendarmerie,* who in the first place might not be inclined to believe the admittedly fantastic story she would be obliged to unfold to them, and on the other hand might well be inclined to believe Mlle. Jusseau if that astute female sought to convince them that the Misses Herington were as deeply involved in Bonapartist schemes as she was herself.

No, Sir Derek it must be; and if Allegra did not ask herself why she had such implicit faith in that gentleman's ability to cope with armed French agents it merely proved that she did have that faith and that Sir Derek no doubt deserved it.

It seemed a very long while to both Hilary and Allegra before they at last again heard the sound of the key turning in the lock, but this time they were rewarded by the sight of Marthe entering the room alone with the tea tray. Hilary pounced upon her at once. Of what she said to her Allegra was afterwards to have only the most confused of recollections, for her young sister unleashed such a torrent of orders and entreaties upon the hapless Marthe's head, coupled with blood-curdling intimations of what would be in store for her if Bonaparte's ravening soldiery were allowed to discover her still in durance vile in Brussels, that even Allegra was struck with awe.

As for Marthe, within a space of minutes she was dazedly allowing herself to be divested of cap, apron, and gown and huddled into one of Allegra's dresses, while Allegra, hastily doing up buttons and pushing her flaming hair into concealment beneath the cap, picked up the tray and hurried out of the room.

"And about time!" Jules growled in French, as she stepped outside. "The less you have to do with those wenches, the better for you, my girl!"—upon which Allegra, slipping quickly past him, her head bent over her burden, merely hunched one shoulder in a Gallic gesture that she had seen the harried Marthe use a hundred times and went off down the stairs.

Jules, to her intense relief, did not accompany her down more than the first flight, but went off on some errand of his own on the floor below, while she continued on down the stairs to the ground floor. As she went, she observed an unusual disorder in the house, doors standing open, boxes lying in the halls, which appeared to confirm Marthe's earlier statement that the pupils had left in considerable haste; but she was too much involved in the present peril of her own situation to do more than take cursory note of this in her mind. If she could but reach the front door, she thought, before anyone saw her. . . .

Joseph appeared suddenly from one of the rooms opening into the lower hall. He was older than Jules and looked as if his feet hurt him.

"Enfin," he said, in an outraged tone, taking little note of the counterfeit Marthe on the stairs above him, whom he appeared to consider merely as a convenient audience, *"dites donc!* She says she must go out. At this hour. In the carriage, and I must take her."

He added a brief and idomatic epithet, also in French and fortunately unfamiliar to Allegra, and marched off towards the rear of the house.

Allegra's heart, which had stopped beating upon his sudden appearance, gave an enormous leap of relief and then settled down more or less dependably to do its usual work, and she came down the remaining stairs, set the tray hastily upon a table and ran out into the night.

Chapter Fifteen

NOT UNTIL SHE had reached the bustle of the Place Royale did she dare to slacken her pace. She was not being pursued—she could be sure of that now—and, if Mlle. Jusseau were indeed going out in the carriage with Joseph, there seemed little likelihood that she would discover Allegra's absence until her return some time later, and perhaps not even then, if she had no occasion to go into the room where she supposed her to be.

Her one concern must now be to reach the house which the Duke of Richmond had hired in Brussels; but this, she discovered, was not so simple a matter as it had seemed to her and Hilary when they had discussed it at the Pensionnat Jusseau. Neither of them had ever visited the house, and obtaining exact directions to it in a city that appeared to be seething with alarm over rumours of the movement of French troops along the frontier, especially when one was a remarkably pretty young woman attired in a maidservant's cap and simple frock, turned out to be almost impossible.

Blank stares and preoccupied faces greeted her first attempts at seeking information, all attention being concentrated at the moment upon a very self-important gentleman in a blue coat and Angola pantaloons, who claimed to have driven into the city from the direction of Charleroi and to have heard the actual sounds of an engagement there. This asseveration then drew an indignant denial from a resplendent officer in the uniform of the

National Militia, who averred that there was not a grain of truth in the report, and that the news that the Prussians had been attacked was only another of the wild rumours that periodically disturbed the city.

On the whole, however, the self-important man was held to have the best of the argument, and three very young Dragoons began to sing *Ahé Marmont* in self-congratulation at the idea of a battle, which led for some reason to a friendly scuffle with several Highlanders, after which they all went off to have a drink together.

Theirs, however, were the only cheerful faces that Allegra saw, for no one else found anything to be pleased about in the notion of a battle's being about to be fought within earshot of the city, and though there was as yet no panic a pall of apprehension and uncertainty darkened the movement and activity that had brought the city to such unusual life at an hour past ten o'clock at night.

All this only sharpened Allegra's anxiety to find Sir Derek and enlist his aid in rescuing Hilary, but enquiries posed to a soldier in a Rifleman's green uniform who passed his arm gaily round her waist and asked what did she want with a duke when the Light Bobs were at her service, and to a proper-looking gentleman who surprised her by making a most *im*proper proposal to her, considerably discouraged her. At last, after traversing the elegantly proportioned square from one end to the other, she came upon a small but knowing street urchin who was quite willing to give her the directions she sought at the price of a coin from the purse she had fortunately remembered to bring with her.

But the information she received was still imperfect enough to cause her to lose more valuable time before she arrived at her goal—a charming house in the Rue de la Blanchisserie, where the sounds of music wafting from the open windows, the brilliant lights shining from every room, and the fashionable carriages drawn up outside, all bespoke a ball in full progress. She drew a long breath and, summoning up all her courage, entered the gates and walked up to the front door.

In describing to Hilary later what happened after that, she was obliged to tell her that she did not exactly know, but that if rumours of the impending clash between the French and Allied armies had not already induced an extraordinary atmosphere of tension and a certain nervous disregard for the conventions in the house, she was sure she would have been driven out with a flaming sword like Adam and Eve from Eden. As it was, after an exhausting series of interviews with several servants, each more suspicious and unaccommodating than the last, she succeeded in bribing a footman, in the confusion occasioned by the arrival of the Duke of Wellington and his party, to carry her message to Sir Derek, and then effaced herself in a corner of the hall, just outside the small anteroom leading to the ballroom, to await his return.

The Duke's arrival, and the word, which spread like wildfire through the house, that he had confirmed the fact that the Allied armies had indeed been ordered to move, let loose the suppressed excitement that had been gathering all evening. Allegra, from the hall, had a glimpse through the anteroom into the ballroom itself, which was a spacious apartment papered with a trellis-and-rose pattern and with French windows open to the hot midsummer night. She could see anxious groups clustering now in corners to discuss the latest intelligence brought by the Duke, while the music, in odd counterpoint to their grave faces, went on as brightly as before and many of the younger guests continued to whirl about the floor in a kind of feverish gaiety that soon affected Allegra to the extent that for a moment she almost forgot Hilary's danger and her own anomalous position and longed to be able to join them herself. Young women in diaphanous, high-waisted, ankle-length ball-gowns of sheerest India muslins or spider-gauzes, amber, blossom, lilac, or cerulean blue, with flowers or plumes in their high-piled, ringletted hair, their feet shod in delicate slippers; their partners gallant in scarlet and rifle-green, with here and there the swinging flare of a fur-bordered, silver-encrusted pelisse—it was as if, Allegra thought in a kind of fascination, the future had ceased to exist for them and there was only this moment, caught in time under a crystal dome of candle-glow and perfume and music and summer night.

All the while the hall was filled with the confusion of officers departing in haste to join their regiments, the coming and going of messengers, and the bustle of servants, so that when Sir Derek, looking as elegantly imperturbable as ever in his long-tailed black coat and satin knee-breeches, presently strode out of the ballroom he did not for a moment perceive Allegra in her corner. She saw him at once, however, and in an instant the queer fascination of the music, the glowing candlelight, the pervading scent of roses and lilies, the brilliant uniforms and the fashionable gowns, seemed to whirl together into a fantastic kaleidoscope and vanish, leaving her once more only a very much harried young woman in a servant's cap and stuff gown, with a young sister in peril left behind her.

She started towards Sir Derek swiftly, and the look of unwonted concern she read in his eyes, behind the imperturbability of his manner, so unnerved her that for a moment she almost lost her dignity entirely, and restrained herself only with great difficulty from hurling herself upon his chest and begging him to help her.

Fortunately, as soon as his eyes fell upon her he began to have his exasperated look again, and she immediately stopped feeling helpless and became as belligerent as one can well be in a servant's ill-fitting dress and cap at a ball.

"I cannot help it, so *do* please stop looking at me like that," she said. "It is about Hilary. Cherry has her locked in our bedchamber at the Pensionnat because we have found out that she is a Bonapartist spy, and she says if we go to the authorities she will say we are spies, too, so you must come at once and help me to get her out."

It was to Sir Derek's credit—or possibly merely owing to his years in the diplomatic service, when he had been obliged to cope with the sort of extraordinary events that somehow seem to occur so much more frequently in remote corners of the world than in England—that he did not immediately dismiss Allegra's words as the ravings of a lunatic and send posthaste for a physician. Instead, he only said to her severely, "The first thing you must understand is that you cannot have a fit of the vapours here. And the second is that I will help you, only you must be considerably more coherent before I can. *Who* is a Bonapartist spy?"

"Cherry—Mlle. Jusseau," said Allegra, giving him a fulminating glance. "And I am *not* having the vapours, only I have been locked up in that room since yesterday and when I was able to get out at last you were at a ball, of all places! It is enough to try the patience of a saint!"

"You are trying *my* patience," said Sir Derek dangerously, "beyond what is permissible, my girl! *Will* you tell me at once what has brought you here in this ridiculous guise?"

Thus adjured, Allegra swallowed her wrath and managed to give him a succinct account of the situation at the Pensionnat Jusseau, at the conclusion of which he said with a resigned air that if ever he had heard of a presumably sensible young woman's landing herself in such a bumblebath he could not recall it at the moment.

"*Oh!*" said Allegra furiously. "It is just like you to say that! As if I could have *known* that Cherry was a spy! But I don't intend to stay here a moment longer pulling caps with you! If you will not help me, I shall go to the authorities!"

"You will do nothing of the kind," said Sir Derek forcefully. He beckoned a footman to him and said a few words to him; then he said to Allegra, "I must leave you for a moment; pray don't run off while I am gone," and walked back into the ballroom.

Allegra, muttering uncomplimentary rejoinders to the circumambient air, remained waiting for him for a space of some four minutes, which seemed an hour and during which she several times decided to go away but didn't. Sir Derek then once more emerged from the ballroom and being informed by the footman that the carriage was at the door, brought Allegra outside and put her into it.

"I have borrowed the Balmforths' carriage." he said, "because I came with them, so we shall be obliged to go first to the Hôtel de Belle Vue, where I shall be able to have my own brought out for us."

"That," said Allegra roundly, "is a completely idiotish thing to do, if you do not mind my speaking plainly, Sir Derek!"

"Not at all," said Sir Derek politely. "You always do. But as it would be even more idiotish for me to appear at the Pensionnat unarmed, in case your friend Jules has an idea of disputing my right to take Hilary away, or to try to send you to Ostend in a carriage for which I have no doubt Balmforth will have pressing need himself, I do not intend to alter my plan."

"Oh!" said Allegra doubtfully, digesting this. "Do you—do you think it will be very dangerous?"

"Not in the least. I have a very good pair of pistols at the Hôtel," said Sir Derek.

"Well, I hope you will be careful," said Allegra, with a certain anxiety in her voice, for, angry as she was with Sir Derek, she did not wish any harm to come to him.

"I shall," said Sir Derek.

"And—and *are* we going to Ostend?"

"Most assuredly you are. That is, if by 'we' you mean you and Hilary. You will then take the packet to England and, I trust, *not* get yourselves into any further scrapes there."

"But—but we cannot go to England!" Allegra protested, her head whirling at the decisive rapidity of the plans being made for her future. "We have nowhere to go—and scarcely any money—"

"You may stay at Rolveston until some more permanent arrangement can be made," Sir Derek said coolly. "It should be quite in order to receive you now, according to the latest intelligence I have received from my agent there. As for funds, you must allow me to be your banker until satisfactory arrangements can be made in that regard as well."

"But—oh no, I could not!" Allegra said, flushing vividly. "Indeed, it will not do, Sir Derek!"

A somewhat ironical smile curled Sir Derek's lips. "And why not?" he enquired. "Are you thinking that Huddleston might be offended and cry off? I can assure you he will think I am doing only what is proper in removing you and your sister from a situation that is certainly uncomfortable and may become dangerous."

Allegra stiffened, and sat up straighter in the carriage. "Let me assure *you*, sir," she said, "that Sir Arthur does not figure in the matter in the slightest degree!"

"What! Do you mean to say he has not made you an offer yet? What a slowtop!" said Sir Derek. "But that accounts, then, for your being so reluctant to leave Brussels—"

"It does not account for it in the least!" said Allegra wrathfully. "I have told you that Sir Arthur has nothing to do in the matter!"

"Lempriere, then?" Sir Derek cast a quick glance at her and, seeing even in the darkness of the carriage the suddenly self-conscious expression that appeared upon her face, said rather roughly, "You are a fool, my girl!"

"I am *not* a fool!" said Allegra, looking daggers at him. "He *has* made me an offer—of marriage," she specified, in case Sir Derek should misinterpret her meaning, "and I said No because I do not mean to marry anyone I do not—I mean, whom I cannot—*Oh!*" she broke off, furious with herself. "I had no intention of telling you that, and I *ought* not to have done so, only you are the most provoking, *abominable* man!"

Sir Derek, instead of resenting these aspersions— which, in view of the fact that he was at the moment engaged, at considerable inconvenience and perhaps some risk, in rescuing her and Hilary from a very disagreeable situation, he might have felt perfectly justified in doing— seemed quite unaffected by them, no doubt because he was fully occupied instead in feeling surprised at her announcement concerning Baron de Lempriere. And as the carriage arrived at that moment at the Hôtel de Belle Vue, no more could be said on the matter, at any rate.

Allegra remained in the Balmforth carriage during the short time that was necessary for Sir Derek to fetch his pistols from his apartments and to give orders for John Holton to bring his own carriage out. This latter was scarcely a vehicle that would have been considered suitable for accommodating ladies upon a journey, for it was the very smart sporting phaeton Allegra had frequently seen him driving about Brussels, and he appologised to her for this fact as he helped her into it.

"*Not* a carriage for a journey," he said. "But it will have to do, I think, because it seems that people are already getting the wind up, with all this war excitement going on. I'll lay odds that tomorrow—or should I say later on today?—there won't be a carriage in Brussels for hire or sale."

He swung himself up beside her and took the reins from John Holton, who then mounted Sir Derek's mare and prepared to accompany them.

"Is it truly war?" Allegra asked in a subdued voice, hearing the muffled sound of drums that had disturbed the city as they had been driving to the Hôtel growing louder and more insistent now. "There will be a battle?"

"Yes," said Sir Derek, his voice quite as calm as ever; but she saw that there was a grim look about his mouth as he gave the horses the office to start. "The Duke says the Prussians have already been attacked. It would appear that Bonaparte has stolen a march on us." He saw the anxious look upon her face and said reassuringly, "Don't be alarmed. I have every faith in the Duke. And I shall see you and Hilary safe out of this, at any rate. John Holton will drive you to Ostend and escort you to Rolveston when you have reached England. He is well provided with money, and I think you are well enough acquainted with him to know that he is absolutely trustworthy. He has been in my service, or my grandfather's, for more than twenty years."

"Yes—oh yes, I know that," Allegra said. "But—"

"You are better out of Brussels now—both you and Hilary," Sir Derek said firmly. "I have no notion to what lengths your Mlle. Jusseau may go to drag you into this affair if she finds herself in serious trouble with the authorities, but if you are safe in England, it cannot signify."

Allegra said nothing, looking about her with a feeling of growing apprehension. When they had been driving from the Rue de la Blanchisserie to the Hôtel de Belle Vue she had been too taken up with her own difficulties and her rather quarrelsome conversation with Sir Derek to pay much heed to what was going on about her, beyond a vague impression that the uneasy calm that had prevailed in the city when she had left the Pensionnat had been shattered into a rather horrendous confusion; but she saw that the confusion was becoming pandemonium now. Huge commissary waggons went rumbling past; gun-carriages hurtled by, pressing a way through the increasingly thronged thoroughfare; a mounted officer, swearing visibly but not audibly because of the din around him, reined in his sweating horse just beside the phaeton, urgent, no doubt, to deliver the despatch he was carrying. And over everything there was the never-ceasing roll of drums and the bright, imperative call of the trumpets.

The phaeton pressed on slowly and persistently through the thronged street. Soldiers, who had been billeted in almost every dwelling in Brussels, were hurrying to join their comrades, forming ranks now in the Place Royale, and Allegra, seeing a young officer tumbling down the steps of a house, buttoning his jacket as he ran, thought with a pang, "That might be Roddy," and then thought of poor, sulky Gilles, and of Colonel Hepworth, and of all the splendidly dressed young officers she had seen dancing at the Duchess of Richmond's ball. They were caught up together now in this horrid maelstrom of war, and she thought unhappily that she might never see them again, or at least not as she had know them, but shattered and maimed if they came back at all.

And at the thought, which, like most thoughts in unnerving moments, was rather unnecessarily melodramatic, for after all they would not all be killed or reduced to the shell of their former selves, she suddenly felt that she had been quite unforgivably rude to the Baron in rejecting his suit and rather wished that, if he had to go to his death, she had sent him there happy in the belief that she adored him.

But this thought and all others were driven from her mind when the phaeton, having at length inched its way through the mass of horses, carts, seething humanity, and military impedimenta crowding the Place Royale, moved on into the comparative quiet of the street outside the Pensionnat Jusseau. She had just said "Thank goodness!" to Sir Derek, and then had begun to think that after all there was nothing much to thank goodness for, since Hilary was not rescued yet and Sir Derek might well find himself in considerable danger before she was, when her eye was suddenly caught by the sight of a travelling britchka with its hood up and a man on the box standing before the Pensionnat. At the same moment the door of the Pensionnat was flung open and two persons, a man and a young woman, the latter struggling wildly with her companion, who held her clasped closely against him, came quickly down the steps to the street. In another in-

stant the female figure had been bundled into the britchka
by her companion and the horses set in motion; but not
before Allegra had ejaculated, "Oh! It's Hilary! They are
taking her away! Oh, *do* something—quickly, quickly!"

The britchka was now moving down the street in the
direction of the phaeton, its driver urging the horses on
so that they were already breaking into a gallop. Without
the slightest hesitation, and with a dexterity that Allegra,
in spite of her fright and anxiety, could not but admire,
Sir Derek swung his own horses across the road, blocking
the exit to the Place Royale and forcing the britchka to
come to a wrenching halt.

A torrent of angry French was let loose upon his head
by the britchka's driver—a man in a bottle-green coat,
Allegra saw, or rather *the* man in the bottle-green coat,
for she had certainly seen that dark face before on more
than one occasion. The diatribe had no effect upon Sir
Derek, however; he merely thrust his reins unceremoniously into Allegra's hands and, jumping down from the
phaeton, advanced purposefully upon the britchka.

At that moment several things, it appeared to Allegra,
happened simultaneously. She saw Jules suddenly emerge
from the britchka with a pistol glinting dangerously in his
hand; she saw Sir Derek launch himself upon him in a
catlike spring that would have considerably astonished
anyone accustomed to seeing that courteous and imperturbable gentleman only in a ballroom; and she saw Jules
go down onto the cobblestones as if he had been felled by
a poleax.

All that, it seemed to her, occurred in one swift moment; in the next, the man in the bottle-green coat, abandoning his horses, had jumped down from the box of the
britchka to attack Sir Derek, Hilary had tumbled out of
the britchka, and John Holton had leaped from his horse
to prevent a staggering but dogged Jules, who had
succeeded in getting to his feet, from making the contest

between Sir Derek and the man in the bottle-green coat a three-sided and rather uneven one.

But only *rather* uneven, it is necessary to state, for Allegra, wholly occupied for the ensuing moments in keeping a pair of spirited horses from taking exception, as the britehka's team was doing, to the stamping, cursing struggle going on under their feet and rearing up in their shafts and bolting, missed as pretty an exhibition of boxing skill as (John Holton was to aver later) had been seen since Cribb, the Champion, had met Molyneux, the Black, at Thistleton Gap in '11.

Sir Derek, who had learned the science in Gentleman Jackson's very fashionable London boxing saloon, and had added to his knowledge in several of the more exotic capitals of the world, had a worthy opponent in height, weight, and experience in the man in the bottle-green coat, but the outcome was never for a moment in doubt. In a space of seconds the bottle-green coat had gone down before the crashing right that Jackson himself had frequently lamented had been wasted upon a gentleman, and Sir Derek, scarcely winded and quite unmarked, was able to turn his attention to restraining Hilary, who had seized the whip abandoned by the man in the bottle-green coat and was endeavouring to assist John Holton in coping with Jules by beating impartially with the stock upon any part of the latter's anatomy that was available to her.

"Very well; you are quite safe now," Sir Derek said to her dampingly, picking up Jules's pistol from the street and pocketing it. Jules, seeing his companion stretched upon the cobblestones, gave up the battle and took himself off at a staggering run, while Hilary threw the whip in the air, jumped up and down, and shouted, "Hurrah!" in the sheer ecstasy of victory.

"John, you had best see to the mare," Sir Derek said, firmly preventing Hilary from dashing up to the phaeton, where Allegra had just succeeded in getting the horses under control, and startling them all over again. A pair of

interested artillerymen, who had witnessed the encounter
between Sir Derek and the man in the bottle-green coat
from the vantage point of a doorway across the street,
here set up three cheers to equal Hilary's, obviously in
appreciation of an English victory over foreign foes, and
then ran on to the Place Royale to join their comrades.
But beyond this the combat had attracted little attention,
having occupied, after all, the space of only a minute or
two from start to finish and the commotion it had given
rise to having been quite outshone by that going forward
in the Place Royale.

Sir Derek, having quelled Hilary and noted that the
man in the bottle-green coat showed no imminent signs of
reviving from the final blow he had received, then turned
his attention to the phaeton, bestowing a—"Well done!
There isn't another woman of my acquaintance I could
have trusted to keep those greys of mine in hand!"—upon
Allegra that she received with great inner satisfaction but
outer calm.

"You may let John take the reins now," Sir Derek continued, observing that John Holton had succeeded in teth-
ering the mare and was now approaching the phaeton.
"Hilary, is there anyone inside the house, to your knowledge?"

"No!" said Hilary, who had been almost dancing up
and down in her eagerness to tell her tale. "Everyone but
Jules and Marthe went away a long time ago, and Marthe
cried all the while and wanted to go, too, only she
couldn't because she was afraid to let Jules know she had
helped Allie escape. But about half an hour ago Jules
came up to the room and found her there instead of Allie,
and he was as mad as fire and she ran away, and then he
said he was going to take me away, too. I kicked him and
he swore," she added proudly, upon which Sir Derek said
very well, that was enough of that, and she might go back
to the Pensionnat now with him and Allegra and put up a

few things in a portmanteau for their journey while Allegra changed her dress.

"Our journey!" Hilary repeated in astonishment. "But—but where are we going?"

Allegra, who was being helped down from the phaeton by Sir Derek, said there was to be a battle and Sir Derek was sending them back to England. But this statement had the unexpected result of causing an expression of the utmost mulishness to settle upon Hilary's face, and she stated firmly that if there was to be a battle she would under no circumstances go anywhere at all.

"But why not?" asked Allegra, with a foreboding feeling of knowing the answer before it was given.

"Because Roddy may be wounded," said Hilary. "And then he will need me."

Allegra, who felt that she had already been through quite enough that evening and was in no mood to be faced with further obstacles now, said not to be silly, and even if that unfortunate event were to occur it was highly unlikely that she would be allowed anywhere near Lord Roderick's bedside. But Hilary had made up her mind, and said with an air of immovable determination that Allegra might go to England if she liked, but nothing would induce her to leave Brussels, even if she had to hire herself out as a kitchen-maid to be able to remain there.

Allegra looked at Sir Derek, thus rather unfairly throwing the whole matter in his lap. And she could not have thrown it anywhere better, for he at once took Hilary in hand with a firmness which, although she vigorously resented it, she could not withstand, telling her in a voice plainly intimating very unpleasant consequences if she disobeyed that she had exactly five minutes by his watch to go into the Pensionnat and pack up a few necessaries in a portmanteau.

Hilary found her feet carrying her, much against her will and rather to her own surprise—to say nothing of Allegra's—into the house and up the stairs to their bedchamber, but said to Allegra rebelliously that Sir Derek could not *make* her go.

"No, darling, but I rather think he will," Allegra said somewhat obscurely, but Hilary perfectly understood what she meant, having seen the look in Sir Derek's eye as he had issued his orders, which had made her feel a little like a midshipman on the deck of the *Victory* facing Lord Nelson.

"Well, at any rate," she said defiantly, "no matter what he says, I shall bring Bluebell with me. He will be drowned, or starved to death, if I leave him behind"— and against this resolve Allegra thought it wiser to raise no objection, only counselling her sister not to draw Sir Derek's attention particularly to her pet's presence in the travelling party, as he might not feel the same anxiety concerning Bluebell's well-being that she did.

Hilary accordingly, having hastily completed a very sketchy job of packing and helped Allegra attire herself once more in clothing suitable to a young lady of quality, pushed the white kitten into the pocket of her pelisse and stalked downstairs with as much of the air of an offended goddess as her small stature permitted her to assume. By this time Sir Derek had succeeded, with an efficiency that appeared to Allegra quite miraculous, considering the disorder in the city, in finding a gendarme into whose hands he confided the still dazed man in the bottle-green coat, and the latter was being led meekly away. Sir Derek then took the portmanteau from Hilary and handed it up to John Holton in the phaeton, after which he helped Allegra and Hilary up, the latter condescending to acknowledge this courtesy only by remarking darkly to him that if he did not look after Lord Roderick if the latter was wounded and write to tell her of it at once, she would never, *never* forgive him.

"I promise you that I shall," said Sir Derek, and then Allegra, bethinking herself of another of her anxieties, asked him what he intended to do about Mlle. Jusseau.

"I? Nothing!" said Sir Derek. "In the state the city is in, it will be wonderful if she does not manage to remain in hiding until she sees what the outcome of the battle will be. And if the Duke is able to carry the day and whip Bonaparte, as I have every confidence that he will, she can do no further harm, wherever she is."

He then moved to the other side of the phaeton to say a few words to John Holton. Allegra felt that she ought to ask him how long she and Hilary might be allowed to remain at Rolveston and when he expected to return to England himself, but all she could think of at the moment was that she was leaving him behind in a city in turmoil, where no one could know what might happen on the morrow, and she had a sudden horrid feeling that if she spoke again she might begin to cry.

So she only sat and looked straight ahead of her, and when he stopped talking to John Holton and stepped back to allow the carriage to start said good-bye to him as if he had merely brought her home from an evening party; and then John Holton whipped up the horses and they drove off down the street.

Chapter Sixteen

THE JOURNEY TO England, under John Holton's competent management, was accomplished without event— which, had Hilary and Allegra been aware of it, would not have been the case had they remained in Brussels until the alarm caused by the news of the military action developing so near its gates had reached panic proportions

on the following day. But to the Misses Herington, both
in the grip of the liveliest anxiety as to what was occurring in the city they had left behind them, the journey
would nevertheless always remain in memory as the most
disagreeable one they had ever made. When they reached
London no accurate intelligence was yet to be had there
as to the outcome of the meeting between the two great
armies, but the preliminary actions at Ligny and Quatre-
Bras were reported in ominous terms in the journals that
the two young ladies avidly perused on the following
morning with their breakfast chocolate at Grillon's Hotel,
where they had put up for the night, and the wildest
rumours were beginning to circulate in town to the effect
that the Allied armies had suffered a crushing defeat and
that Bonaparte was already in Brussels.

With such dire news to take with them into Cambridgeshire, it was not likely that Allegra and Hilary
would be in good spirits as they approached the end of
their journey, and to Allegra, at least, the pleasure of returning home was marred, in addition, by the thought that
Rolveston was no longer their home and by the dread of
seeing the beloved grounds and house altered by a
stranger's taste. When the chaise turned in at the gates
she even closed her eyes for a moment in what she told
herself severely was a perfectly cowardly fashion; but
when she opened them again, prepared for disagreeable
changes, no changes met her eye—except that the lawns,
the shrubberies, and the Italian garden that her mother
had loved and that had fallen into such sad neglect of late
years seemed to have been restored, as if by the wave of a
magician's wand, to the trim beauty that had been theirs
in the days of her childhood.

Even Hilary, who had convinced herself that Lord Roderick had lost at least an arm or a leg, if not his life, in
battle, and had accordingly fallen into a state of such unwonted depression that not even Bluebell, who was finding more ways to divert himself in a post-chaise than one

would have dreamed it possible for one small kitten to do, could rouse her from it, gasped with pleasure as she gazed about her.

"Oh, Allie, do look!" she cried. "It's just the way it was when we were small; they've even cleaned the fountain and it is playing again! I wonder if there are fish in the pond?"

Allegra almost said of course there were, because it was obvious that a magician's wand that had missed nothing else would not have missed them; but there was a prickling behind her eyes and it occurred to her that she had best not say anything at all just now. Then the chaise drew up before the front door, and before she and Hilary could step down from it a serious-looking young man came hurrying down the steps to greet them, saying that he was Cairnes, Sir Derek's agent, and he hoped they would find everything in the house properly in readiness for them.

"Holton's message with Sir Derek's instructions arrived only this morning," he said to Allegra rather anxiously, "and the staff isn't quite complete yet, but I do hope we shall be able to make you comfortable."

By this time a very respectable-looking butler and housekeeper had also appeared upon the doorstep, and a footman had come up to take their portmanteau. Allegra, with a feeling that she had stepped into an enchanted dream and that if it did not go away at once she would become ten years younger and find her father and mother in the drawing room when she went inside, responded mechanically to their greetings, and then she stepped over the doorsill and her heart almost stopped.

All, all the same—the cool, gracious hall with its noble staircase freshly painted and carpeted, the glimpse through an open doorway of elegant Chippendale and silver-striped paper in the dining room, the pale yellow brocade of draperies and furniture in the drawing room looking as she remembered them from earlier, golden years, before age and neglect had tarnished them. Over the fine carved mantel there was even hanging her own portrait, painted when she was seventeen, in all the glory of her first real evening frock, just as it had hung since the day it had left the artist's hands and her father had invited half the county to come and admire it.

"And the very first thing Miss Dianeme Hardison will do when she enters this house as its mistress will be to have it taken down," the thought flashed across her mind as she looked at it through eyes that had grown momentarily dim with tears—a blighting thought, which cleared sentimental memories at once from her head. A very beautiful house it was that she was standing in; but it would belong to another woman, not to her.

So she smiled at young Mr. Cairnes, and assured the housekeeper that she and Hilary would be pleased to have a refreshing cup of tea after their journey up from London, and within a space of minutes she was upstairs in the room that had been hers since she had left the nursery, where a tidy little maid unpacked her few belongings from the portmanteau the footman had carried upstairs and then went across the hall to do the same with Hilary's there.

Hilary herself, seated on the four-poster bed watching Bluebell exploring his new surroundings with an air of mingled suspicion and disdain that might have become an adult cat but seemed a trifle pretentious in one who had not yet outgrown kittenhood, gave vent to a luxurious sigh as the door closed behind her.

"Oh, Allie, isn't it *famous?*" she said. "I mean being home again and finding everything just the same! I *do* think Sir Derek is a great gun—or he would be," she added, her brow darkening slightly, "if he hadn't obliged me to leave Brussels in that abominably high-handed way! But you *do* think he will take care of Roddy if he should be wounded, don't you? Because he *promised*—"

Allegra patiently assured her sister for perhaps the

dozenth time that she was certain that he would; but her own pleasure at being "home" again, like Hilary's, was subject to these same intrusions of nagging worry over what might be taking place at that moment in or around Brussels, and conversation lapsed while each young lady brooded over the particular anxiety closest to her own heart.

They came downstairs again after a time to partake of a dinner that gave eloquent testimony of Sir Derek's having succeeded in engaging the services of an excellent French chef, and afterwards Mr. Cairnes looked in again to enquire if they were quite comfortable and being well taken care of by the staff. He was such a civil, pleasant young man that Allegra, who had come to Rolveston prepared to dislike him cordially for taking Mr. Rudwick's place, found herself liking him in spite of herself, and had a very interesting conversation with him on the subject of crop rotation, for she was not her father's daughter for nothing and knew almost as much about farming as any country squire in tne neighbourhood.

And the *coup de grâce* to all her intentions to hate Mr. Cairnes came when it developed that he was himself on excellent terms with Mr. Rudwick, who, he said, had insisted on moving out of the agent's house, although Sir Derek and he, Mr. Cairnes, had agreed that he was to continue living there for as long as it suited him, while the new agent was accommodated in the rehabilitated *cottage ornée* that an eighteenth-century Herington had built on the estate for a lady of doubtful virtue who had been his companion for many years.

"But Mr. Rudwick said that the house was too big for him now and he would be better off in the cottage himself—not but what I should have been quite as happy to have gone on with the original arrangement," said Mr. Cairnes earnestly. "And I'm bound to tell you, Miss Herington, that I don't know how I should have got on without him, for he knows Rolveston like the back of his hand

and has been most helpful about giving me the benefit of his advice when I run into difficulties of any sort. But of course I needn't tell that to *you*," he finished, blushing slightly as he apparently recollected that Miss Herington was far better acquainted with her father's former agent than was he.

Allegra said she was very happy to learn that Mr. Rudwick was still living at Rolveston, and promised to visit the old agent herself the very next day; but she did not look particularly happy as she went off upstairs to her bedchamber. To say the truth, she was feeling most unaccountably depressed, perhaps at the remembrance of how very wrong she had been on that morning at Chatt Park when she had accused Sir Derek of ruthless inhumanity in driving Mr. Rudwick from Rolveston and had therefore been led on to quarrel with him and to reject his suit—though why one should be feeling depressed over having rejected a gentleman who obviously did not care about one in the least and had immediately gone and got himself engaged (or as near it as made no difference) to another young lady, she could not imagine.

All the same, it was with a feeling that everything had gone so irretrievably wrong that it could never come right again that she got into bed that night. She rather expected that, between her depression and her anxiety as to what was occurring on the other side of the Channel, she would sleep badly; but the fatigue of her journey overcame both, and she awoke in the morning feeling much refreshed, and ready to face the uncertainties of her own and Hilary's future with a good deal more optimism than she had been able to summon up on the previous day.

This mood was much enhanced a little later by the irruption of a very flushed and excited Mr. Cairnes into the breakfast parlour with the news that had just come from London.

"A glorious victory!" he stammered out, too much stirred even to apologise for his intrusion. "The Allied armies have met Bonaparte at Waterloo and won the day—rompéd him completely! Isn't it splendid? I *knew* the Duke would do the trick!"

Allegra, feeling as if a great weight had suddenly been lifted from her heart, said so had she, while Hilary jumped up from her chair and, obviously restraining herself from doing a sort of victory dance only because of Mr. Cairnes's presence in the room, contented herself with picking Bluebell up and kissing him enthusiastically several times, much to that intelligent feline's disapproval.

In a few moments, however, she recollected her previous anxieties concerning Lord Roderick, and enquired of Mr. Cairnes with some apprehension whether there had been many casualties in the battle. His face too grew more serious, and he said he was afraid there had been.

"Do you—do you expect to hear from Sir Derek soon?" Hilary asked him, turning such hopeful eyes upon him that Mr. Cairnes, though not of a particularly romantic turn of mind, suddenly wondered if there was an attachment between his employer and the younger Miss Herington—which might account, he thought, for the rather puzzling circumstance of her and her sister's descent upon Rolveston in Sir Derek's absence.

So he explained as kindly as he could that he had no way of knowing when Sir Derek would next communicate with him, but could, of course, get in touch with him if necessary—a reply that gave Hilary little satisfaction. She said to Allegra when they were alone that naturally Roddy himself would write her all about the battle, ignoring so determinedly the possibility that Lord Roderick had been killed or too seriously wounded to write that Allegra's heart ached for her and she was glad to be able to suggest a visit to the Dowager Lady Warring at Questers as a means of distracting her sister's mind from her worries.

Having already ascertained from Mr. Cairnes that the Colbridges were all still in London for the Season, they felt no need to include Chatt Park in their morning-calls—a great relief to Allegra, who was well aware that explaining their presence at Rolveston to her aunt and uncle might present some difficulty. And she was equally relieved, upon arriving at Questers, to hear from the butler that the younger members of the family there were also in London, leaving only the Dowager at home. The latter was sitting in the garden, the butler informed them, and thither Allegra and Hilary at once repaired.

Her ladyship, who had been in receipt of a hasty scrawl from Allegra sent from London, was not surprised to see them, nor that they had left Brussels in view of what had been happening there; but she was bursting with curiosity as to how they came to be at Rolveston. She had been aware, from Allegra's letters, that they had seen something of Sir Derek in Brussels, and had even built a few small hopes as to the possibility that the match she had tried to make might prosper there as it had not in Cambridgeshire—hopes that had quickly been dashed by the news, conveyed to her in letters from other friends in Brussels, that an announcement of Sir Derek's betrothal to Miss Hardison was momentarily expected. The only solace left her was the impression that at least Allegra's rejection of Sir Derek's suit had not caused him to wash his hands of the Misses Herington's claims of relationship upon him. And this impression Allegra, seeing her ladyship's curiosity, took pains to foster, as being the easiest way to explain their presence at Rolveston.

Unfortunately, Hilary was not so reticent. She favoured Lady Warring with such a complete account of her attachment to Lord Roderick Buccan, Sir Derek's opposition to it, and the manner in which he had praiseworthily rescued them from Mlle. Jusseau and her henchmen and blameworthily bullied her into leaving Brussels, that Lady Warring was able to perceive that a great deal more had occurred in Brussels than she had ever imagined.

So she took in everything that Hilary had to say, noting

on several occasions that Allegra was making an attempt to head her sister off from disclosures that involved Sir Derek, and at last said in a deceptively incurious voice that they seemed to have had a very gay and exciting time in Brussels.

"So many English there, too," she said, "which made it particularly agreeable for you, I have no doubt. Did you tell me that you met Colonel Hepworth there?"

"Oh, yes!" said Hilary readily. "And I think he made Allie another offer, though she won't admit it, because the last time I saw him he pinched my cheek and asked me how I should like to have him for a brother-in-law, and when I said I thought he was rather old for that he laughed and said he was sure he was, but that didn't stop him from wanting to make a fine fool of himself every time he clapped eyes on my red-haired baggage of a sister."

"He doesn't mean it seriously, you know," Allegra hastened to say, blushing a little, but Hilary said stoutly that of course he did, because any gentleman, even if he was as old as Colonel Hepworth, would be glad to marry her if she would have him.

"She had an offer from a baron, too, just before we left Brussels," she said to Lady Warring. "He is a Belgian, and very handsome and romantic, and in the army, but I don't think I should want him for a brother-in-law, either. And, at any rate, Allie didn't—I mean want him for a husband—so that is that."

Lady Warring, fixing Allegra with a rather enigmatic look, observed that it appeared to her that her goddaughter was very hard to suit.

"Yes, and there is Sir Arthur Huddleston, too," Hilary went on, apparently determined to display all her sister's triumphs to Lady Warring; "that is to say, he hasn't made her an offer yet, because he is a dreadful slowtop, but he was on the verge, I am sure, and will probably get round to it when he returns to England. But if I were Allie," she went on, considering the matter critically, "I should rather have had Sir Derek than any of them, because he is the nicest when he isn't bullocking one into doing something one doesn't in the least wish to do. Only he is going to marry Miss Hardison now, so I daresay she hasn't the chance any longer."

Lady Warring, who had known her goddaughter from the day she had made her first appearance in public at the font, a fine, healthy baby, already exhibiting a will of her own, looked at her now and her heart almost failed her, for there was an expression in Allegra's eyes as her sister uttered these last words that she had seen there before, on the day the news had been received of Lieutenant Neil Alland's death, and had hoped never to see there again.

"Oh, dear!" she thought in great distress. "Not again!" But aloud she only said that she had never met Sir Arthur, but hoped to have the pleasure of doing so if he came into Cambridgeshire.

"You won't like him," Hilary said disparagingly. "He is dreadfully prosy, besides being a widower and always giving one good advice"—which made Lady Warring smile and say she could see he must appear to disadvantage beside a romantic Belgian baron.

She was glad to see that Allegra had recovered her countenance by this time, but judged it wise nevertheless to turn the conversation, which she did by enquiring what their plans were, now that they had returned to England.

"I don't really know," said Allegra, at once beginning to look practical and worried. "Everything happened so suddenly in Brussels that we hadn't time to make any plans, which was why I was obliged to accept Sir Derek's offer to come to Rolveston. But of course we must not impose upon him by staying there any longer than is necessary. So I have been thinking that I should write to Aunt Hatherill today—"

"Oh, no!" exclaimed Hilary, looking quite revolted. "You *won't*, Allie!"

"But I shall—indeed, I must," said Allegra, glancing at Lady Warring for her approval. "She may very well know of someone among her acquaintance at Bath who may require the services of a governess or a companion, which will solve my immediate problems, and perhaps, if she sees what a well-conducted young lady you have grown into, she will decide that she does not hold you in such aversion any longer that she will not be willing to give you a home."

Hilary gave a little shriek of dismay. "Oh, Allie, you *wouldn't!*" she gasped. "I *won't* go to live with Aunt Hatherill! Oh, it would be far better if you married Baron de Lempriere, or even Sir Arthur—"

Lady Warring, in a peremptory tone quite foreign to her usual gentle manner, said not to be impertinent, and then remarked more mildly to Allegra that there would be time enough for her to consider what she was to do when she had had a few days to settle her thoughts. She then turned the conversation to the garden, and to some particularly fine damask roses that were just coming into bloom at the other end of it. Allegra, pretending an interest that she did not in the least feel, rose and walked down the box-bordered path to admire them, while Hilary, still looking rebellious, remained in her chair, biting her underlip rather sulkily. Lady Warring rounded on her as soon as Allegra was out of hearing.

"Hilary, I do not wish to scold you, but you really must not plague Allegra by being difficult and childish now," she said decisively. "You *must* know how unhappy she is—"

"Unhappy? Allie?" Hilary's eyes widened, her sulkiness forgotten in a moment. "But she isn't! I mean, of course things are in a pucker just now, but they will come right again—"

Lady Warring sighed exasperatedly. "Oh yes, for you, perhaps," she said, "for, though I *cannot* think that Lord Roderick's parents will be overjoyed at the idea of his marrying a girl without a penny, they are really very nice, reasonable people and if you and he continue in your attachment, something may be worked out. I *should* think, though, that your own feelings for Lord Roderick would give you *some* insight and sympathy for Allegra's!"

"For—Allegra's?" Hilary looked at her blankly. "But—but Allie is not in love with anyone!"

Lady Warring's mild eyes flashed. "Oh, you stupid child, can't you see that she is head-over-ears in love with Derek Herington!" she exclaimed. "One has only to look at her face when his name is mentioned. And the dreadful part of it is that it is not of the least use, for he will certainly marry Dianeme Hardison and my poor Allegra will dwindle into an old maid!" She dabbed at her eyes fiercely with her handkerchief. "Oh, don't talk to me!" she said, as Hilary, still looking stunned, opened her lips to speak. "I am a foolish old woman, but it was the dearest wish of my heart to see her married to Derek and settled at Rolveston, and now it has all gone wrong—so dreadfully wrong—and I really do not think I can bear it!"

Chapter Seventeen

HILARY RETURNED TO Rolveston with Allegra a little later in an unwontedly subdued mood—so subdued, in fact, that she even had the wisdom to forbear endeavouring to draw her sister into a discussion on the subject of the revelation that Lady Warring had made to her. She had been so absorbed in her own feelings for Lord Roderick that it had never occurred to her that Allegra was having her own romantic difficulties, but now that the matter had been brought to her attention she was able to look back and recall a good many instances when her elder sister's behaviour where Sir Derek was concerned had seemed more than a little odd to her.

Being a young lady who favoured direct action she at once decided that she ought to do something about the matter; but what she was to do, with Sir Derek still in Brussels and Allegra at Rolveston, had her in a puzzle. And then, before she could come to any decision at all, something else occurred that put her sister's problems quite out of her head for the moment.

This was the arrival, on the morning following their visit to Questers, of a brief communication from Sir Derek, informing them merely that Lord Roderick had taken a fragment of shell in his left leg during the engagement at Waterloo, that the wound was not serious but was sufficient to lay him up for a time, and that he himself would bring his young cousin back to England as soon as Lord Roderick was able to travel.

Upon first perusing this missive, Hilary at once flew to the conclusion that it was Sir Derek's way of breaking it to her gently that Lord Roderick had been killed, or at least so seriously wounded that his life was despaired of. But upon Allegra's pointing out to her that, in all their acquaintance with him, Sir Derek had never been known to indulge in sentimental or even civil evasion, she consented to cheer up slightly, and even presently to speculate as to whether it would be to Hadfield that Sir Derek would bring his cousin for his convalescence.

"I should think it very likely," Allegra said, her own heart quite unaccountably beginning to beat a little faster at the thought of Sir Derek at Hadfield, not twenty miles distant from Rolveston.

"Then I shall go there to see him," Hilary stated instantly.

Allegra, amused in spite of herself at the imagined picture of her determined young sister presenting herself at Hadfield with the demand to be conducted to Lord Roderick's bedside, said that she had best wait to be invited.

"Pooh!" said Hilary. She added, "At any rate, I *shall* be invited, because Roddy will ask his mother to, and she will be so glad he is alive that she won't be able to refuse him."

This comforting thought was sufficient to keep her in reasonable tranquillity during the ensuing four days, during which nothing further was heard from Sir Derek, and at the end of that time her spirits were raised still further by a brief and rather shaky communication from Lord Roderick himself, informing her that he was coming along splendidly and would be at Hadfield by the middle of the following week if all went well, as he had every confidence that it would. Accompanying this missive was one to Allegra from Sir Derek, corroborating Lord Roderick's hopeful account of his progress and stating that he hoped to see her and ascertain how she and Hilary were getting on as soon as possible after his arrival at Hadfield.

"Well," said Allegra resolutely, as she refolded the letter, "that will be more than a week from now, and I hope by that time I shall have heard from Aunt Hatherill and she may have some suggestion as to a position I may take. It will certainly not do for us to remain here at Rolveston any longer than that, for Sir Derek will wish to have his house back and—and our staying here has already made us the subject of enough gossip in the neighbourhood, at any rate."

This, Hilary knew, was in reference to an encounter that had taken place on the previous day at Questers, when she and Allegra, paying their daily visit to Lady Warring, had found Mrs. Brownridge there and had been subjected by that estimable lady to a searching enquiry as to how they came to be established at Rolveston—an enquiry that had been prevented from becoming exceedingly embarrassing only by Lady Warring's firmness in putting an end to it.

"I expect they all think that Sir Derek has made you another offer and you have accepted him this time," Hilary had been unwary enough to remark to Allegra as they had walked back to Rolveston together; and then could have bitten her tongue out as she saw the suddenly stricken look upon her sister's face.

So out of deference to Allegra's feelings she did not now say—as she would have liked to—that she would never, never go to live with Lady Hatherill, but contented herself instead with remarking with a very grownup air that when she had seen Lord Roderick she would be better able to discuss her future plans.

During the ensuing period of waiting they finally had the pleasure of a letter from Lady Hatherill—if pleasure it could be called when a good half of it was taken up with pointing out serious flaws in the manners, conduct, and general character of its recipients. But it ended with a grudging offer of a home for both Hilary and Allegra "until better arrangements can be made"—"which sounds," Hilary said irreverently, "as though she hopes to have us transported to the colonies at the end of a month or two, only I don't think even she can do that." Lady Hatherill added that, as she was just on the point of leaving Bath to spend a few weeks at Worthing, where she hoped the sea air would be beneficial to her nerves, it would not be convenient for her to receive them until her return, and she named a date somewhat past the middle of July as the time when she would expect them at her home in Laura Place.

"Good!" said Hilary, when Allegra had read this part of the letter aloud to her. "That means that I shall have plenty of opportunity to see Roddy and make plans with him, and to become acquainted with the Duke and Duchess. And then we shall see if I must go to Bath," she concluded, with such ferocious confidence in her own powers of persuasion that Allegra had a fascinated vision of the ducal pair meekly submitting to seeing their youngest son married by special license from his bed of convalescence and Hilary confronting Lady Hatherill triumphantly as Lady Roderick Buccan and daring her to make her go to Bath.

As a matter of fact, Hilary's previously expressed confidence in the malleability of Lord Roderick's mama in the hands of her wounded son was indeed justified later in the week by the arrival at Rolveston of a note from the Duchess, inviting both the Misses Herington to come to luncheon at Hadfield as soon as Lord Roderick should have recovered from the fatigue of his journey from Brussels. No explanation of her reason for desiring this visit was forthcoming, but Hilary was undeterred by this from falling into the most optimistic plans for the future.

These included, although Allegra did not know it, a determination to do something about her and Sir Derek as well, though exactly what there was to be done when Sir Derek was by this time probably betrothed to Miss Hardison did not at once appear. But Hilary was quite certain that she would think of something before it was too late, and on the day appointed for the visit to Hadfield attired herself in her most becoming frock of flowered muslin—which had providentially arrived from Brussels only the day before, owing, she could only suppose, to Sir Derek's having arranged for the things they had left behind at the Pensionnat to be sent on to them—with as much buoyancy of spirit as if she had just read the announcement of her betrothal to Lord Roderick in the columns of the *Morning Post*.

Allegra's feelings, as she sat in Sir Derek's carriage behind Sir Derek's coachman, watching the summer landscape with its heavy dark foliage melt and change around her, were far more mixed. She would be glad to see Lord Roderick, but she dreaded being obliged to face the Duke and Duchess as Hilary's guardian and admit to them how entirely unprovided Sir Thomas Herington had left his daughters in this world's goods. And then there was Sir Derek. She wished she had not to see him, but perhaps on the whole it would be better to do so at Hadfield, where there would be other people present, than at Rolveston.

And, as it developed, this was true, for there were not only people but dogs, the Duchess having no inhibitions about mingling pets and guests, and in the confusion of disentangling one from the other while introductions and greetings were being exchanged, the flush that arose to Allegra's cheeks when her eyes fell upon Sir Derek's tall form went quite unnoticed.

The Duchess, who was a large, masterful woman, quite overtopping the Duke's mild, stooping form, at once seized upon Allegra and swept her off into a corner of the saloon where she had received her guests, an apartment dominated by a huge family piece by Lely of the Duke's ancestors and ancestresses.

"I like your sister," said the Duchess, her eyes resting with instant approval upon Hilary, who, her dark eyes sparkling with happiness, had seated herself on a sofa across the room beside Lord Roderick. The latter was looking pale, and had limped rather badly as he had stood up and come forward to greet Hilary and Allegra upon their arrival, but seemed otherwise quite unaffected by his recent disagreeable experiences. "An engaging child," continued the Duchess, "and with plenty of spirit, too, I should think, to cope with Roddy's. But I am scarcely surprised at that, because I knew your father. Best man to hounds I ever saw, always excepting Assheton Smith. I've met you, too, haven't I? In the field? Excellent seat and hands, I remember."

Allegra said that would have been some years ago, and moved to make room on the sofa between her and the Duchess for a young King Charles spaniel to sit beside her, as she seemed to be expected to do.

"Does she like dogs?" the Duchess asked abruptly.

"Like—? Oh, you mean Hilary! Yes, very much," said Allegra, feeling an insane desire, inspired by the Duchess's unorthodox conversational methods, to say that the reason she did not show it particularly at present was that she liked Lord Roderick more. But she succeeded in suppressing it and instead told the Duchess the story of a King Charles Hilary had owned some years before who wished to go to church with her every Sunday and, persistently eluding capture, sat outside the church door and howled whenever he heard her voice uplifted in song, so incensing the organist that Sir Thomas, to keep the peace, had finally been obliged to order Hilary to remain mute during the hymns. This anecdote was very well received by the Duchess and she riposted with several tales concerning her own pets, after which the Duke, who had been talking to Hilary and Lord Roderick, or, rather, listening to them eagerly talking to each other, came over and sat down opposite them.

"Dear me, Miss Herington," he said in his gentle, absent voice, "you have a head of hair exactly like your mother's. I remember seeing her at a ball once and thinking that it lit up the room. Rather a pity it isn't you Roddy wants to marry. I always fancied having red hair in the family."

"Don't make personal remarks, Ethelred," said the Duchess firmly but kindly, rather, Allegra thought, as if he had been six years old instead of sixty. "Of course Roddy cannot marry Miss Herington; he is in love with her sister. Not," she added, looking critically across the room at the young lovers, "that it makes the slightest degree of sense for him to be wishing to marry *her,* either. They are a pair of babies." She looked at Allegra. "How old is your sister?" she enquired.

"She is turned seventeen, ma'am," said Allegra, feeling rather guilty, as if it were somehow her fault that Hilary was so young.

"And Roddy has turned twenty," said the Duchess.

"Much too young to settle, and so the Duke will tell him, of course. But when he is twenty-one he may tell *us* that he will do as he pleases, which I naturally *wish* him to do, because nothing is more odious than people making their children marry people they don't in the least care to. That sounds rather tangled, but you know what I mean. Do you think your sister would like being the wife of a marching officer? Because that is what she would have to be, of course, if she married Roddy. He has *no* prospects, except for my aunt Dorothea, who makes a new will every month, and sometimes in his favour."

Allegra, gathering her wits under this onslaught, said that she thought Hilary was better equipped than almost anyone she knew to be a marching officer's wife, as she had an optimistic disposition and very little attachment to material comforts, but she added with determined candour that her sister had no fortune.

"None," she added firmly, as she saw the Duke look slightly disappointed, "or what I am sure you would call none. And I," she added defiantly, "have been a teacher at a school in Brussels, and must try now to find a new position—"

But at this the Duchess only laughed comfortably and, Allegra thought, with a kind of *grande dame*'s coarseness.

"Oh, as to *that*," she said, "I can find you a husband easily enough, my dear. You've a good figure and a fine complexion, and you come from excellent stock. Remiss of your relations not to have done something about you before this."

It was at that moment that Allegra noted that Sir Derek, like the Duke, had seen fit to leave the young lovers to their own devices and stroll across to their side of the great room, where he was now standing with his shoulders propped against the massive mantelpiece and had obviously heard every word of the last several remarks that had been made. She coloured up like fire, and her confusion was not made less by Sir Derek's observing, with what she could only characterise as a saturnine glance in her direction, that the list of Miss Herington's admirers in Brussels had been endless but that she evidently preferred single blessedness, at least for the present.

"Nonsense!" said the Duchess. "Everyone ought to be married; it saves so much trouble for their relations. And especially you, Derek," she added, turning on her nephew in what Allegra considered a quite unfair fashion, in spite of her relief at having attention drawn away from herself. "You ought to have married years ago—only not a Russian or a Turk, of course, which I can see *may* have made it rather difficult for you."

Sir Derek said that fortunately he had never wanted to marry a Russian or a Turk, and then it was time for them to go in to luncheon, which was a simple, even rather Spartan meal of cold meat and fruit, much appreciated by several of the Duchess's particular pets, who accompanied her into the dining room and ate quite as much of it as any of the guests.

Allegra, who was relieved to find herself between the Duke and Lord Roderick, initiated a conversation with the latter on the subject of the battle at Waterloo, which he seemed quite willing to talk about for a time, though rather anxious to get on to something else.

"I didn't see much of it myself, you see," he said apologetically, "because I was wounded almost straight off, and they took me to the rear. I wouldn't have minded being wounded nearly so much if it had happened at the end instead of in the beginning, because I'd never been in a battle before and now it doesn't look as if I ever will be. At least just now," he said, with youth's perpetual optimism. He then added, as if he were obliged to say it at once or burst, "I say, Miss Herington, I've talked to my father and mother and I don't think they'll kick up much of a dust if Hilary and I get really engaged now. Then we can be married when I am twenty-one—as long as you agree."

And he gave her such an anxious glance that it went to her heart and made her look at him rather helplessly. She had talked the matter over with Lady Warring, who was of the opinion that nothing definite should be done until Lord Roderick had reached his majority; but in the face of a clear lack of opposition by the Duke and the Duchess she felt that she would be a black-dyed villainess if she set her own face sternly against the engagement.

In this dilemma she found herself looking across the table at Sir Derek, who should have been talking to his aunt but was allowing her instead to feed her clamoring pets without interruption while he eavesdropped on the conversation between Allegra and Lord Roderick.

"If you have the slightest degree of prudence," he said firmly, in answer to her unspoken plea for support, "you will certainly not agree to such an outrageous engagement, Miss Herington. But as I realise full well that Hilary has her heart set upon it, and that it will make not the slightest difference to her if you tell her that she is not to be engaged to Roddy, or if anyone else tells her so—"

"Except you," Allegra thought but did not say, remembering Brussels and the way he had made Hilary leave that city when she had just declared that wild horses could not drag her away.

"—I should advise you," continued Sir Derek, unaware of this mental interruption, "to forget all about it and let Nature take its course, which it undoubtedly will, and there will be a wedding in June. Which you," he went on, to Lord Roderick, "will probably regret bitterly when you are billeted in America or India with a wife who has all the determination of a cyclone and several children to support and no money so you can get out of the house now and then for an evening with congenial friends." He added reflectively, "If I had the least degree of conscience myself, I should tell my aunt that Hilary prefers cats to dogs, and so put an end to the matter at once."

Lord Roderick laughed and said Lord, his mama had no objection to cats—or monkeys or parrots, either, specimens of all of which had enlivened Hadfield at one time or another; and Allegra sat wishing that Sir Derek would stop being humorous and charming and go back to being overbearing and odiously critical as he had been in Brussels, so that one could dislike him as one should.

As it happened, she was soon to have her wish. Since it was a fine day, they did not remain indoors after luncheon was over, but were taken by the Duchess to view the kennels and the handsome litter recently produced by her favourite Italian greyhound; and Allegra found herself walking beside Sir Derek. Now was the moment, she told herself, to thank him properly for all he had done for her and Hilary in Brussels and for the hospitality he had offered them at Rolveston, and also to apologise to him for having accused him so unjustly of driving Mr. Rudwick from Rolveston; but she found it unaccountably difficult to embark upon either of these subjects with a gentleman who, when she fleetingly raised her eyes to his face, appeared to be contemplating her with an ironic gleam in his dark eyes, as if he already knew everything that she wished to say.

"Sir Derek—" she began at last, in desperation.

Sir Derek flung up a hand, the gleam glowing even more pronounced.

"No, pray don't go on, Miss Herington," he said. "I know exactly what you feel obliged to say to me, and that the words are sticking in your throat. Odious to be under the necessity of expressing gratitude to a person one dislikes—don't you agree? But you may make yourself easy; you owe me very little, and that little may well be written off under the obligation of relationship."

Allegra, confused and uncomfortable—and could it have been that she was more uncomfortable about the phrase, "a person one dislikes," than about anything else?—said in a rather muffled voice, "Oh, no! I mean, I really *am* grateful to you for getting Hilary to leave Brussels, and lending us John Holton and Rolveston, besides all the money, which I shall certainly repay as soon as I am able—"

"My dear Miss Herington," said Sir Derek, looking amused, "don't you know that refugees are never required to repay anyone for anything done in their behalf? In fact, it would be considered quite improper and ungrateful of them if they did."

"Yes, but we are not—" said Allegra, feeling still more confused.

"There I disagree with you. And as you will admit that I have had far more experience in such matters than you have, you will kindly drop the subject and not say anything more about it in future. Shall I give you news of your friends in Brussels, instead? I am afraid that I have none of Mlle. Jusseau, for she appears to have dropped quite out of sight since the night she incarcerated you and Hilary in the Pensionnat. But Colonel Hepworth, whom I saw just before Roddy and I left Brussels, is in high gig, went through the entire battle without a scratch though he is lamenting a pair of horses shot under him, and asked to be remembered to you. Gilles de Lempriere—"

"Yes?" Allegra was able to say quite composedly as he paused, his dark eyes fixed rather penetratingly upon her face. "I hope he too suffered no injury at Waterloo?"

"None at all. But I cannot recall," said Sir Derek thoughtfully, "that *he* entrusted me with any kind messages for you."

Allegra gave a gurgle of laughter. "No, I expect he did not," she said. "He is very cross with me still, I daresay. If he had been killed I was prepared to be very remorseful for having treated him so badly, but now I suppose it does not signify, and he has already set up a new flirt—"

"As a matter of fact, he has," Sir Derek acknowledged.

"A very dashing Bruxelloise, a brunette—not in the least in your style."

By this time, owing to Allegra's apparently finding it impossible to walk and talk at the same time, they had dropped quite behind the others. This gave her a splendid opportunity to say what she wished to say about her injustice to Sir Derek in the matter of Mr. Rudwick, a subject she would not have cared to broach before others; but before she could bring herself to begin upon it Sir Derek, looking down at her, enquired whether she had really any serious objections to Hilary becoming betrothed to Lord Roderick.

"It is an excessively imprudent match, of course," he said, "but I am beginning to feel that it will require more effort than I, for one, am willing to expend to try to keep them apart. You can have no notion how trying it is to be assured by a halfling a dozen times a day of his undying devotion to a young lady!"

"Oh, but I have!" Allegra said, with a smile, "for you must know that I have undergone much the same thing with Hilary. But I must say that I do believe those absurd children are in earnest. After all, I was not much older than Hilary when—"

She stopped abruptly, aghast at what her unwary tongue had been leading her on to say. She could only hope that Sir Derek would not take her meaning, but that hope died almost as soon as it had been born.

"—when you entered into an engagement with a young man not much older than Roddy, whose death, I gather, was a misfortune from which you have never recovered," Sir Derek finished her sentence for her evenly.

Allegra glanced up into his face, astonished. "But—but how can you know of that?" she stammered.

Sir Derek shrugged. "I believe the engagement *was* publicly announced," he said.

"Oh yes, but—" She was about to say that his having

taken sufficient interest in such an announcement to have kept it in mind all these years seemed quite unlikely, when she suddenly realised that doubtless Lady Warring had seen fit to inform him of the matter at the time he had been considering making her an offer of marriage. Colour rose in her face, but she managed to say with an appearance of calm, "That was a great many years ago, and is quite beside the point now. The thing that disturbs me is finding the Duke and Duchess so—so very unworldly, quite unlike what I had expected them to be. That seems to put the whole burden of the decision upon *my* shoulders—"

"And you have no desire to be the one obstacle set in the way of true love, on the one hand, or to take the responsibility of sanctioning a marriage that may turn out very badly, on the other," said Sir Derek, who seemed to accept with equanimity the necessity of finishing her sentences for her. "Very well. Then I, in the capacity of my relationship to both young people, will take the burden upon *my* shoulders. You had as well tell your sister that, if she continues for a year in her attachment to Roddy, she may marry him—and then pray that when my greataunt Dorothea finally passes to her reward she will be found to have done so at a time when she has made her will in Roddy's favour. And now," he continued, in a slightly altered voice in which, if Allegra, had not been entirely occupied with her own feelings, she might have discerned a kind of quite uncharacteristic anxiety, "having disposed of Hilary's future, we shall turn to yours. Have you made any plans since you have arrived in England? I am much afraid I hurried you out of Brussels far too rapidly for you to have made any there, and it is quite out of the question, of course, for you to return there."

"Yes, I think so, too," Allegra said, wishing that something was not impeding her breathing in such a way that she found it extremely difficult to talk in anything but very short sentences. "So I thought I should go to Bath. I mean Aunt Hatherill has asked me. Or rather she agreed to take Hilary and me when I wrote to her. Only temporarily, of course—"

She broke off, wondering what she could have said to make Sir Derek look suddenly so contemptuous and thunderous.

"I see," he said after a moment. "To Bath. I heard before I left Brussels that Arthur Huddleston was contemplating an extensive visit to his mother there upon his return to England. When may I wish you happy, Miss Herington?"

Allegra choked. "Oh!" she said. "As if I—! What an *odious* man you are!"

"Am I?" said Sir Derek rather harshly. "Because I choose to speak plainly to you? But I cut my wisdoms long ago, my girl, and I have seen more than one unconsolable female console herself very satisfactorily, when it suited her, with a dull, complaisant husband who was content to live under the cat's foot."

"You—are—*abominable!*" said Allegra, standing stockstill in the middle of the path and confronting him with blazing eyes. "As if I were the kind of overbearing, contentious female who only wanted a husband to manage—" She broke off, mastering her wrath, and went on after a moment, in a voice of ominous sweetness, "And when am I to wish *you* joy, Sir Derek? I understand that the announcement of your betrothal to Miss Hardison is hourly expected! But allow me to warn you, sir, that if *you* do not intend to live under the cat's foot you had best assert your own mastery—as you know only too well how to do, I am aware!—at the very outset of your marriage. Miss Hardison has no milk-and-water disposition, you know!"

"Miss Hardison," said Sir Derek scathingly, "has far too much conduct to allow herself to engage in such unbecoming brangling as seems to appeal to *you,* Miss Herington!"—at which exact moment, rounding a turn in the kitchen garden wall, they ran into Hilary and Lord Roderick, who had turned back to see what had become of them.

One look at the two angry faces—Allegra's flushed, Sir Derek's almost white—and Hilary's own face grew serious. She cast a speaking glance at Lord Roderick and, taking Allegra's arm, walked on with her, prattling to her about the new puppies, and meanwhile making up her mind with what Sir Derek had rightly characterised as the determination of a cyclone to take a hand herself in what appeared to her to be her sister's highly unsatisfactory affairs.

Chapter Eighteen

MID-JULY, and the time set by Lady Hatherill for receiving her two nieces in Bath, arrived with unnerving rapidity. Hilary, who, as Lord Roderick's at least semiofficial betrothed, had enjoyed two more visits to Hadfield, was, Allegra considered, taking her forthcoming banishment to Bath with such uncharacteristic docility that, if Allegra herself had not been in an unwonted state of depression at the idea of leaving Rolveston, it would have seemed cause for high suspicion to her. As it was, she was so low-spirited that she did not even object when Hilary displayed to her a small sapphire ring that had been presented to her by Lord Roderick in quite unauthorised recognition of their engagement, and roused herself from her dejection only to quarrel with Sir Derek, when he rode over from Hadfield to Rolveston on the Friday before their departure, about his desire to send them to Bath in his own travelling-chaise.

"We have already accepted far to many favours from you, Sir Derek," she informed him, with what she was sure he was characterising as her Lady Hatherill manner. "Thank you very much, but we shall do quite well in the coach."

From this determination she was not to be moved, and, upon Sir Derek's becoming exasperated, she became warm, with the result that it was finally Hilary who was obliged to coax Allegra into at least allowing Sir Derek to drive them in to Huntingdon, where they might obtain seats on the night-mail. A compromise to this effect was accordingly arrived at, and Sir Derek, though none too well pleased, it appeared, by Allegra's obstinacy in rejecting the use of his chaise, engaged himself to eat an early dinner with them at Rolveston on the Monday following and then to drive them to Huntingdon.

"What an overbearing creature he is!" Allegra, still flushed with controversy, said as he departed. "I fancy it is not often that he is baulked of having his own way—which is no doubt why he is looking so particularly grim today!"

"Well, you know he only meant to be kind, Allie," Hilary protested mildly, but looking at her so penetratingly as she spoke that Allegra was moved to ask if her hair was wrong

"Oh, no," said Hilary, colouring a little. "It is only—well, you see, I was thinking about something. A—a sort of problem I have. Allie, if *you* knew someone who was ruining her—*his* whole life because he thought things were one way when they were really quite different, wouldn't you do something to help him, even if—if it was something he might not *quite* like?"

Allegra, who was still thinking about Sir Derek and his nefarious habit of trying to arrange one's life, said rather absently that she expected she would.

"Well," said Hilary, with an air of mingled relief and resolution, "that's all right, then."

And she went off, saying that she had a letter to write, leaving Allegra, coming out of her own reflections, to wonder with some amusement what her sister was up to now, and to arrive at the conclusion that she was probably set upon bullying Mr. Cairnes or one of the Rolveston staff into doing something they had not the least desire to do, simply because she had taken it into her head that it would be good for them.

The days ran on swiftly to Monday, and Allegra, hearing no more about the matter, forgot it. She was, in truth, so heartsore at the idea of leaving Rolveston for a second time—no more than that, she assured herself!—that Hilary appeared to find her a most unenlivening companion, and at last suggested, on the Monday afternoon, that, as they had no further preparations to make and had already paid their farewell visit to Lady Warring, Allegra go up to Mr. Rudwick's cottage and bid him good-bye. She herself declined accompanying her, saying that she must take Bluebell for a ramble, as he would be shut up in the coach for so long very soon; and Allegra, after vainly trying to represent to her once more that Lady Hatherill's ancient pug, to say nothing of Lady Hatherill herself, might object to Bluebell's becoming a resident of Laura Place and that she had best leave him at Rolveston with Mrs. Simmons, the housekeeper, gave it up at last and went off alone to see Mr. Rudwick.

When she returned shortly before dinnertime, having been detained by the old agent in reminiscing conversation for so long that she was aware she would have scarcely time to change her dress before Sir Derek arrived, she was met in the hall by the housekeeper, who enquired with a worried face if she might speak to her for a moment.

"Yes, of course—but only for a moment, Mr Simmons; it is growing late," Allegra said. "What is it?"

The elderly housekeeper hesitated, a look of embarrassment appearing upon her face.

"Why, miss, I hardly know how to put it!" she said, after a moment. "It's Miss Hilary, you see. She's—she's gone off with Lord Roderick, and she's not come back."

"With Lord Roderick?" Allegra stared at her incredulously. "Nonsense! You must be mistaken, Mrs. Simmons!"

The housekeeper shook her head positively. "Oh, no, miss, I'm not mistaken," she said. "Driving the Duke's phaeton and his bays, he was—which Simmons knows as well as any of Sir Derek's horses, for you know his cousin Roger is head groom at Hadfield. And—and Simmons says Miss Hilary had her portmanteau with her, *and* the kitten—"

Allegra, her face by now perfectly white, made a supreme effort and managed a careless smile.

"Oh, what a naughty child she is!" she said, with what she could only hope was a convincing air of sangfroid. "She has been teasing me to allow her to dine in Huntingdon with Lord Roderick before we leave, and I see now that she has taken matters into her own hands. When Sir Derek arrives, Mrs. Simmons, will you have Simmons tell him not to stable his horses, as we shall of course wish to go on to Huntingdon at once ourselves and dine there with my sister and Lord Roderick."

Mrs. Simmons, looking surprised, was moved to utter a protest concerning the nice pair of turkey poults even now roasting in the oven, to say nothing of the fricando of veal and the fresh-made cheesecakes; but Allegra, waving cheesecakes, veal, and turkey poults aside, ran up the stairs to her bedchamber, where, closing the door behind her, she pressed her hands to her pale cheeks and attempted to bring some order out of her whirling thoughts.

This, then, was the explanation of Hilary's unwonted docility about going to Bath: she had never had the least intention of going there at all! Instead, she had persuaded Lord Roderick (that it was *her* idea Allegra had not the least doubt) to elope with her, for that the pair were even now on their way to Gretna Green seemed the only logical interpretation of Mrs. Simmons's revelation.

Only the thought that Sir Derek must arrive at Rolveston within half an hour prevented Allegra from giving way to panic. Upon him all her reliance was placed; for he must be as anxious as she to prevent a scandal in a family with which he was so nearly connected. And if it were possible to overtake the imprudent young lovers, he would know how to do it. For her own part, she could do nothing better now than to put herself in readiness to depart with him the moment he arrived at Rolveston.

Fortunately, she had not long to wait. By the time she came downstairs again, her dress changed for travelling and a footman following with her portmanteau, Sir Derek was already entering the house, an expression of considerable surprise upon his face as he listened to Simmons relaying her message begging him not to stable his horses.

"What has happened?" he demanded as Allegra came towards him, her hands unconsciously outstretched to him in greeting and appeal. He took her hands and led her into the drawing room, closing the door behind him. "What is it?" he repeated, with concern. "You are as white as a ghost. Shall I fetch some wine?"

"No, no! I am perfectly well. It is Hilary," said Allegra, collecting herself with a strong effort and rejecting an ignoble impulse to fling herself upon Sir Derek's chest and burst into tears. "She—I came home not half an hour since to learn from Mrs. Simmons that she has gone off with Lord Roderick in the Duke's phaeton—and she has taken a portmanteau with her, and her kitten—"

"The devil she has!" said Sir Derek. Exasperation rose in his face. "Good God, have you *no* control over that little minx?" he demanded.

Allegra stiffened, her lachrymose mood deserting her upon the instant.

"I can scarcely keep her under lock and key until she is one-and-twenty, Sir Derek!" she retorted. "And if *your* only response to the situation is to rake *me* down, I see that I shall be obliged to seek help in other quarters!"

She attempted to step past him impetuously to the door, but a hard grasp on her wrist brought her up short.

"Don't fly up into the boughs—hornet!" Sir Derek's voice advised her. "Have you any notion where they have gone?"

She stared at him. "Gone? Why, to the Border, of course!" she said. "Where on earth else should they go? They certainly cannot be married in England!" She attempted to pull her wrist free of his grasp. "Oh, do let me go!" she implored impatiently. "Can't you see we must not waste a moment? You *must* wish to bring them back as much as I do!"

"I do—but we shall waste more than a moment if we go haring off with tired horses without the least notion in what direction we had best go!" said Sir Derek. He released her and, saying peremptorily, "Wait here!"—strode out to the hall, where she heard him issuing rapid orders to Simmons. He then returned to the drawing room and said briefly, "I am having my Welsh greys put-to. Simmons says Roddy was driving only a pair, and I doubt very much, at any rate, that he will make off with his father's phaeton if he has determined to take Hilary to Scotland. It is more than likely that they will travel post, and that he will leave the phaeton and the bays at Huntingdon." He broke off. "Did Hilary leave a note for you?" he enquired abruptly.

"A note?" Allegra looked at him blankly.

"Yes, a note! I know she is a shatter-brained chit, but surely even she would scarcely have set off without leaving you some word—"

"I never thought to look," said Allegra guiltily, and she ran off upstairs at once, returning in a few minutes with a sheet of paper in her hand and a rather odd expression upon her face. "There is only this; I discovered it in her bedchamber," she said, handing the paper to Sir Derek.

Sir Derek scanned it rapidly. "Darling Allie," it read, "I know you will not *quite* like it, but I have gone off with Roddy. You said yourself, you know, that one shouldn't let anyone ruin his life if one could help it, and this is the only way I could think of. Pray don't be angry. And if you will tell Sir Derek, I am sure he will help you, because Roddy says he thinks he really does not wish to marry Miss Hardison. Your loving Hilary."

"What on earth do you make of it?" asked Allegra in a mystified voice, as Sir Derek raised his eyes from the note. "How can she believe that it will ruin Roddy's life if he is obliged to wait until he is twenty-one to marry her? Or is it possible that the Duke has changed his mind about permitting the engagement?"

She did not add, "And what can Miss Hardison have to do with it?"—feeling that at this point, in the haste and excitement of preparing for flight, Hilary must certainly have lost her senses completely, for it was obvious that Sir Derek would do his possible for her in these straits whether he wished to marry Miss Hardison or not. And why Hilary should *wish* him to help her, when it must have been apparent even to her muddled mind that that help would take the form of hot pursuit of herself and Lord Roderick, was another puzzle.

She was glad, at any rate, that Sir Derek did not choose to pursue this matter, either, for he only said, as he refolded the note and restored it to her, "My uncle cannot have done so; I left him not two hours ago discussing with my aunt whether there might not be a house on the estate suitable for Roddy when he marries your sister." He added, "But the horses will have been put-to by this time, so let us waste no more time in talking but go on to Huntington at once. If they are indeed making for the Great North Road, they will certainly have passed through there, at any rate."

Allegra, who was herself only too anxious to be off, at once agreed, and in a few moments she was being handed up into Sir Derek's phaeton, in which light sporting equipage it was apparent that they would have a considerable advantage in speed over a heavier post-chaise. She had, in addition, every confidence in Sir Derek's skill as a whip, having had a number of opportunities in Brussels to observe his handling of a team, but she could not forbear saying in an anxious voice as they set off, "You *will* make haste, won't you? Such a scandal must follow Hilary all her life, and I cannot bear to think of her being ruined by what is only youth and heedlessness."

"Pray let us have no more talk of ruined lives!" Sir Derek said brusquely, as he lightly felt his leaders' mouths and gave them the office to start. "If it is your intention to enact me a Cheltenham tragedy over this, I give you fair warning that I shall leave you here. I shall have enough of that, I don't doubt, when I come up with that precious pair!"

Allegra gave a gasp of indignation, and was launching into a vigorous rejoinder when she saw that it would have little effect, since Sir Derek was obviously not attending to her. There was a frown between his brows, and a decided expression of dissatisfaction upon his face.

"What is it?" she asked involuntarily.

He did not at once reply, only looping a rein dexterously as the greys came up with a slow-moving gig on the road and letting it run free again as they shot past it. He turned his head briefly then to glance at her.

"That note," he said. "Does it occur to you that there is something deuced queer about it?"

"Yes, of course there is—but I daresay if *you* were

seventeen and setting out upon an elopement you might write something every bit as queer: I know *I* should!" Allegra said impatiently. "What does it signify, at any rate? She has certainly gone off with Roddy; she was quite clear upon *that* head!"

Sir Derek looked as if he might have pursued the subject further, but evidently thought better of it after a moment and concentrated his attention instead upon arriving at Huntingdon as expeditiously as possible. Here he declared his intention of making enquiries about the fugitives at the several posting-houses the town contained, and a brief but spirited debate thereupon ensued between him and Allegra, she declaring that it would be folly to waste time in doing so when it was plain that the young lovers would have taken the Great North Road, and Sir Derek pointing out with equal force that they did not at present even know whether they were to pursue a phaeton or a post-chaise, nor had they the least assurance that Scotland was actually the pair's destination.

"Well, she is *my* sister," Allegra finally capped her argument, "and *I* say we should go on at once. And if you will not take me," she added dangerously, "I shall hire a post-chaise and go on by myself!"

Upon this Sir Derek capitulated, although with a look of distinct exasperation and a curt comment that he hoped she might not be sorry—"which is not true," Allegra said unkindly, "for you really hope that I may be, so that you will be proved right"—and in a short time they had passed through Huntingdon and were bowling north in the direction of Norman Cross and Stamford.

It was Allegra's hope—a slim one, she was aware—that the eloping pair would not travel by night, and that she and Sir Derek might therefore come up with them at some posting-house along the road as soon as the long summer hours of daylight had failed. It was still far from dark, however, being only around seven in the evening, when, as they entered Stilton, Sir Derek briefly announced to her that he would stop at the Talbot Inn for a change of horses—a necessity which, in spite of her impatience at the delay, she was quite ready to acknowledge, for Sir Derek's greys had already covered a distance more than equal to two full stages.

But when he stated as well that, if he could obtain no news of the fugitives at that hostelry, he was prepared to delay their journey for further enquiries at the Crown, and Woolpack, and the Bell, complaisance vanished, and she demanded to be told why he should wish to do such a cork-brained thing as that.

"It is certainly far too early for them to have halted for the night as yet," she said. "You cannot hope to find them at any of the inns here."

"I do not hope to do so," said Sir Derek. "What I *do* hope to do is to learn whether they have changed horses here, or whether they have passed this way at all. *You* may be quite certain that the trail must lead to Scotland, Miss Herington, but the farthest I go upon this wild-goose chase, the more convinced I am that it is exactly that."

"Nonsense!" said Allegra. "How could it be?"

She turned a stormy, anxious face upon him, prepared to do battle in defence of her theory, but as they swept into the inn-yard at that moment and Sir Derek, jumping down, occupied himself in issuing instructions to the ostler who came running up as to the care and stabling of his own horses and the putting-to of a fresh team, she had no opportunity to say more to him.

This business having been satisfactorily concluded, he did approach her again, but merely with a polite invitation to her to step down from the phaeton and enter the inn, where she might procure some refreshment while he pursued his enquiries after the eloping pair.

"I shall do nothing of the sort!" said Allegra. "We shall not stop here, Sir Derek! I insist that we go on at once."

Sir Derek looked quite unmoved. "Well, if you are determined to starve, you may do so, of course," he said, "but I scarcely think it will benefit Hilary in any way if you do. And if you intend to hire a post-chaise when my back is turned and go on alone to the Border, I should warn you that the charges will not be inconsiderable, so that you may well find your pockets to let before your journey's end. And I shall *not* lend you the money," he concluded firmly, as she opened her mouth to speak.

He then extended his hand to help her down from the phaeton, which, after a moment's seething hesitation, she accepted, for obviously she could not advance their progress in any way by remaining seated in a stationary carriage in an inn-yard. He thereupon conducted her inside the inn, saw her comfortably established in a private parlour with the landlady in attendance, and departed, apparently quite oblivious of the coldness with which she accepted these attentions.

Fortunately for the state of her temper, she had scarcely had time to swallow a glass of lemonade and eat a modest repast of bread and ham when he returned. He had been unable, he said, to learn of any vehicle bearing a young couple answering to the description of Hilary and Lord Roderick that had changed horses at any of the posting-houses in town.

"Nor," he said, "do I think that we shall have better luck at Norman Cross, Miss Herington. In fact, the more I consider the matter, the more certain I am that we are following a false scent. May I see the note Hilary left for you again?"

Allegra, who had had a few private reflections of her own upon that puzzling missive, which she was for some reason beginning to wish she had not showed to Sir Derek, said mendaciously that she believed she had left it at Rolveston.

"No, you did not," said Sir Derek inexorably. "You put it into your reticule."

"Well, and if I did," said Allegra hastily, "it can tell us nothing at all that we do not already know. *Do* let us go on now!"

"When I have seen the note," said Sir Derek maddeningly.

Allegra, biting her lip, opened her reticule, took out the bone of contention, and threw it upon the table. Sir Derek calmly picked it up and reread it.

"I wonder if you will explain to me," he remarked after a moment, "exactly what your sister means by her reference to my *not* wishing to marry Miss Hardison."

He raised his eyes, as he spoke, to Allegra's face, which she would at once have liked to exchange for someone else's face that would not so basely betray her by looking self-conscious and utterly foolish, as she was certain her own was doing.

"I have not the least guess," she said, snatching the note out of Sir Derek's hand and putting it back into her reticule. "*Now* will you go on—?"

"No," said Sir Derek, not contentiously but with complete decision. "I will not. As a matter of fact, I am going back to Huntingdon."

"To Huntingdon? But you cannot!" Allegra stared at him, aghast. "You *could* not be so—so—"

"Dastardly?" said Sir Derek kindly. "Oh, but I can. But if you think that in doing so I am condemning your young baggage of a sister to a life of ostracism, you are fair and far out. Of course I *may* be mistaken, but the conviction has been growing upon me for some time that she and Roddy had no more intention of eloping when they drove away from Rolveston today than you and I had."

"No more intention—? But what can they have had in mind, then?" Allegra protested, feeling a faint sinking sensation as she uttered these words which she hastily repressed, as being caused by a suspicion too horrible for words.

Sir Derek was looking at her quizzically. "I do not know," he said candidly. "But I most assuredly intend to find out. And if I can discover no trace of them by enquiries at every pike we pass on our way back to Huntingdon, I shall be certain of one thing, at least—that they have *not* set out for the Border."

He thereupon advised her that he was ready to start if she had finished her repast, and Allegra stood up, feeling suddenly quite numb, and wondering, because of that ghastly suspicion that had got into her head, if one could disown sisters as one could children, if they had placed one in a position too horrid even to contemplate.

In such a state of mind she was in no condition to lodge any more protests with Sir Derek about his intention not to proceed any farther northward, which, indeed, was the last thing she wished to do if that suspicion in her mind were correct. In the meekest of silences she allowed herself to be helped up into the phaeton once more in the busy inn-yard, where the long summer dusk was just beginning to draw on and the first candlelight to wink out from the latticed windows of the inn, and in silence she saw Sir Direk turn the new team southward.

Had she somehow betrayed herself to Hilary? was the thought that was now occupying her mind to the exclusion of all others. And *had* Hilary, in an excess of sisterly zeal, plotted to place her and Sir Derek in a position so compromising that he would feel called upon to offer her marriage?

"If she has, I shall kill her," thought Allegra simply, feeling herself quite capable of the deed at the picture of herself and Sir Derek, far from Rolveston at an advanced hour of the night, and with no trace to be found of the fugitives they were pursuing, obliged to put up at an inn where, by fell chance, they would be recognised by a travelling acquaintance, upon which Sir Derek would offer her the *amende honorable* to save her name from tarnishment.

"I *knew* I should not have allowed her to read all those ridiculous French romances while we were in Brussels!" she thought, in deep despair. "I daresay, after all, it is all my fault—and if I had had the slightest degree of sense I should have hired a post-chaise and gone after her alone, without waiting for Sir Derek. I wish I was *dead*," she thought bitterly and quite unprofitably, and was slightly consoled only when she stole a glance at her companion's profile and saw that he had not in the least the appearance of a gentleman suspecting that he might be about to be entrapped into marriage with a female he detested. On the contrary, he only appeared intent upon the management of his new team, so that she was able to nourish the comforting thought that perhaps the dreadful suspicion that had come into her mind was quite absent from his, and that if Providence was with her he might never think of it.

But that this was a forlorn hope she was well aware, for whatever undesirable traits one might attribute to Sir Derek, a lack of perspicacity was not one of them.

It was hardly to be expected that, under these circumstances, the drive back to Huntingdon should have been an agreeable one for her. She scarcely knew, in the first place, whether to be relieved or cast into even higher fidgets by the fact that none of sir Derek's enquiries along the way could elicit the least news of Hilary and Lord Roderick. Apparently no travellers answering to their rather remarkable description—for surely few young gentlemen with a very noticeable limp were undertaking journeys accompanied by a young lady carrying an obstreperous white kitten—had been seen upon that stretch of road, and Allegra was gradually forced to admit to herself that

Sir Derek's theory that the pair had not eloped to Gretna Green seemed to be borne out by the facts.

But if not to Scotland, where, then had they gone? The answer to this question was supplied, at least in part, at the Crown in Huntingdon, where Sir Derek, after drawing a blank in his enquiries at two other posting-houses, the George and the Fountain, was finally rewarded with news of the fugitives.

The Duke of Wyon's phaeton? a grinning ostler, his tongue unloosed by the bestowal upon him of a half-crown, said. To be sure he had seen it; as a matter of fact, it was drawn up behind in the yard of the inn at that very moment, and the Duke's bays in the stables.

"And the young gentleman who was driving it?" Sir Derek enquired.

The answer came promptly. "Hired a po'shay, guv'nor."

"To take him—where?"

"To take him *and* the young gentry-mort," said the ostler, with a very meaning wink. "to Thrapston. A turtle-pair they was, if ever I seed one—"

"Yes. Very well," said Sir Derek dampingly. "And the phaeton and horses? What instructions had you about them?"

"Said we was to keep them here till he came back for them."

"No indication as to when that might be?"

"Said it would be tonight, guv'nor—and give me a crown to keep me chaffer close if anyone was to come asking me about it," he added, looking up at Sir Derek with such limpid expectation of his willingness to bestow an even superior largesse for this betrayal of trust that Sir Derek felt himself honour-bound to reach into his pocket again. The ostler looked gratified, and said he knew a gentleman when he seed one. "And if you're wishful to know what *I* think," he added helpfully, which Sir Derek had in no wise indicated that he was, "I'll tell you. I'll cap downright him and that 'dentical young gentry-mort be ee-loping, and their lay is to throw you off the scent. I wouldn't go off to Thrapston if I was you, guv'nor. The Great North Road is what you want."

Sir Derek, ignoring this advice, instructed him to have a fresh team put-to in the phaeton, and then, jumping down, came round and extended his hand to Allegra.

"I think—a council of war?" he said, looking up at her with a slight gleam in his dark eyes, as if he rather expected hostilities to begin at once.

But Allegra, who had the spirit quite taken out of her by the ostler's confirmation of all her worse fears—or rather, her second worst ones, for the worst of all, of course, would have been if Hilary had really gone to Gretna Green—allowed herself to be handed down and led into the inn without demur.

Inside, in a private parlour, Sir Derek, who had not, as she had, partaken of any refreshment at Stilton, ordered beer and a sandwich for himself and endeavoured without success to interest her in tea or a glass of sherry.

"Nothing, thank you," she said, feeling as hollow and numb as if her last hour had come, and casting about desperately in her mind for something to say that would lead Sir Derek's thoughts in any direction except the one where her own had fatally settled. "I—I wonder," she said at last, in a highly uncertain voice, "what they could have wished to do in Thrapston."

"Have dinner, I should imagine," said Sir Derek equably. "They keep a very tolerable table at the White Hart, I have heard."

"Oh!" said Allegra doubtfully. "Do you—do you think we should go there, then?"

"Not in the least," said Sir Derek. "I doubt if we should find it at all an interesting excursion. Do you know Thrapston?"

"Not very well," said Allegra, feeling by this time that

either she or Sir Derek had gone mad, or that they were reciting a scene from a play, of the plot of which neither had the least idea. "I have passed through it once or twice, I fancy, when I went into Leicestershire with Papa on a visit."

"A very uninspiring village," Sir Derek assured her. "I cannot conceive what should have given Roddy the notion of taking Hilary there. Except, of course, that it is *not* on the Great North Road. Ah—here is my dinner!" he added, as the landlord came into the room bearing a tray upon which a foaming tankard, a fresh-baked loaf, and a cheese wrapped in a napkin reposed invitingly. "Can I prevail upon you to join me, Miss Herington?"

Allegra said in tones of distinct repulsion that she could not touch a bite, and watched with some bitterness, in view of her own state of high discomfort over the situation in which she found herself, as Sir Derek addressed himself to his bread and cheese and beer with every appearance of enjoyment.

"Where *are* you going, then, if you do not intend to go to Thrapston?" she demanded after what seemed to her an interminable time, during which Sir Derek made no attempt to renew the conversation.

Sir Derek looked at her amiably. "Back to Rolveston, of course," he said. "Where else?"

"To Rolveston? Oh! Do you—do you think we shall find Hilary there?"

"Most assuredly," Sir Derek said. "I have not the slightest doubt that by this time she has concocted some outrageous Banbury tale with which to account to Simmons and Mrs. Simmons for her reappearance there. By the way, you need have no concern about the ability of that estimable couple to hold their tongues, though I think it unfortunately very likely that what bits and pieces of the affair the rest of the staff may be able to gather will

be spread about the neighbourhood, for what anyone may
be able to make of them."

Allegra said, "Oh," which was not a very valuable con-
tribution to the conversation, and fell silent again,
wondering not what the neighbourhood would make of its
imperfect knowledge of the events of that day, but what
Sir Derek was making of his. But as he still looked quite
cheerful she could not believe that he was experiencing
any fears that his presence with her at the Crown at the
comparatively innocent hour of nine o'clock in the evening would make it necessary for him to offer her his hand
in marriage in the event they should be discovered there
together; so, still clinging to the shreds of her hope that
Hilary's reprehensible behaviour that day had had nothing
to do with her, or that at least Sir Derek would not think
it had, she waited with great impatience for him to finish
his meal and then they drove back to Rolveston together.

Chapter Nineteen

IT WAS PAST ten o'clock when the phaeton drew up before the front door at Rolveston. Allegra, who had been
much relieved during the drive from Huntingdon to find
that Sir Derek seemed no more inclined for conversation
than was she, though in a quite cheerful way, was moved
to steal a glance at his face as he handed her down from
the carriage, with a view to ascertaining whether his
period of silent reflection had given him any new and disturbing ideas about Hilary's peculiar behaviour, and was

disconcerted to see that it apparently had. At least, he looked at her very steadily in return and with what she felt was a distinctly menacing expression in his eyes—not menacing in the ordinary sense, but in the sense of knowing exactly what was going through her head. For perhaps the dozenth time in her acquaintance with him she wished that he were a peacefully slow-witted sort of man instead of being all too diabolically perceptive; but this was sheer cowardice, she told herself, and, raising her chin defiantly, she met Sir Derek's glinting dark eyes squarely and walked into the house with him.

Simmons, who opened the door for them, appeared to accept with a praiseworthy lack of astonishment the reappearance at Rolveston of a young lady who, to his certain knowledge, had concluded her visit there and should be on her way to Bath. He took in charge her light wrap and Sir Derek's hat and York tan driving-gloves, and said in a detached voice, as one giving information to whom it might concern, that Miss Hilary and Lord Roderick were in the drawing room. Allegra, preventing herself only just in time from uttering a fervent—"Thank God!"—looked at Sir Derek and, seeing the amused glance he shot at her, found the overcharged emotions of sisterly relief that Simmon's words had roused swept away on the instant by a feeling of high dudgeon over the realisation that, though too much the gentleman to put it into words, Sir Derek was saying, "I told you so," to her.

All he actually said, however, was, "Thank you, Simmons," after which he walked across the hall to the drawing room door and, opening it, stood aside for her to precede him inside. She did so, and found herself confronting a pair of flushed, astonished, and—she was somewhat surprised to find—angry faces, for she had evidently interrupted the young lovers in the midst of a flaming quarrel.

"Allie!" Hilary gasped, while Lord Roderick, seeing his

cousin's tall form in the doorway behind her, jumped up, exclaiming, "Derek! Oh, this is famous! So we *didn't* succeed in gammoning you, after all!" He turned an accusing face on his betrothed. "You see! I told you Derek wasn't such a green 'un as to rise to that fly," he said to her, obviously too warm with the dispute that had been taking place between them to deny himself, as Sir Derek had done, the ignoble satisfaction of pointing out to his opponent how wrong she had been. He turned back to Sir Derek. "How far did you go after us?" he demanded with great interest. "I wagered Hilary anything she liked you wouldn't go beyond Stamford."

"Only to Stilton," Sir Derek murmured, with a glance from under his lids at Allegra that made her say warmly, "Oh, very well! You had as lief say it—that you would not have gone *that* far if I had not prevented you from making enquiries at Huntingdon when we first arrived there, as you wished to do!"

"No, did he?" said Lord Roderick, pluming himself anew. "Hilary *would* have it that he would drive straight through."

"How you underestimate me, my child!" said Sir Derek, coming across the room in a leisurely manner and, taking Hilary's hand, drawing her down beside him upon a Chippendale sofa. "But I shall forgive you all if you will now inform me exactly why you felt it necessary to stage this elaborate and rather overly melodramatic charade."

"Hilary," said Allegra hastily, "you need explain nothing to Sir Derek! It is not his affair. *I* shall deal with this."

Sir Derek looked at her reproachfully. "No, really!" he said. "This is unhandsome of you, Miss Herington! After I have been dragged about the countryside for hours on the veriest wild-goose chase, provided with nothing better than bread and cheese for my dinner, and obliged to expose my greys to the no doubt quite incompetent ministrations of strange ostlers, surely I may claim *some* rights!"

Hilary, who had been looking rather apprehensively at her sister, here said in a small, defiant voice that she had meant it all for the best.

"I am sure you did," said Sir Derek soothingly. "And if I may say so, a very good job you have made of it. I beg you will pay no heed to your sister's injunctions, Hilary. It is obviously her intention to get you alone and drag the whole story out of you while I remain in total ignorance, which I will tell you here and now that I consider grossly unfair. Come now, cut line! For what fell purpose did you embark upon this pernicious scheme?"

Hilary gazed at him uncertainly; then her eyes flew to Allegra's flushed, imploring face. Obviously matters had not turned out as she had hoped, for here was Sir Derek at his most urbanely ironic, quite untouched, it seemed, by any softer sentiment, and there was Allegra looking as if she would have liked to murder everyone in the room and then go upstairs and have a good cry. Hilary, with her usual uncompromising loyalty, made up her mind on the instant and said to Sir Derek very clearly, "Well, I won't tell you."

"You won't?" said Sir Derek, looking disappointed but not overly so. "Then I shall have to ask Roddy."

He looked enquiringly at Lord Roderick, who at once coloured up very red, looked at Hilary, who gave him no help at all except for a minatory glance from beneath frowning brows, and at length stammered exculpatorily that he didn't know anything and it wasn't really his affair, after which he appeared to find his cravat too tight and ran a desperate finger around between it and his throat. Sir Derek looked at him kindly.

"No, no, you underestimate yourself, Roddy," he assured him. "After all, you, it seems, were the person who made the fascinating disclosure to Hilary that I do not re-

ally wish to marry Miss Hardison—a piece of perspicacity
upon which I sincerely congratulate you. In point of fact,
I do *not* wish to marry Miss Hardison; indeed, I never
did, although, owing to a severe disappointment, I may
have been led to act in such a way as to cause certain
persons to leap to the quite unwarranted assumption that
I did."

"Including," said Allegra, feeling herself upon firm
ground upon this point at least, "Miss Hardison herself, I
have no doubt, Sir Derek!"

"Not at all," said Sir Derek politely. "Or no—perhaps
I am not being quite accurate upon that point. I imagine
Miss Hardison *did* believe that I wished to marry her—
but if you will stop looking at me as if you consider me a
hardened seducer of innocent maidens I will tell you that,
while she no doubt found the notion rather pleasing, she
had not yet by any means made up her mind whether she
wished to marry *me* the last time I had the honour of
seeing her in Brussels. There is always Alding—he *is* a
marquis, you know, so much more satisfactory than a
mere baronet. Yes," he concluded thoughtfully, "I rather
believe she will have Alding—especially when she learns
that I am to marry someone else."

"Oh! Are—are you going to marry someone else?"
enquired Hilary, looking exceedingly taken aback and
casting an anxious glance at Allegra.

"I *think* so," said Sir Derek judiciously, not looking at
Allegra at all. "But I can't be sure, you see, until I can
find out from you or Roddy exactly why you felt it incum-
bent upon you to stage a mock-elopement in order to
prove to your sister that I really do *not* wish to marry
Miss Hardison."

At this point Hilary, whose face had been almost puck-
ered with the intense mental effort of following the meaning of this speech, suddenly brightened visibly and, clap-
ping her hands together, exclaimed, "Oh, famous!"—

while at the same moment Allegra turned and walked out of the room. Sir Derek looked after her, an expression in his eyes that Hilary had never seen there before.

"I am no doubt a rogue and a villain to tease her so," he said, with an attempt to speak lightly, "also a coxcomb to insinuate that she might look favourably upon my suit—especially since she has already told me once that she would not have me. And *that*," he concluded, with sudden candour, "shows the state to which I have been reduced—to be discussing such matters with a pair of infants. But the truth is that we have been coming to cuffs with each other since five o'clock and I believe I am in need of reinforcements."

"Well, you have them now," said Hilary, doing a complete volte-face and coming down stoutly upon Sir Derek's side, "that is, if you really *do* wish to marry Allie, which is what I think you mean. I daresay she has gone upstairs to her bedchamber. Shall I make her come down and talk to you?"

"Can you?" enquired Sir Derek, looking skeptical.

"Yes," said Hilary matter-of-factly. "I can, if I tell her that you will come upstairs to her yourself if she doesn't."

Sir Derek gazed at her with considerable respect. "Thank you!" he said. "I *told* you I was in need of reinforcements. And to think that the best I was capable of was to send a message up to her that I should remain here until she consented to come down!"

"That is because you are a gentleman, and have scruples," Hilary said kindly. "But it won't do with Allie, you know. She has even more of a temper than I have, and I fancy that you may be obliged to speak to her quite as you did to me in Brussels before you can bring her round. But I have forgiven you for that," she added magnanimously, "because you took such good care of Roddy when he was wounded."

She then rose and walked out of the room, leaving Sir

Derek looking at his young cousin with an amused expression upon his face.

"Halfling, there is not the least doubt of it—you are destined to become a marshal!" he said. "I can see no obstacle to it that will not yield to that chit's determination."

"Yes—isn't she splendid? Awake upon every suit!" said Lord Roderick enthusiastically. "I didn't like it above half, you know, when she was so set upon our carrying out this hoax, but I can see now that it was the very thing!"

Sir Derek's face grew a trifle stern. "Yes, that is all very well," he said, "but I warn you that if you try such a thing again, you will have me to reckon with, Roddy! You may have brushed through this business tolerably well— though God knows what sort of scandal-broth will be stirred up in the neighbourhood when the story of your peregrinations today gets about—but you must understand that I shall not stand idly by if you try such a scheme *au sérieux*."

"No, no—upon my honour I shan't!" said Lord Roderick earnestly. "Good God, what kind of loose-screw do you take me for? *I* know what such a scandal would mean for Hilary!"

"Well, see that you keep that in mind when your Delilah next tries her wiles upon you," Sir Derek recommended; but as his mind was taken up almost entirely at the moment by his own affairs he did not continue the subject, and instead asked his young relation if he would not like to go into the library and find something to read or go for a stroll upon the terrace.

Lord Roderick, who could take a hint, thereupon departed and left his cousin alone in the drawing room, where he did not long remain solitary, however, for in a very few moments the door was opened and Allegra came hastily in.

"Sir Derek, this is intolerable!" she began, looking at

him with such a magnificently stormy face that he was quite certain Hilary had delivered to her verbatim, as coming from him, the message she had suggested, and could think of no other way to express his admiration of the results than to take both her hands in his. "*Quite* intolerable," continued Allegra, furious to find her voice failing her as she felt her hands taken in that strong clasp. Her eyes, which had been fixed indignantly upon Sir Derek's face, abruptly fell and she said in a much lower voice, in fact a scarcely audible one, "Don't, pray! There's no need. Those stupid children—Oh, I could *beat* Hilary!" she exclaimed, suddenly finding her fury again and wrenching her hands free of Sir Derek's. She walked away across the room swiftly to the windows. "Sir Derek, *pray* go away!" she said in a muffled voice, her back to him. "I am very tired—and this is all *quite* unnecessary—"

"I am sorry, but I am *not* going away," Sir Derek said, coming across the room and firmly turning her about so that she was obliged to face him again. "Not until I have said what I have to say to you, at any rate. And if you think I am saving it because of anything those children have done, it is all your fault, because if you had not made me believe that you detested me and were going to Bath to marry Arthur Huddleston I should have said it long ago. Allegra, my dear, *will* you marry me?"

Allegra, with the horrid consciousness of tears swimming in her eyes and her heart battering against her ribs so violently that it made her extremely uncomfortable, summoned all her willpower and said in a voice that she tried to make entirely indifferent, "Sir Derek, if you have taken it into your head that I have a—a *tendre* for you, I can assure you that you have quite mistaken the matter! Nor will you convince me that your sentiments towards me are any different from what they were on the—on the former occasion when you made me an offer—"

"No," said Sir Derek unexpectedly, "they are not, I was in love with you then and I am in love with you now." Allegra's eyes, startled, flew to his face, and what she saw there made her heart begin to batter her even more remorselessly than it had before—an expression of such warmth of feeling as she had never thought to see upon that cool, ironic face. "Only so much more in love with you now," said a voice that matched the look, "since I know you so much better, my sweet, distracting termagant—and who is to say that I should not have been warned at the outset by that flaming hair?"

Allegra, who felt as if the whole world was suddenly turning topsy-turvy around her, gasped, "Oh, but you can't be—you weren't—"

"Was I not and am I not?" said Sir Derek, taking her into his arms and proceeding to reply to this question with a kiss that so ruthlessly resisted any attempts she felt obliged to make to counter this most unconventional means of continuing a conversation that she soon abandoned them. Sir Derek appeared to find this submission praiseworthy, for he kissed her again and then murmured several rather disjointed statements into her crown of bright curls, against which at the moment his cheek was resting. Allegra, feeling quite delirious by this time, suddenly realised that she was imagining all this or that Sir Derek, in an access of remorse over his many rudenesses towards her, had chivalrously determined to counterfeit an affection for her that he did not in the least feel, and, regaining partial control of herself, pulled away from him with some violence.

"*Now* what is it?" enquired Sir Derek, looking at her reproachfully. "Just when I thought we had everything nicely settled—"

"We haven't settled anything at all!" Allegra said, giving him a harassed glance. "You—you are not speaking the truth, Sir Derek! You know you only took the notion of marrying me in the first place because you thought it would be s-suitable——"

"That," said Sir Derek firmly, but with an air of great patience, "is what I allowed you to think, my enchanting pea-goose, because I was quite aware that you would not have believed me had I tried to convince you that it was otherwise with me at that time. But my grandfather could tell you—or he would if he could, only unfortunately he can't because he is dead—that he and I had the most monumental battle of our lives when I came home from my one and only visit to Rolveston and announced that if I ever married—which at that point seemed a rather remote possibility to me—a red-headed chit named Allie Herington who could ride like an amazon and looked at me as if I were several degrees lower than the boot-boy would be the girl for me. I think it was that that decided him to push me into the diplomatic service, where I should be abroad most of the time and out of the way of temptation, and, being very young, I promptly forgot my air-dreams and fell in love, seriatim, with a variety of other females who had the advantage of being several years older than you and thus of a suitable age to—er—reciprocate my affection. But I never *quite* forgot those dreams, I am proud to say; and when I found myself in London in '08 and heard you had made your come-out I looked forward with the greatest interest to seeing you there. I *did* see you once—at a ball at Almark's, where you looked gloriously out of place among all those simpering, insipid beauties and I tumbled into love with you all over again until someone kindly informed me that the *on-dit* was that you and the young lieutenant you were dancing with were to be married. And so I went home without so much as speaking to you, and the next day into Leicestershire. I read the announcement of your engagement in the *Morning Post* while I was there."

He paused for a moment, a rather odd expression in his

eyes, which appeared to be searching her averted face for some sign that he apparently did not find there, for when he went on it was in an altered, brusquer tone.

"Of course that sent me nicely to grass," he said. "It was obvious that a boy's romantic fancies were to remain only that—not that they merited anything better, for I had never lifted a finger to fix my interest with you, considering you far too young. I might have done so after young Alland was killed, of course, except that I have been very little in England since that time, as you know, and on one of the few occasions that I was, Lady Hatherill informed me, when I enquired about you, that you had not consoled yourself for your lieutenant and probably never would, since you had rejected more than one advantageous offer for that reason. So it was only when Rolveston fell to me, when I came into this part of the country again and this house, your portrait"—his eyes went briefly to the vivid young face looking down at them from over the mantelpiece—"put me very much in mind of you once more, that the idea came to me that perhaps, after all, it was possible—" He broke off abruptly; after a moment he went on, with a rather twisted smile. "Well, we are boy and girl no longer, Allegra, and it is folly, I know, to expect from you what you gave once and can give no more. But since Hilary and Roddy, at least, appear to believe that your happiness might be served by our marrying—that you no longer hold me in that strong aversion that you once let me know of so unequivocally—"

"Oh, stop—stop!" Allegra cried suddenly. She raised her eyes, brimming with tears, to his face. "It—it isn't like that at all," she said, her voice unsteady but her eyes fixed with painful candour upon his. "I *did* love Neil—I loved him dreadfully, and when he died I thought for a while that I should die, too. But I didn't. I grew up. I'm not a girl any longer, Derek, and I—I've learned that you can love someone else just as dreadfully—only I c-couldn't *bear* it when I thought you were offering for me only because you were s-sorry for me—"

At this point she found herself quite unable to continue, owing to the fact that two very strong arms were encircling her so tightly that she could scarcely breathe, much less talk, and even breathing became impossible when Sir Derek kissed her very ungently and then said several things that might have appeared to an impartial observer to express something less than his usual keen intelligence consisting as they did chiefly of such phrases as, "My darling!" and "My little love!"

How long he might have gone on saying them is debatable, for he showed no signs of falling into a more rational mood, but perhaps fortunately the drawing-room door was opened presently and Hilary's anxious face appeared in the aperture. It brightened at once, however, at the sight of her sister, who was now seated upon the Chippendale sofa with Sir Derek's arms about her and her head upon his shoulder.

"Oh—famous!" she exclaimed, causing Allegra, who had not heard her come in, to jump and disengage herself hastily from Sir Derek's arms. "I thought you might have come to dagger-drawing again," Hilary went on, advancing into the room and planting herself before the lovers with her arms akimbo and an expression of great satisfaction upon her face, "so I thought I should just look in and see if there was anything I could do. But I see you are going on like winking—"

"We *were* going on like winking, until you interrupted us," Sir Derek said severely. "Go away, you abominable brat. Can't you see that you're not wanted?"

"Yes, but—tell me first, are you *really* going to marry Allie?" Hilary demanded, standing her ground. "Because if you are—will you let me live here with you at Rolveston until I marry Roddy, instead of going to Aunt Hatherill? *Do* say yes! Because I simply shall not be able to *bear* it if I must go to Bath, and I promise I shan't be the *least* trouble to you!"

Sir Derek, with praiseworthy patience, said that if he had his way he and her sister would be married on the following day by special licence, and that though he barred her presence on the wedding journey she might consider Rolveston her home for as long as she liked. But to this plan Lord Roderick, who had entered the room in Hilary's wake, uttered a shocked and decided negative.

"No, I say, Derek," he protested, "you can't do that! Marry Miss Herington by special licence, that is. Not at all the thing, you know! Much better to have the wedding at St. George's, and an announcement in the *Morning Post,* and bride-clothes, and all that flummery. Don't you think so, Hilary?"

Hilary said decidedly that she did, adding a rider to Allegra to the effect that if Sir Derek was trying to bullock her into marrying him in any such scrambling way, she had only to say the word and he would have her to deal with as well.

Allegra looked in helpless amusement at Sir Derek. "Derek—" she appealed.

"Yes," said Sir Derek, rising. He took Hilary's arm with one hand and Lord Roderick's with the other and escorted them politely but firmly to the door. "Bless you, my children," he said, "but you will have to learn that there are times when a man prefers to be alone. And when I say alone, I use the word in its looser sense, which does not preclude the presence of female company. Do I make myself clear?"

Hilary seemed inclined to rebel at this summary dismissal, but Lord Roderick, with a grin, said perfectly clear, and they would be on the terrace when they were wanted.

"Good!" said Sir Derek. "And that, I may warn you,

will probably not be for a very long time." He closed the door behind them and turned again to Allegra. "Now as I was saying, my love," he remarked, with a gleam in his eyes, "when we were so rudely interrupted—"

He resumed his seat upon the sofa beside her; but as the conversation that ensued was of much the same nature as it had been before, there is little point in dwelling upon it further, beyond stating that it did indeed go on for quite some time, but that as Hilary and Lord Roderick were engaging in exactly the same kind of dialogue on the terrace, they did not much object to waiting.

About the Author

Though she was born in Ohio, Miss Darcy is so at home with her chosen period, Regency England, that readers of her novels could easily believe she was born and raised in the best society of the day. Romantic, gay, spirited, her books, *Georgina, Cecily,* and *Lydia* are an enchanting delight.

Have You Read These Bestsellers from SIGNET?

More Bestsellers from SIGNET

☐ **MACLYON by Lolah Buford.** A turbulent novel of flaming love and uncontrollable passion . . . "Dashing, dramatic, romantic and highly sexed!"—*Publishers Weekly* (#E6634—$1.75)

☐ **PHOENIX ISLAND by Charlotte Paul.** A towering novel of disaster and survival . . . of passion, power and savage excitement. (#J6827—$1.95)

☐ **THE BRACKENROYD INHERITANCE by Erica Lindley.** A legacy of peril . . . a dazzling young beauty . . . a fire storm of passion, and possession. (#W6795—$1.50)

☐ **MISSION TO MALASPIGA by Evelyn Anthony.** From New York to Rome to Florence—love and deadly danger by the author of **Stranger at the Gates** . . . "Surpasses Helen MacInnes!"—*Bestsellers* (#E6706—$1.75)

☐ **MAGGIE ROWAN by Catherine Cookson.** An unforgettable novel of a passionately driven woman who paid the price of heartbreak for a dream. (#W6745—$1.50)

THE NEW AMERICAN LIBRARY, INC.,
P.O. Box 999, Bergenfield, New Jersey 07621

Please send me the SIGNET BOOKS I have checked above. I am enclosing $＿＿＿＿＿＿(check or money order—no currency or C.O.D.'s). Please include the list price plus 25¢ a copy to cover handling and mailing costs. (Prices and numbers are subject to change without notice.)

Name＿＿＿＿＿＿＿＿＿＿＿＿＿＿＿＿＿＿＿＿＿＿＿＿＿＿＿

Address＿＿＿＿＿＿＿＿＿＿＿＿＿＿＿＿＿＿＿＿＿＿＿＿＿

City＿＿＿＿＿＿＿＿State＿＿＿＿＿＿＿Zip Code＿＿＿＿＿
Allow at least 3 weeks for delivery